The Last Memory

T. T. Faulkner

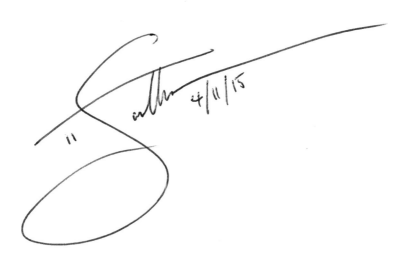

To my family, who gave me a candle.
To my teachers, who gave me a match.
To my friends, who made sure I didn't burn it all down.

CONTENTS

One is for Culture,
and from it we share.
Two is for War,
spoils to whom dare.
Three is for Magic,
which flows twixt all life.
Four is for Art,
a pen stronger than knife.
Five is for Technology,
the advancements we make.
And from all these numbers,
one man shall take.
Fire and brimstone will rain in the air,
'til the only knowledge left is despair.

PROLOGUE

Wet socks make it harder to run. Splashes echo off the decayed concrete walls as the young girl patters through the creeping darkness of the tunnel.

All the while, he silently pursues her. He never quickens his pace; he limits himself to a meandering stroll yet never seems to lose ground. He moves effortlessly—the air pushing him forward, eager to rid itself of the unnatural presence. His black coattails slither behind him like two serpents writhing along in malevolent joy. His clothes remain spotless and pressed, even through the dripping, filthy tunnel. It's almost as if the surrounding murk knows better than to harass him.

The young girl presses on—blood turning her moldy socks a deep auburn. A glance back reveals her pursuer's toothy grin—like a cat eying a frightened mouse. Her shoulders droop with an unyielding weariness. It has been days since this chase began. Her muscles burn from running and her sides ache with hunger. She fights back the memories of that day—the fire and screams replaying endlessly in her mind. Everything she cares for has been lost.

She considers giving up—letting him take her. How easy it would be to just end this suffering now. A dim glow pours in from the streetlights ahead and it gives her the strength to push on.

She quietly prays that what she's doing is right, but it is too late for such thoughts. The course has been set—the chain of events is unfolding. She lowers her head and runs faster. Twisted laughter fills the stagnant air, reverberating off the walls and echoing in her mind.

Her time is running out.

I

I nervously passed the counterfeit license between my hands, feeling the smooth plastic slide across my fingertips. This was it—another bar and another insurmountable challenge.

The object of my dread stood before me. The bouncer was a huge bald man wearing a black shirt that clung to his bulging muscles as if it was painted onto his flesh. After the last few bars, I was starting to think that there was some secret bouncer clothing store that only sold one kind of obscure, black, skin-tight T-shirt. It didn't help that he was eying me under his massive forehead long before I got to the front of the line.

When I finally stood in front of him, he reached out with a meaty paw and plucked the small card from my hand. He eyed it over his crooked nose, glancing from the picture to my face over and over again.

A deep-rooted heat rose in my cheeks. *Cool it. This is how it always goes. The worst thing that can happen is he smashes you into paste.*

The giant gave the card one last squinted look and nodded. With a sigh of relief, I retrieved the forged ID and walked through the smoky doorway.

I surveyed the crowded landscape and wondered what I was doing here. The odor of cigarettes and lemon-scented cleaner wafted across my nostrils. I wasn't even a big fan of bars. In fact, I had never been to one until recently.

David thought it was important we go out every night this week since my twenty-first birthday was coming up. "Seriously, Noah, life's over once you hit twenty-one. There's nothing left to look forward to after that. Don't even bother going to clubs once you're legal. The chicks can sense that kind of thing. When you turn twenty-one, you're just another creepy college guy."

David and I had been friends since I'd moved to central Florida. I had just started middle school and hadn't been used to the city or the sun. While most of the kids had avoided the pale newcomer, David had waddled right up and introduced himself—we'd been best friends ever since. Despite being a big lug, he'd always been there for me. He would pull me down from coat rack wedgies, and being friends with one of the popular boys definitely had its privileges. When college had rolled around, we'd decided to go to the same university and had been roommates since our freshman year. So when he remembered my birthday was coming up he suggested taking our party on the road with fake IDs and a map of the coolest bars in Orlando.

The neon glow from the entrance lights cast shadowed images across my vision at each new stop. At first, the adventures had been exciting. We'd sneak into the clubs, laugh, and throw back a few drinks. But as the week had progressed, I'd started to dread the nightly outings into the seedy underbelly of Orlando. I took solace in knowing that after tonight, the festivities would be over and I'd just have my actual birthday to look forward to.

I spotted David on the other side of the room. He raised an empty glass to the heavens and pointed at it like a sad puppy. I nodded and pushed my way past two overweight frat boys in an attempt to order a few more beers.

The loud bass of some foreign techno beat thundered in my ears as I approached the counter. I held up two fingers and the bartender ducked away to siphon whatever watered-down brew they were selling that night. I slapped some money on the bar as the barkeep placed two full glasses in front of me. I clutched them close—like a mother guarding her children against wolves—and surveyed the mob I would have to wade through to reach David's booth. Moses parting the Red Sea was nothing compared to this. I took a deep breath of the pungent tavern air and plunged into the squall of drunken students and the morally oblique. If life really did end at twenty-one, these people hadn't gotten the memo. It wasn't surprising, though—David's advice usually proved faulty.

As the night wore on, I began to sink into a funk. It wasn't the lack of atmosphere or the sour taste of the beer that was bothering me. It was more that while David was enjoying the company of two gorgeous blondes, I was practically sitting alone without even a wandering glance to acknowledge my existence.

I tilted my mug to the side and examined my distorted reflection, seeking some sort of respite from their constant prattling. I observed a distinctly scruffy image staring back at me. My thick, brown hair fell to about my ears and I had a complete lack of a tan. But, I thought, I'd dig me if I was a chick.

It wasn't like I'd never had a girl interested in me. Some would say I had a mysterious quality about my appearance—like the handsome stranger that rides in to save the captured princess, except thinner and most likely falling off his horse. It probably didn't help that my idea of a conversation starter was pointing out one of my many around-the-world novelty shirts.

I continued to sit alone on the old, uncomfortable cushion while David smiled and laughed with his new female friends. The clock ticked away and my seed of depression quickly grew into an annoying weed. David's "you are not the father" dance had just landed him one hundred percent more attention than my "VISIT DENVER" shirt. But was it his fault I was spending the night before my birthday as a wallflower, or was it my own social awkwardness that had brought me here?

I noticed a girl across the bar looking in my direction and smiled at her. She rolled her eyes and said something to her friends that was apparently very funny. Suddenly, I found that the large crowd and loud music was too much.

I unknowingly made the most important decision of my life.

"David... uh, I'm gonna head out."

He looked back with his usual dumbfounded expression. "Whaaat? Why would you want to leave a hot joint like this?"

"You know, it's just getting late and tomorrow's gonna be a big day. I don't want both of us to have a hangover on my birthday."

One of the two educated young ladies was obstructing David's mouth at that point, but I'm pretty sure he said something along the lines of "you gotta do what you gotta do."

I waded through the thick fog of cigarettes, past the menacing security guard, and out into the night. I'd like to say the refreshing burst of a cool nighttime breeze greeted me, but this was downtown Orlando. Instead, the grimy smell of the city welcomed me as I stumbled outside. Florida air isn't like other places; it creeps under clothes and pulls the sweat from bodies. Whenever possible I tried to stay in it for as little time as I could manage. With this in mind, I took a brisk pace as I maneuvered down the dark streets. As I walked, I pondered the important things in life—like where gelatin comes from, or why superheroes always wear full body costumes while villains are cool with wearing nothing more than a simple lab coat. Then David's words trickled through my consciousness. His predictions always had a peculiar effect on me, and I found his most recent revelation a heavy burden. Luckily, the things he said usually tended to be more cruel than correct. For my twentieth birthday, he'd told me something special was going to happen. When school ended that day, I found out that the "something special" was having my entire car wrapped in toilet paper like an ancient, metallic mummy—Highway-ho-tep, the four-wheel drive sports sedan of golden Egypt. Stunts like that made me wonder why I ever believed anything he said.

I glanced down at my watch as I quickly walked through the night air. A friend of mine had once asked me if I would rather be the most hated man on earth and be remembered forever, or just be Noah Lane and be forgotten to time. I couldn't answer the question then and I still hadn't come up with an answer.

I looked back at my watch. 11:59 p.m. with the second hand making its final lap. I sighed and counted down to David's sordid prophecy.

"I guess this is it. Five, four, three, tw—"

I was interrupted by a sudden impact that sent me tumbling across the concrete. I was about to give the culprit the most threatening apology they would ever experience until I saw who had just leveled me.

She was the most beautiful woman I'd ever seen... that is, for a dirty, homeless person. She had snowy, white skin that seemed to shimmer in the moonlight—where it wasn't spotted with dirt and filth. The matted nest on her head was strawberry red and was elegantly tied back with a cross made from a bendy straw and a small, single-leaved twig. I couldn't tell much about her figure—the shirt she wore was baggy to the point of being comical. It hung like a blanket all the way to her knees and folded freely about her frame. On her feet, she wore red, striped knee-high socks, like you would wear in a baseball game.

She was an angel.

"Um, sorry," I managed to choke out. "Do you need some pants?"

She spun to face me, her face growing red with her screams, but her words were lost as I was drawn into her eyes. They were like staring at the moon—not the actual moon, but what I *wanted* the moon to look like. It was like seeing it through the eyes of a child for the first time, before it had all been spoiled with science and reason.

Looking into her eyes was like looking into all the wonderful things that I couldn't understand and therefore considered miraculous. Her irises enchanted me and held my breath hostage. I lowered myself back into reality and noticed the girl was punching me in the chest.

"Get *off* me!"

"Oh... sorry. Let me help you up."She ignored my outstretched hand, springing instead onto her dirty socks with the lightness of an elf. Wait. Were her socks bloody?

"I am fine. Get away." She tumbled back onto the pavement, dislodging the twig from her heavenly crown.

"Come on. Let me help you."

"I-I can get up on my own." Her voice was a spring breeze but held an edge of authority. She had a touch of an English accent. It was the way her words seemed to be spoken—with gentle care, like each one was valuable.

There was a sound in the distance and the girl's head snapped to attention, staring into the darkness. It was strange. Her eyes seemed to shift from a beautiful hue to a cloudy white. It made her already pale skin seem shades lighter. I followed her gaze as the eerily-controlled sound of footsteps falling in perfect rhythm began to echo off the buildings.

That's when I saw him.

He was a combination of history professor and male model—sculpture-like and full of wisdom. His pace was relaxed, yet he appeared to be moving unnaturally fast. His face was chiseled into violent angles and his opulent black hair was combed straight back, reflecting the light from the lamps above. It was actually difficult to call his hair black—just as I couldn't say his tuxedo jacket was black... or his pants or shoes. The same way his white shirt wasn't white. In fact, they weren't true colors at all—they were purer than that. They had a fury that burned my eyes, like staring directly into the sun. But it was his smile that unnerved me the most. It stretched a little too far—like invisible hooks were tugging at the edges—and it contained all the joy one would get from watching a starving man die.

I helped the homeless girl up and she looked at me for what must have been the first time. Her eyes grew wide with shock, becoming the moon once again. She whispered one word to me, "Run."

II

This was one of the greatest moments of my life. Well, it would have been better without the creepy stalker trailing behind us. But despite that minor setback, I was running hand-in-hand with the prettiest girl I'd ever met.

We took off down the street. She hobbled along on her injured leg and I did my best to act as her crutch. As we ducked through dark alleyways and crooked side streets, she quickly called out the next set of directions without hesitating whenever we hit a fork in our path. It was as if she already knew exactly where she wanted to go. I figured she must have been from the area to know her way around so well.

I chanced a glance behind us, thinking we must have lost our pursuer, but he was still there—a mechanical soldier with a never-ending power supply. He drifted through the winding path without missing a beat. I pushed over a silver trash bin as we rounded another corner. The strange man carried on—the large cylinder simply drifted past him like debris caught in a boat's wake. The edge of his smile grew tauter.

I could hear the homeless girl beginning to breathe harder and knew we couldn't keep this pace for much longer. I had to make a decision.

"Can you move on your own?" I was surprised how winded I was.

"Maybe." Her voice was strained with exertion and pain.

"Good, then GO!"

I pushed her forward and circled around on our pursuer, letting my angel go on without me.

The statue in the tux stopped abruptly, surprised. The toothy grin melted away into a strange, sympathetic frown. In three seemingly-normal strides, he covered a four lane street and stopped two car lengths away from me.

"Well, well." His refined, educated voice was reminiscent of the history buffs I'd heard on those civil war documentaries I'd watched when I'd pretended to be sick and stayed home from school. "It seems a son of man has decided to see the world as it is. Then see well, Son of Man. You are playing with forces you do not understand. Forgive my lack of manners." He swooped into a low bow. "I am Colere, keeper of the world's culture. I apologize for what has to be done."

He raised a single cuffed arm to the sky and pressed his stony middle finger to his thumb. The space around it began to shake and distort like heat contorting the air above a flame. I could feel the world tense up as those two fingers pressed harder together. Somewhere deep within me, something stirred. A part of me awakened from a long slumber and looked out, confused by its surroundings. I took a step toward the rippling tide and felt my gut lurch. My vision began to blur, sending the whole world tumbling into swirling agony.

Then he snapped his fingers.

The sound was the deepest bass tone I had ever heard. It was like someone had struck a tuning fork made of pure darkness, which I believe is an accurate comparison considering the whole street became enveloped in a cloud of the very same blackness, vibrating in my ears. The inky mist continued to eclipse my sight until all that was left was Colere's candent smile. Then there was silence.

Vast, empty, earsplitting silence.

A hand pushed forth from the gloom and the dark mist slid across the pavement. Below my feet, the earth began to shake—gently at first and then more fiercely. Out of nowhere, a white pillar burst from the ground in front of me. It grew twenty feet tall, missing my head by inches as it climbed upward. I stared in awe at the shining monolith that had almost just killed me. It stood huge and perfect, with ornate carvings from top to bottom. I reached a trembling hand out to touch the cold, marble surface. It was real.

Suddenly, a hand clamped firmly onto my shoulder. I reeled around to find the homeless girl still by my side. She pulled me away from the rumbling sidewalk just as another marble pillar sprouted to our left, smashing through the first pillar. The two columns exploded into a hail of sharp rocks. I ducked away as projectiles clattered against buildings and bushes. I flinched as a heavy fragment hammered my skull. Warm liquid trickled down the side of my face and the world took a red tint as the sticky blood dripped into my eye.

The pull of a pale hand jolted me back into the present. "Why did you come back for me?" I managed to squeak through the delirium.

"I never left."

"I don't understand. Why did you stay?"

"Because I have seen too many people die in the past few days."

Her voice wrapped around me and I began to feel the anxiety fall away. It seemed an odd time for me to be swooning, but there was something about the way she spoke that seemed to force confidence into my body. She grasped my arm and we sped down the sidewalk again. Even in the cloud of darkness that had settled on the street, her directionality seemed to prevail. I could barely see my feet, yet she still managed to deftly navigate alleyways and intersections.

"Are you from around here?" My words shriveled in the thick fog.

"Not exactly." Her eyes flashed and she quickly darted to the right. Another huge pillar ruptured through the concrete, almost kneecapping the nimble redhead. I cautiously maneuvered around the obstruction and pressed on.

We swung around to the next side street and passed by the skeletal remains of some old, condemned building. The windows and doors were barricaded with thick, wooden planks and a musty smell drifted through the alleyway.

The homeless girl paused for a moment in front of the large, barricaded entrance. Frustration painted her dirt-smudged face. "This is not where we are supposed to be," she stammered.

The ground began to quake violently and another pillar birthed from the cement. It was much larger than the others, and neither the quick, moon-eyed girl nor I were able to move in time. The impact sent a shockwave through my entire body. I tumbled into the air, gravity ceasing to care about its rules. The world shifted and spun as I was thrown back, crashing through the decayed, wooden boards covering the entrance to the old building.

I rolled across the dusty floor, and then pushed myself up and tried to look through the dirt and darkness that was settling around the room. The red-haired girl lay crumpled on top of a pile of splintered debris. She was unconscious—helpless. All I knew was that I couldn't let that... whatever he was... get to her. I couldn't bear to think what intentions a man like that would have for someone like her.

I surveyed the remains of the building for some kind of weapon and picked up a busted metal pipe. One serrated end had been flattened to a sharpened point. I'd once brushed my arm against something like it while exploring an old building with David. It had sliced my arm wide open and I'd had to get a tetanus shot.

I tested the weight of it in my hand and wondered if monsters could get tetanus. I used the makeshift saber to straighten up and face the broken threshold. There was nothing there save the slow, methodical rapping of shoes hitting the ground outside. I pushed myself forward, cringing through the electric shocks delivered by the cuts and bruises that plagued my every step. I stumbled once, dropping my gaze to the floor then looked back toward the entrance, which was no longer empty.

There he stood. Flawless features bored into me as he leaned coolly against the inside frame, obviously amused by the pathetic boy in front of him.

"Do you even realize what you are doing, Son of Man? What forces you are facing? I do not wish to learn from you, but I am sure you could impart some of your knowledge on me."

"I won't let you touch her." I tried to sound brazen, but there was too much fear in my voice to pull it off.

He laughed—cold, civilized. "Your kind is so mindlessly chivalrous. You know nothing about her or what she has done."

"Tell me what she did to deserve this." I pointed toward the fallen figure, battered and broken on a heap of ruined wood and mortar.

"Her?" he replied quizzically. "Nothing but live." He waved his hand and sent rippling sparks dancing across the stagnant air. "Much like the others I have taken, I am more interested in what she knows. But if it is wrongdoings you require, you merely must examine the curse she has laid upon your head, child. I can see you fading from your world even as we speak. Fear not though, Son of Man. Once I take from her what is mine, I will spare you the grief of losing everything you hold dear." He lowered his hand back to his side and the frolicking lights shattered into dust.

"Why are you doing all this? It's not right."

"Not right?" he replied tersely. "Boy, right and wrong are not merely words with which to attack your enemy with. I take little joy in anything but the pursuit of knowledge, and now you are boring me, which is impressive for someone who has lived as long as I." He straightened his obsidian jacket.

Now was my chance.

I hefted the pipe forward and swung with every part of my being. I'd never been in a fight—hell, I didn't even play fighting video games—but for some reason, this just felt right. As it cut through the air, I could feel all of my muscles acting in unison. I pictured gladiators performing the finishing blow on savage beasts and soldiers striking down their enemies with deadly bayonets. My whole body propelled the wicked extension forward with a raw force that would strike with the power of the heavens, killing any foe in its path.

Or it would have if it didn't pass harmlessly in front of my assailant's face, missing it by inches and landing solidly against the wooden door frame. I made a silent promise to forever say that he dodged the blow if I managed to live through this.

With a deafening clatter, the impact of steel against rotting wood sent a painful vibration through my body. My arm reeled back instinctively away from the shock, but then something strange happened. Everything seemed to slow down. The wild recoil steadily became more controlled and a hazy pull aligned itself within me. The retreat was abruptly ended by the wet sound of tearing flesh. I let go of the pipe to find where I'd been hit, but I wasn't the injured one.

Colere stood, shocked—the jagged piece of metal lodged deep in his neck.

I was surprised to see fresh blood flow from the wound. How had I even hit him with such a clumsy backward swing? Hesitantly, I took a step away and looked at the man.

A mask of utter confusion covered his perfect face. Then his shoulders dropped and an eternal sadness washed over him. He stared straight at me—straight through me. His eyes seemed to hold eons of weary travel. Visions of an ancient city aflame assaulted my mind. Families poured out of their homes, running in terror as fire scorched everything they owned. A building crumbled to dust, choking the life from a small child hiding under the floorboards. He had stopped hearing the gentle breathing of his mother lying on the floor long ago and welcomed the quiet relief. Somewhere nearby, a statuesque man climbed the long set of stairs to an old castle that had protected these people for so long. He read from an aged book, paying no mind to the large bricks crashing around him or the strange creatures screaming for mercy or vengeance.

When the strange vision subsided, I no longer saw the calm predator who had watched a city burn. There was no toothy grin or confident swagger; the only discernible feature I could see now was sadness.

Colere strained to open his mouth. His voice was strangely calm. "Father, why?"

I was amazed at how clearly he spoke, especially with a rusted chunk of metal jammed in his throat. Then I noticed he was glowing.

Beginning at the tips of his black hair, he began to turn gold. It flowed over his brow and down his neck—like liquid pouring over hot steel. His tux began to shimmer brightly, and his perfectly pressed pants took on a metallic sheen. Soon, the flowing river of light encompassed his entire body. In front of me stood a perfect, golden statue of a sad man with a tarnished shard of iron jutting from his neck like the handle of a pot. Light bent around the idol as it started vibrating. In a bright flash, the statue turned into a golden man-shaped cloud. At first, it seemed oddly beautiful—like some glittering deity. That image was quickly shattered when the cloud shot forward and tore through my body like a thousand tiny knives. The assault lifted me off my feet and tossed me across the room.

I made a sizable dent in a stone pillar and collapsed onto the pile of debris next to my ivory angel, who was still unconscious. My body screamed in agony and I felt a sharp pain in my side, but what gave me the most fear was the possibility that the homeless girl might already be dead. Even if she wasn't, who would call an ambulance to help her? Though I had done my best to save her, it seemed it just hadn't been enough. I lifted my left hand and pain tore through my side. I reached out and touched her face.

"I'm sorry." I winced as I spoke. "I guess David was right: life does end at twenty-one."

The irony of the statement wasn't lost on me and I suffered through a pathetic chuckle. My eyelids grew heavy and darkness crept into the corners of my vision from somewhere in the back of my skull.

As nothingness overtook me, I mumbled to myself, "Happy birthday."

ONE

I was sitting in the corner of a room larger than any I had ever seen—a cavernous audience hall decorated with architecture from every era. Pillars lined either side of a huge, red carpet that led onward into the endless chamber and faded into the shadows somewhere in the distance. The pillars stood taller than buildings—soaring skyward into the barely-visible white ceiling. Something was strange about them. I squinted and studied them. They were all very impressive, but it seemed as though none of them were exactly the same as the last. All of them were built in different architectural styles and in some cases, out of different materials altogether.

In fact, no two features of the huge room looked exactly alike. It was as if architects from every era in history had been allowed to design exactly one piece of the chamber. Gothic spires cut through the air next to Roman archways that leapt from the cold, tile floor. Log cabin staircases led to small adobe huts, and an array of unique, flying buttresses lined a corridor in the distance attached to nothing but air. Nothing in this room made any sense—I knew then I had to be dreaming. But it wasn't the strangeness that solidified the thought; I just knew, like knowing how to breathe.

I examined a collection of strange bricks that comprised the structure I was now sitting against. Despite the jumble of mismatched building materials, it seemed sturdy enough. I tried to push against it—to prop myself up—but my arm wouldn't move. Actually, I couldn't feel any part of my body. Instead, I felt an essence was trapped inside—like my skin was some kind of hollow casing made to imprison my spirit. I started to panic, screaming inside the husk of my body that sat silently against the wall. Something moved in front of me and I followed it with my eyes. I wanted to look away, but my will was gone. I wasn't even sure if I had chosen to examine the room earlier or if I had been told to by some unseen force.

After a few moments of silence, a man in a long, black robe stepped into my sightline. He was fairly young—only a few years older than me—but his eyes betrayed his body. They were the eyes of someone who had seen too much and lived far too long. His voice was thick with pure power and dominated everything else in the vast chamber.

"There you are. Welcome, Noah."

Footsteps echoed through the Escher room, and four figures lined up behind the man with the timeless eyes. The shortest one spoke; his high-pitched voice pecked at my ears.

"So, a son of man somehow managed to kill our brother? We should show him the same courtesy." Even though the squat man was standing right in front of me, he paid me no attention. It seemed as though only the one in the black robe knew I was there.

The man with the powerful voice turned to face the speaker. "In due time, but I would like him tested first."

"And if we break the toy?" A gleeful female voice spoke.

The man looked to the source of the comment and something heavy hit the floor. The remaining figures took several steps back. The man returned his attention to me and leaned in close.

"I would like to see what you can do, Noah Lane. I would appreciate it if you did not die before your use is fulfilled."

He pushed down on me and I felt myself fall deeper into my body until the room, the strange figures, and the man with the timeless eyes were all gone.

III

Light crept over my eyelids. I rolled onto my side. My back ached from sleeping on the uncomfortable sofa. Morning sun peered in though the apartment window, casting a long shadow over the stack of textbooks in the corner. The old air-conditioning unit kicked in and its low whirr brought life to the silent den. That had been the weirdest dream I'd ever had and I hadn't even drunk that much.

"Oh, Noah. You are awake. I was worried you were going to sleep all day."

I sat up, shocked. "Holy crap! You're real?"

"Of course I am real. However, I do not believe I ever introduced myself. My name is Luna."

My angel's name was Luna.

I scanned the room and saw her leaning against the bathroom door. Her red hair was still wet from the shower; it flowed over her shoulders like sun-dappled water over stones. Her skin was now polished porcelain. Dripping water traced angular lines down her strong arms. I could barely make out her petite frame under the towel she had coiled around her body.

She blushed a visible red at my stares. "I think I might have to take you up on the clothing you offered me last night."

"Last night!" The series of events flashed through my head. "Oh, my God! Are you all right? Did all that really happen?"

"Yes, I am fine. I am... um... a fast healer." Her tone was quiet. "And last night did happen. About that... we really need to talk."

"So, wait a minute. How did we get back to my apartment?"

"I carried you."

"How did you know where I live? And how do you know my name? And how on earth could you carry me?"

"You had a small leather folder in your pocket." Luna fidgeted, avoiding my gaze. "There was an identification card inside."

Something was off. I'd been carrying a fake ID because of our bar hopping. If she had gotten the information from my license, she would have called me Duff McWalen and we would've been somewhere in Ohio right now. But before I was able to point this out, I was interrupted by keys clanking together outside the door and the sound of tumblers moving in the lock.

"That must be David." Relief washed over me. "He is *not* going to believe all of this."

Luna took a step to restrain me, but it was too late. I rushed forward and jerked the door open to a very confused David. He looked straight at me, then at his hands, and then at his key. After this awkward exchange, he returned his gaze to me.

"Noah?" he called out, holding the "oah" for a few extra seconds.

"Of course, it's me, David. Who... else... would it..." my greeting was cut short as he brushed past my shoulder and wandered into the apartment, still calling my name.

"Noah? Are you home? C'mon, man. This isn't funny."

I looked at Luna, who avoided my eyes. She was pretending to show a deep interest in the kitchen table's varnish. I followed David into my room where he checked under the bed.

"Son of a— Where *are* you Noah?" His desperation hung in the air.

"I'M RIGHT HERE!" I shouted into his ear.

He perked up at that, and all my anxiety fell away as he stood to face me. He reached into his pocket and pulled out a small, vibrating cell phone. After glancing at the glowing screen, he put it to his ear. "Yeah, Sam. I still can't find him. No, he's not at the house." David turned and walked back to the front door, stopping to take a last look around the apartment. "You're right, but I've never seen him take any interest in bar girls. With the way he acts, I don't think he could land one, anyway. I'll call his parents if we can't find him soon." He walked out the door, slamming it behind him. Muffled footsteps faded out of earshot.

I stared at the space where David had been. Why hadn't he seen me? Was this some kind of birthday prank? And what did he mean I couldn't get a bar girl because of the way I acted? I could totally get one if I wanted; they just weren't my type.

I spun around to Luna, who was still staring at the table. The look on her face immediately told me something was very wrong.

She took a deep breath. "I think you should sit down, Noah. We need to talk."

IV

I sulked at the table, cradling my head in my hands while Luna went into the kitchen and made us both tea. She sat down opposite me and shifted the steaming cup between her palms. The smell of the warm liquid roused me from my stupor and I glanced at her through the gaps in my fingers.

"So, why can't David see me?"

"Well," Luna began, "mainly because you do not exist on the same plane as him anymore. When I ran into you, you kind of... well... left that world."

I set both my hands on the table and looked hard at her, just to make sure she was serious. She was a random homeless person, right? Some of them were prone to spouting nonsense. But everything that had happened last night was so real, and the way David had looked at me—like I wasn't even there—made me know in the pit of my stomach there was truth to what she said. I gave in.

"All right. Explain."

"Okay." She took a deep breath. Her cosmic eyes began to glow softly. She reached over the table and stirred the contents of my cup.

Once it was swirling quickly—like a fragrant whirlpool—she sat back. I looked down into the cup and images began to swim through the dark liquid, rising as the steam drifted upward. "There are two dimensions to our world. The one you come from is called the Plane of Man, and the one I come from is called the Plane of Gods. A long time ago, these worlds were one and all beings lived together."

I watched as an oddly shaped creature mingled with a small human. They laughed and played together, running up and down the hovering cloud of steam.

"That was until a great war between your kind and the magical creatures broke out."

Suddenly, a wind blew past and both were wearing armor. They charged at one another, unleashing brutal strikes with their weapons.

"The sons of man—your people—were too easily swayed by the powers of light and dark to be allowed to roam free with the more powerful beings. With the rate at which your kind multiplies, you could have easily shifted the scales to one side or the other. So, the gods separated the two planes to protect themselves and their creations. Are you with me so far?"

I stared at her blankly as the tea settled and her eyes mellowed back to their usual slight luminescence. Apparently, she took this as a yes.

"I will continue, then. Very rarely do the two worlds interact. Creatures from the Plane of Gods tend to just ignore your kind, and your kind tends to do the same. They drift about as ghosts, rarely noticing each other. Sometimes, your species will make claims of things like Bigfoot or other such monsters. That is an example of the two realms clashing—"

"So, wait. Bigfoot is real?"

Her beautiful eyes narrowed, irritated at the interruption. "Well, yes. But they are not quite as your kind perceives them to be."

"And Nessie?"

"What is a Nessie?"

"Never mind. What about vampires?"

"Yes, there are an abundance of vampires on this side, but-"

"Leprechauns?"

"No, those are fake. Now, would you like me to finish, or not?"

"Yes, please continue."

"Anyway, places where these sightings happen tend to be weak spots in the two worlds. These are caused by incidents of high emotions by residents on either side. When I ran into you, we must have been near one and... well... I accidentally pulled you out of your world and into mine."

"Then when that monster said you had put a curse on me and I was going to lose everything, was that true?"

Luna looked down at the table and sipped her tea. "Colere... yes... he is an especially powerful creature—a Chronographer. They are a particular breed of monster that thrives on murder and destruction. He was referring to your departure from the Plane of Man. Now that you are a part of the Plane of Gods, your friends and family will no longer be able to see you."

I sat in silence for a moment. "What will they think happened to me?"

"The same thing they always think when a son of man suddenly disappears. They will look for you for a while and then perform whatever death rite your people follow."

My heart started to ache. A pain in my stomach pulled my shoulders down until my forehead rested on the table.

"Then... my mother, my sister, my father, and all my friends... they'll... they'll think I'm dead?"

"Yes."

"Then you have to put me back!" I slammed a fist against the table. "You have to put me back into my own world!"

"I cannot, Noah." She offered me a pitying glance. "Once one of your kind crosses over to the Plane of Gods, they can never go home."

Heat rose into my face as fury welled up inside me. Then, with a crashing wave of defeat, it faded from my body. I fell back into my seat, deflated. "How often does this kind of thing happen, Luna?"

"More often than it should." She reached across the table and rested her hand on mine. "If it makes you feel any better, most of those who pass over do not last long enough to suffer. Some do not even live long enough to find out what has happened to them."

That didn't make me feel better, but another thought did. "I was able to see David."

"Yet he could not see you. You are still transitioning. The people from your old home will fade from view with time."

I slouched deeper into my chair. Everything was just so... heavy. I used to only have to worry about sleeping through my calculus class. Now there were alternate planes of existence and monsters bent on destruction. I glanced up at Luna and saw a new determination about her.

She stood, walked across the room, and looked out the window. "How did you kill him, Noah? It should not have been possible."

It took me a minute to realize what she was talking about. "I swung a sharp piece of metal at him. He tried to dodge it and I stabbed him in the neck." I felt bad for editing the story, but a promise was a promise.

"No one has ever killed one of the five Chronographers, and they have used things much worse than a piece of metal. It does not make any sense. How can a son of man accomplish such a thing?" She went quiet, focusing on something down the street.

I moved to stand next her. The smell of lavender wafted from her rose-colored hair. I tried to find what she was looking at, but couldn't see anything of interest. Whatever she saw must have been very far away. It was almost like she was in some kind of trance.

Abruptly, she jerked her head back, almost as if she had been struck—but there was no one else in the room.

"Are you okay? You look pale... er."

She turned toward me, fear pushing her words. "We should go. The others are coming soon."

I dug through my clothes drawer, throwing two pairs of jeans and five pairs of underwear into a backpack. Luna was back at the window. She had changed out of the towel and was now wearing a pair of plaid pajama pants I hadn't worn in years and a white tank top my sister had left at the apartment after visiting me a while back. Her hair was tied back in a neat ponytail and her feet now sat in a pair of black running shoes. Above them, you could just make out the beginnings of her newly-washed red, striped knee socks. Despite the odd combination, she pulled it off quite nicely. It was the first time I had seen her out of baggy clothes. She was stunningly beautiful. Under that white skin was lean muscle, and although she looked like she couldn't have been any older than me, she exuded an aura of preparedness and experience.

I stared at the pile of clothes in my bedroom. I didn't know how much to take, but assumed I should pack light. Of my T-shirt collection, I took a France, Ireland, Saskatchewan (since it had brought me such good luck in the past) and, finally, a shirt that read, "Welcome to the Sunshine State." I wasn't sure how long it would be before I saw Florida again and the picture of the ocean on the front always calmed me.

After I stuffed the clothes into my backpack, I went into the bathroom and grabbed my electric toothbrush, toothpaste, and whatever other meager necessities I could find. I looked up at my reflection in the mirror. My hair was messy from sleeping on the couch. Knowing Luna had seen me like this was embarrassing. I splashed some water on it and straightened it out with my hands. When would I be able to look into a mirror again? I winked at myself and turned out the light.

I threw a pack of beef jerky in my bag and slung it over my shoulder. There wasn't much in the kitchen I could take with me. I figured potato chips would just get destroyed, and warm soda had never been my thing. I wished my sister would have left some granola bars after her visit. She was a bit of a health nut and it would have been the only thing I was sure my roommate would never touch.

I closed the fridge and plucked a picture of my family and me at Disney World off the door. We were standing in front of the castle—my mom, dad, sister, and I—all smiling while some actor dressed as a chipmunk gave a thumbs up to the camera. The thought of never seeing them again was almost too much to handle. I braced myself against the counter, wishing I could hear their voices one last time. I knew Luna had said no one from that world could interact with me in this one, but I decided it was worth a try.

I dropped the photo into my bag and picked up the cordless phone mounted on the wall. With a deep breath, I dialed my parent's number. I crossed my fingers as the first ring went by. On the second, I said a silent prayer. On the third ring, I heard the receiver pick up, but there was silence on the other end.

"Hello? Mom?"

Instead of the reply I was expecting—which frankly was none—a heavy mechanical sound began to chirp. I spoke louder into the receiver. "Shelly? Is that you?"

The chirp continued to rapidly grow in volume until I had to hold the earpiece out in front of me. The sound evolved into an earsplitting shriek. I dropped the phone and reeled back as every glass surface in the apartment began to vibrate. The noise was so intense, I could barely stand it. I cupped my hands over my ears. The whole apartment seemed to be shaking.

Suddenly, glasses exploded off the shelves. Shards rained down from every direction, battering my skin. The noise slithered its way between my fingers and attacked my senses. After it coiled itself around my head, it crawled all the way down my spine. It wasn't until I felt the stinging pain on my arms and the warm trickle of blood on my skin that I realized the sound had stopped.

Luna rushed into the kitchen, confusion and worry on her face. "What just happened?"

"I tried to call my parents," I yelled through the ringing in my ears.

"You WHAT?" The concern in Luna's face quickly turned to anger, and her comforting eyes darkened several shades.

"What were you *thinking*? It is not like she would have been able to hear you. You *do not* use phones, you *do not* use computers! Now he knows our location. There is little time." Luna ran over and pulled me forward.

I grabbed my backpack as she flung the front door open and raced into the hall. We hurried down the dilapidated corridor. The whole thing was painted an ugly brown and flakes chipped from the walls as we stomped by.

She stopped in front of the elevator and proceeded to jam the "down" button incessantly. "Why are these machines so slow? I swear. Your kind makes the most useless gadgets."

I didn't have time to be offended. A bright blue electric spark flickered from the button, lapping at Luna's finger. She quickly withdrew her hand as it burst from the console, rippling through the musty walls around us. We stood in silence as the lights flickered with the same contaminating blue glow. The generators whirred to a halt and the gentle hum of florescent lights faded to silence.

I looked at Luna through the azure dusk and saw terror on her face, the same look she'd had the night before when the smiling Colere had stepped onto the street corner with murder in his stride.

Luna stared at me. The color in her eyes had drained to a faint white and I knew there could only be one thing coming up that elevator.

Colere's relatives.

V

Even with all the power off in the building, the small elevator light was still blinking. Its red glow pierced through the dark room like a watchtower's warning—something's on its way, clear out the villagers.

I tapped Luna on the shoulder and she shook the frenzy from her head. With a deep breath, she grabbed my wrist and we headed back down the path. I had always thought it was stupid that the builders had put the emergency staircase on the opposite side of the building from the elevator, but right now I took comfort in the distance.

Luna turned to me as we hurried away from the rising elevator. "If it is who I think it is, we are in for some real trouble. He must have found us when you used the phone."

"Who is it?" I regretted asking as soon as I'd said it.

"Lojo," she spat, as if the word tasted awful. "He is one of the five Chronographers. He spends a lot of time on your side of the barrier."

"Luna, I don't understand. What exactly are the Chronographers?"

She looked back at the elevator, its light slowly approaching our floor. "It is a long story and there is not enough time to tell it now. Just know they are immeasurably dangerous and none of them can be killed."

"But I killed one." My voice sounded shrill and weak.

Luna stopped dead in her tracks. "That is correct. You did. That means that there are only four left. Now all we have to do is find out how a son of man can kill one of the most feared immortal creatures in existence and we shall be fine. Until then, I suggest we continue to run."

I couldn't tell if she was being serious or sarcastic. Besides, I was more concerned that she had said, "four left," but even that thought was pushed aside by the ominous ding of an elevator arriving at its desired floor.

We slowly turned as the double doors ground open and another blue spark sped from the aperture. It crawled spiderlike down the walls, detonating every light fixture and reducing the worn, chipped paint to cinders. The destruction was followed by a sudden gust of wind that knocked both Luna and me to the floor. The gale roared into the small space, scooping all the fallen debris into the air. I shielded my face from the second barrage of broken glass I'd faced today. The hail battered my arms and legs, renewing old wounds and opening fresh cuts in its wake. As the harsh beating of falling objects died down, I saw the epicenter of the storm that had just torn through the sixth floor of my former home.

In front of the elevator stood a strange man surrounded by light, but it wasn't from any lamp in the building. It was as if he was generating his own glow—fluorescent, like the kind used in old hospitals. I struggled to see the man through the eerie phosphorescence.

Lojo was wearing a pair of worn blue jeans and a gray hooded sweatshirt. The hood was up, resting over his face and shrouding it in darkness. However, in that darkness, his eyes—lambent in the shadow—glowed like two blue LED lights. The only skin visible on the strange killer's body was on his hands and bare feet, which poked out from underneath his frayed pants. His flesh looked pale to the point of translucence. Blue veins traced over his skin—deep and protruding—like a tangled mess of wires. He might've been tall if he didn't slouch so profoundly.

Electricity crackled as Lojo raised his head and the two shining lights grew brighter under the hood. His arms dangled lazily at his sides—palms forward—as tiny sparks resonated from his fingertips. With a heavy sway, Lojo ambled forward. His bare feet dragged across the stained carpet and he teetered drunkenly with every laborious step. His arms swayed with the momentum. Static-charged lightning jumped from the carpet to his fingers as he bobbed to and fro like an electrified metronome. He lurched ahead unnaturally—like his backbone was made from springs—and whenever he brushed close to the walls, the paint would turn black and crumble to ashes. The smell of ozone burned in my nostrils.

"Hello, Luna." His voice was emotionless and mechanical. It sounded like two pieces of metal being scraped together. "It would be easier if you did not flee."

I leaned over to Luna and whispered in her ear, "Don't listen to him. He's lying."

Luna rolled her eyes. "Thank you, Noah. You should be a military strategist."

We both sprang to our feet and bolted down the hallway. Another rippling shockwave roared behind us.

I swung open the door to the stairwell and together we ducked inside. I pressed a shoulder against the door as electricity and debris collided with the wall.

Luna nodded and we took to the stairs four at a time, leaping over garbage and using railings to make tight turns onto the next set. "Do you know if there is an overpass near here?" she asked as she nimbly dodged an abandoned bag of trash.

"This is Orlando. They're more common than trees. There's one a few blocks from this apartment."

Three flights up, the door to the stairwell exploded off its hinges and tumbled down the gap between the stairs, splitting the concrete as it slammed into the floor at the bottom. We both stopped and looked up as electricity crackled against the handrails like a Tesla coil. Two piercing LEDs looked down at us. A single translucent hand raised, blue veins shifting underneath the skin as muscles flexed. Our eyes met as the creature snapped his thin fingers. The stairs shook with the weight of the sound and the after-effect was immediate. As the deep baritone echoed off the walls, the air got thicker and dark mist crept in from the corners.

The hooded figure raised a lazy hand to the sky. The mist swirled over his arm and shot out, coiling together and spreading outward as it left his pale fingertips.

"We should probably move faster." Luna's matter-of-fact tone was scarier than if she'd screamed at the top of her lungs.

As we turned and ran down the remaining steps, a strange whirring rang out in the small space. Above, three thin pillars of smoke raced toward us, changing shape as they fell. Tiny, metal wings sprouted from the clouds and spinning propellers grew from their fronts, blowing the remaining mist from their sleek exteriors and revealing three small, silvery biplanes.

Nothing made sense anymore.

They maneuvered skillfully toward us in the cramped stairwell. The lead plane weaved through railings, barreling straight toward me.

I ducked at the last second and it careened into the adjacent wall. As the toy crumpled into the concrete, it unleashed a massive explosion. I lost my balance, flying forward into Luna. We tumbled down the stairs in a tangled pile of limbs and crashed onto the final landing.

Luna coughed violently and I cleared a large rock from my legs. Above, two vivid, blue lights peered through the gray shroud. Despite their lack of expression, I could tell there was nothing good behind them. Luna lifted me by the shoulder and we tumbled out the door into the bright sunlight. I'd never been so grateful to feel that humid, Orlando air. Luna took the lead and we made our way to the street.

I paused to look at the flickering phantoms blinking in and out of existence. They looked like normal people, but blurred, like ghosts. Was this what it was like to lose the ability to see other humans?

I did my best to ignore the strange apparitions and pointed Luna in the direction of the nearest overpass. Behind us, the whirring of the two remaining biplane explosives began to grow louder. I glanced back and saw one making its kamikaze dive straight for Luna. I lunged forward and pulled her to the sidewalk just as the deadly projectile soared past her head. The vehicle lost control and careened sideways into the road, exploding a few feet away from a ghostly pickup truck casually driving down the street. Shocked from the seemingly random explosion, the driver jerked the wheel, steering the truck directly toward us. Luna grabbed my collar and hoisted me out of the way as the rogue vehicle plowed through a fire hydrant and continued into the storefront of a crowded coffee shop.

Suddenly, the people who were barely visible flashed into full color. Frightened customers stampeded from the shattered building, stumbling over each other, away from the chaos. The broken fire hydrant sent a torrent of liquid into the air. The third biplane barreled into the stream, rocketing upward and detonating in the sky.

Luna and I continued to run as the crowd scattered around us. As they ran past, I could already see them fading from my vision. This allowed me to catch a glimpse of the man in the hooded jacket. He was turning the corner and heading straight toward us. We raced to the overpass, now just a block away. Behind us, muffled screams and the sounds of lampposts and neon signs exploding filled the air. I looked back and saw Lojo falling behind.

He stopped at the hydrant. Water rained from above and dissolved into a sizzling mist before it touched his papery skin.

I thought he had given up, but then I saw his eyes look toward the remains of the wrecked truck. With a nod, the engine began to screech back to life. The gears ground into reverse and the vehicle backed out of the crater it had made in the side of the building.

Lojo leaped nimbly into the truck bed. He placed a hand on the roof and the tires began to squeal. The high beams flicked on—like the eyes of a hungry predator—and it let out a vicious honk. It lurched from its grave and careened toward us.

"Luna, he's coming and he has a car."

"It is fine. We are almost there." She pointed to the overpass, now about fifteen feet away. The truck barreled toward us. Even if we did make it to the overpass I wasn't sure how it was going to help. Generations to come would see our imprint in the asphalt.

"Close your eyes," Luna called over the rumbling engine of the oncoming death machine as we reached the stone overhang.

The truck was so close now, I thought I could make out bits of Lojo's face from underneath his hood.

"Why?" It seemed like a silly question when I was about to die.

"Just trust me." She clasped her hand around mine.

It was more of an order than a request and I couldn't help but oblige. At the very least, I would die next to this beautiful girl.

I closed my eyes as we ran under the bridge. The sound of the truck was so loud it could have been on top of us already. It welled up and oppressed every one of my senses, and just when I was sure I could feel the steely teeth of the ruined vehicle, it grew quiet. The shrieks of the phantom people and roar of rushing water faded from our ears. The deep rumble of Lojo's zombie truck seemed to fall farther and farther behind us until all was replaced by the chirping of birds and a soft, dry wind.

VI

I opened my eyes. A rustic, dirt road surrounded by lush, green woods stood where the hard concrete and sprawling cityscape used to be. I was standing on the other side of an old, unused overpass. Thick ivy grew over the sides of the bridge and large chunks of worn rock lay dejectedly under their former home. I scanned the horizon but aside from the archaic road and seemingly endless expanse of woods, nothing extraordinary caught my eye. Evening shadow crept over the stone overhang and it looked as though dusk was settling in. I wondered how we had just lost a whole day.

Then I noticed the air.

It didn't have the same wetness that it should have had. It was actually fairly pleasant.

Questions stirred restlessly in my mind, but they were interrupted by the sudden flipping of my stomach. I slumped onto the ground—supporting myself on my hands and knees—and began to vomit.

"I am sorry. Traveling such a long distance by wishing bone often has unhealthy results for first-timers." Luna reached down and pulled a small, white "Y" from her striped sock. Down its center was a large crack. "Shoot! Barely one jump left in this one. It looks like we must travel on foot from here."

"What're you talking about?" I managed to say between heaves.

"Oh, right." She continued to examine the small bone. "I keep forgetting you are unfamiliar with this. Hmmm... how to explain? Traveling—as well as many other things—is based entirely on choices. When these choices are made, alternate universes are created based on the decisions not made. These universes only last a few seconds, but leave behind a lot of magical energy. At places where choices are made often, like near an overpass, someone can use that residual energy to jump great distances to other points of similar conductivity. That is, as long as they have one of these." She held up the wishbone.

I tried to listen to her explanation, but my attention wavered as I tried to remember if I'd eaten anything orange in the past day.

"In other words," she continued, "these places are gates and this wishing bone is the key. With it, we can cover great distances in very little time. Your kind has always been very keen at finding objects with magical properties. It is too bad you were never very good at using them. Then again, if the sons of man ever found out what a rabbit's foot could really do, there probably would not be as many of you around." Luna's laugh was a gentle chime but her sarcasm cut me to the bone.

"I am sooooo done with this," I grumbled, finally gaining some composure. "In the past day, I've been hit with a piece of the Parthenon, impaled by a cloud of light, thrown through a concrete wall, cut apart by glass *twice*, run down by the truck of the undead, and blown up by hobby shop toys. I'm staying right here."

"Oh, please." Luna looked at me like an amused mother. "You would not last an hour out here. I doubt you could even win a fight with gelatinous globster. If I were you, I would be more concerned about the injuries you sustain from constantly falling over. I swear, if I did not have to pick you up off the ground so much, we would have reached safety much earlier."

She turned away and headed toward a row of trees. "Besides, if you wait here, the vampires will pick up your scent and bleed you dry."

"Well, is there anything else I should hate here, Luna? You know, 'cause the list is getting pretty long."

"Stop it. You look fine. Now come on, I have a friend who can help us find out where to go next."

I wobbled to my feet—defeated—and followed her into the woods. As we left the old road behind us, I examined myself and found that she was right. I barely had a scratch on me, yet I had vivid memories of a few nasty cuts sustained in the last day or so. Luna had said that jumping between places of great choices put us there quickly—wasting only a little time. Our trip had only lasted an afternoon, not nearly time enough for me to heal. I had once scuffed up my knee falling off my bike and that had continued to bleed for over a week. So how had the deep scratches on my arm healed without even leaving a scar in such a short time? Not to mention the distinct memory of broken bones after the fight with Colere. There was so much going on that I didn't understand.

I looked back toward where the dusty road had been. All I could see now was an army of trees standing at attention in their green and brown uniforms. We plowed through the overgrown brush and ventured deeper into the woods. I wondered how it had been possible for Lojo to find us so quickly. The phone thing was pretty obvious, but Luna had known he was coming long before that. So what was stopping him from appearing out of a rabbit hole and asking us for the time? Despite Luna's obvious annoyance with me, I decided now was as good a time as any to get the answers to some of my questions.

"Luna, I think it's time you told me who these Chrono guys are. What do they want?"

She stood still for a moment and after a long pause, she began to tell the story. "A long time ago—before the world was separated in two—there was a small village of men... but there also lived one man in particular. He was blessed with great intelligence and was revered by all those around him. One day, he told the townspeople that he would journey out in search of the gods and ask them to share their knowledge with all the people. The town rejoiced and off he went.

"After a great journey, the man found the gods and made his request. They deemed it honorable and decided it was time to share their gifts with mortals. The gods gave the man fire and sent him back to his people. When the man returned, he claimed he had stolen the fire from the gods himself. The townspeople celebrated and all shared in this great knowledge."

I was captivated by the way she spoke. I hurried over a tangle of roots to get closer, but it seemed like her mind was somewhere else. Her radiant eyes gazed upward through the gaps in the canopy. I fell in beside her as she continued.

"But time passed and the man became accustomed to the constant praise. He began to fear that his people would one day forget about his contribution. He decided it was time to return to the gods. When the man reached the gods once more, he demanded they give him all the world's knowledge—that it was only fair for them to share. The gods were already angry that the man had lied about their first gift, but they were fond of meddling in the affairs of mortals and decided to make him a deal. They would not give him all the knowledge at once—that would be too much for one man to bear. Instead, they would grant him immortality. He would have to spend his life acquiring all the knowledge in the world and to aid him, the gods created the five Chronographers."

I tripped over an exposed root but caught myself before I hit the ground. "So that's who we've pissed off?"

"Precisely." Luna smirked at my bumbling. "The five Chronographers were made to collect all the knowledge the world has to offer. They are invulnerable and immortal. They are ruled by the singular desire to accomplish this task, and when they have gathered all the knowledge to be obtained from a certain place, they destroy it to prevent further knowledge from accumulating—Rome, Atlantis, the Lemurian Empire, all destroyed by the Chronographers. The one you saved me from, Colere, demolished those three empires. He was known as an extremely thorough and precise worker." She cringed at some unspoken memory. Before I could ask what was wrong, she stopped and looked right at me. "You killed him, though. Somehow, you were able to kill a... a thing that I once watched walk through an entire army without sustaining as much as a scratch." Wonderment dazzled about her.

I tried not to blush, but I could feel the warmth in my cheeks. I changed the subject. "What about the little Red Barons we faced down on the stairs? Where did those come from?"

The diversion worked. Luna shook the dreaminess from her eyes and pushed a large branch out of her way. "We do not know everything, but it seems like whatever a Chronographer takes, he can call back—like how Colere brought up those marble columns from the sidewalk. As long as they destroyed the object themselves, they can re-create it simply by snapping their fingers and summoning the nostalgia."

"The nostalgia?" I hopped over a medium-sized rock, concentrating hard to retain my footing.

"It is the strange mist that the Chronographers call to their aid. Inside the nostalgia is everything they have ever taken. I have even heard they have specific things they like to collect. Colere was a fan of architecture and the ways in which all creatures interact. The customs of other species fascinated him, as well. This interest made it easy for him to gain others' trust. The second one we saw—Lojo— seems to favor technology. There is a story where he—"

She was interrupted by the loud rustling of branches to our left. We both stopped dead in our tracks. The low snarl of a creature carried on the warm, night breeze. I started to move in front of Luna, but everything happened too fast. Something plopped to the earth from the canopy above. It landed in a small poof of dust and looked up at us with its large, adorable eyes.

I had never seen a koala in real life before, and none of the wildlife documentaries could do it justice. The gray, chubby ball of fur propped itself up onto all fours and flopped onto its large butt. It pawed about a pile of leaves and raised one to its black, oval nose. Its face crinkled as it sniffed.

I clasped my hands over my mouth to avoid making involuntary cute noises. "Awwwwww! It's adorable." I knelt down to get a better look. The koala tilted its head in amusement. "Luna, are you seeing this? I didn't even know there were koalas in North America." I looked back and saw the look of sheer horror on Luna's face. She was slowly backing away from the fluff ball, reaching down to pick up a large stick.

"Get. Back. Noah."

"Oh, come on. He's no threat. He's just a cute ole' koala bear." I began walking toward the little guy, even though I could hear Luna's protests behind me. I reached down to pat the critter's head, but it jerked away before I could touch it.

"Noah, watch out!"

The koala let out a hiss and its head opened like a Pez dispenser. Four rows of razor sharp teeth snapped at my outstretched hand. Luna lunged forward and batted the demonic marsupial away.

Just another entry in the list of things I hated here.

"What did I tell you? I have no idea what a 'koala' is, but that is a drop bear."

"A what?" I was still trying to regain my composure after what I'd just seen.

"A ravenous creature that likes nothing better than tearing flesh from bone. They drop from trees and eat your head."

The creature wiggled back up the thick tree trunk from which it had come. As it climbed, several more trees began to shake with an unknown weight. I snatched up a branch to defend myself. Something heavy dropped from above. I looked up and saw the white glimmer of teeth rapidly descending.

Luna's bat swung above my head, launching the creature into the woods. Several more bears began falling from the branches, gargantuan teeth chattering as they waddled toward us. Gracefully,

Luna began twirling and weaving through the attackers, striking them as she passed by.

I watched her nimbly dodge the falling piranha and riposte a strike in return. Meanwhile, two drop bears fell in front of me. I swung wildly at the first one, which clamped its jaws onto the stick. I lifted the pole and swung it upward in a wide arc, sending the bear soaring into the bushes. I kicked toward the second but it snapped back, almost grabbing my shoe.

"Do not use anything but your weapon," Luna called over the thumps of falling sacks of fur. "If they bite you, it is over." She rolled through two lunging bears, which collided into one another. As soon as they latched on, they began to tear each other apart. It wasn't a pretty sight.

More and more drop bears filled the small outcropping. I continued my efforts but the koalas just kept coming. Even Luna's precise and powerful strikes seemed to do no more than temporarily stun the creatures. Soon, we were standing back to back as a mob of toothy carnivores tottered around us.

"I don't think we're gonna make it through this one," I warned while poking the remains of my stick at the lead koala.

"Do not talk like that. We will fight until it is over."

Her confidence was nice, but the scene seemed self-explanatory. Even as the gray wave of fur grew closer, more drop bears continued to pour from the trees, snapping their grotesque jaws as they advanced.

Somewhere in the forest, a howl rang out. All the bears stopped and looked around, confused. Others immediately started scrambling back into the surrounding brush. Something large burst from the undergrowth and barreled through a group of attackers.

Claws flashed and two drop bears went limp. The thing careened back into the woods, tumbling the small creatures out of its way. The remaining bears turned fluffy tail and ran. In a matter of seconds, we were alone in the clearing once again.

I was about to breathe a sigh of relief when—quick as an arrow—a brown blur leaped from the bushes. It plowed into Luna, pinning her to the forest floor. I whipped around, brandishing the large piece of wood, but it was too late.

Luna let out a high pitched scream followed by series of shrill... giggles?

I regrouped and looked again.

A large dog was lapping at Luna's face and she was laughing like a little girl. "Chip!" Luna gasped between laughs. "Please, I cannot take it."

"Sorry," the dog whimpered in its strange accent that seemed vaguely Russian. "We are just so happy to see you again." The dog released her and began to stand... and stand... and continued to stand until he was seven feet of hairy man/dog creature. Actually, he was more like a wolf. He was covered in thick, brown fur from head to toe, and muscular in the same measurements. His strong back tore upward and curved sharply forward like a furry question mark. He had the long snout of a wolf and his mouth was filled with sharp teeth, but his face was intelligent and caring, like a child. He turned his gaze on me. His nose twitched and a flash of anger wrinkled his snout.

I raised my weapon in defense and his demeanor... changed to joy?

"Is that a stick?" Chip's tail wagged uncontrollably. "Please throw it! We love to chase the stick."

I obliged and threw my splintered weapon into the bushes. Chip bounded happily after it—a large, giddy two-legged dog.

"So who is this guy?" I asked Luna while watching Chip leap an overturned tree to return the stick.

"He is a werewolf. They have... um... personality issues. They have the mind of both a human and an animal, which is why he refers to himself as 'we.' He may be a little odd, but Chip is a friend of my family."

I had never thought of Luna's family before. I wondered what they were like and if they might be worried about her. Thinking back, I realized she had never mentioned them until now.

When Chip brought the stick back the third time, I refused to pick it up. A slimy film had enveloped the entire branch and the game was no longer fun on my end.

Luna approached the huge beast and scratched the side of his face. One large foot thumped the earth, shaking the forest around us. "Chip," Luna cooed, "would you mind taking us to your home?"

"We would do anything for the Lady Luna, especially if the rumors are true." Then Chip looked at me and his kind voice became rugged and angry. "We don't approve of this one, though. We would like to tear his flesh apart and pick our teeth with his bones. He reeks of the unspeakables."

Luna looked at me hard, like she was seeing something that hadn't been there before. "He can be trusted, Chip. He saved me from one of them."

"We do not argue with the Lady Luna. We will bring her home safely." Chip turned and lumbered off, gesturing with his long muscular paw to follow.

Luna hurried to his side. They laughed and joked in a way I had not seen since I'd met her.

I wished I could have been up there with her. The exchanges between them seemed like something coveted and it made me feel lonely in this strange world. As we continued onward, I noticed Luna looking back at me several times—studying me as we batted away low hanging branches and climbed over old rocks. I tried not to look at her as we continued on. I walked silently behind them the rest of the way.

* * *

Night had fully set in when we reached a clearing. I didn't know what to expect from Chip's home—a log cabin or possibly a cave. What I saw was an old, boxy Winnebago—complete with satellite dish and folding lawn chairs. It was white in the places it wasn't dented or covered with dirt. Black stripes were crudely painted down the side—presumably to make it go faster—and a large awning was pulled out over the passenger side.

Chip opened the door and ducked down to enter. I gave Luna a cautious glance and she nodded.

The inside of the vehicle was actually pretty nice, considering an animal lived in it. Faux wooden cupboards and counter tops lined the edges of the mobile home. The tan walls were adorned with several pictures of mountain scenery, and the single, small, blue couch that pressed against the wall looked comfortable enough. In the back, a small alcove led to a bedroom, but I couldn't see inside because of the beaded curtain that hung in front of the entranceway. Overall, the mobile home was fairly mundane... except for the pillows. Almost every inch of the old carpet was covered with pillows of every shape and size.

I stepped over a large green one with frilled edges and almost slipped on the rubber chew toy underneath.

Chip masterfully weaved through the pillow gauntlet and opened his fridge. He handed Luna and me bottles of water then lowered his huge, hairy body onto a set of cushions in the corner of the bus. He gestured for us to sit on the blue couch.

I brushed a half-chewed bone off the seat—wondering what it could have possibly come from—and sat down.

As Luna took her place, Chip smiled. "It makes us happy to have the lady in our home, even if she brings us vermin as well."

This time Luna smiled. "He is my friend, Chip, and I told you, he saved me from one of the five."

"It's true then? A man-son has killed one of the unspeakables?" His voice grew deep as he turned toward me. "Did you rip out his throat, Man-Son?"

"Not really." I gulped. "I kinda hit him with a pipe."

"Really?" He pondered my words for a moment and then nodded. "It makes sense. We don't think anyone has tried that before."

Luna cleared her throat to get his attention. "Chip, I assume you know what has happened to my family."

Chip's shoulders sank and he began to whimper. "We are sad to hear what has happened to the children of the moon. Much howling we did when we heard."

Luna nodded and spoke with a tenuous composure. "Well, then, I would appreciate your help. I believe what is left of the Five will continue to pursue me until the celestial bloodline is destroyed and our powers are stolen. We must seek out the one who hears all. You were once the greatest tracker our family knew, and although you have been away all this time, I would like your aid in finding him."

Chip's ears rose and he stiffened to attention. His head brushed against the mobile home's ceiling. "We do not like to leave here. Much peace these woods have brought us. Tennessee has been kind."

"Tennessee? You mean like the sixteenth state? Is there a souvenir stand nearby? I don't think I have a shirt from here." Both of them stared at me. "Or not."

Luna turned back to Chip. "I know you are at home here, but I need your help. It will be like old times."

Chip sat for a moment, and then the large, doggish smile appeared again. "We will find the listener for you and we will rip out the throats of those who get in our way."

"Good!" Luna clapped her hands together. "I would like to leave in the morning. Noah and I have had a rough day."

"Then we will gather supplies for the trip." And with that, Chip stood up as much as he could in the small space and walked out the door into the forest.

I turned to Luna. "Seriously, are there any T-shirt stands around here?"

She rolled her eyes and walked toward the back of the bus.

I rinsed my electric toothbrush off and spit into the sink. I had insisted that Luna take the couch while I slept on the floor with Chip's pillows. They reeked of dog and I had to rub them against the counters to get all the hair off. I dug a small trench in the mountain of cushions and created my own little cocoon on the floor.

This is what my life has become.

In the blink of an eye, I had gone from a sub-par college student to a fragile "son of man" wanted for the murder of an immortal history professor. Still, there was something cool about being in Tennessee. I'd never even driven out of the state and now I was teleporting halfway across the country using nothing more than a wishbone. I lay there for a while, listening to the melodic sound of crickets chirping and the soft hoot of an owl. It was so different than the city. I felt bad I wouldn't be spending more time here to get to know the place.

I tossed and turned for most of the night. It wasn't that my makeshift bed was uncomfortable, I just couldn't fall asleep—something quite odd for me. Normally, falling asleep was almost too easy. It wasn't unusual for David to have to shake me awake for my turn at the bowling alley. I was such a deep sleeper that my mom used to come into my room in the morning to see if I was still breathing.

After a while, I leaned on my elbow and looked toward the couch were Luna slept. I decided to ask the question that had been on my mind since Chip had left. "Hey, Luna." There was a grumble from somewhere above. "Are you awake?"

"I am now, Noah. What do you want?"

"I just wanted to know what happened to your parents. You said something was wrong with your family."

She remained silent for another minute. A waning crescent moon floated loftily outside—its light drifting down to meet Luna's eyes, which mimicked the appearance of the celestial body. It was an eerie look, but also strangely appealing—like looking into the sky of an alien planet with foreign orbs staring back.

"They were... killed, not too long ago."

"By Colere." It was a statement more than a question.

Luna said nothing for a moment, and then she sighed. "Yes, my family has a particular gift. We can see things—brief glimpses into the future."

"Like when we were being chased last night; it was too dark to see the road but you knew where to go."

"And I also knew Lojo was coming before you made that phone call. The ability is spread throughout my bloodline. The larger my family is, the weaker the ability tends to manifest. Because of this, my people are hesitant to have children. My parents and I were the last of the celestials. We tried to remain hidden but Colere found us. When he arrived, not even the entire castle guard was able to stop him."

I remembered the vision I had seen when Colere had died—a crumbling castle village and towers falling to the earth. Was that where Luna had come from? Actually, she did have a very regal quality about her. The way she spoke and moved were of a higher class. Was it because I'd first seen her dirtied and beaten that I'd missed it for so long? I stared at her for a moment, stunned. "Luna, are you royalty?"

She gave a small, wry smile.

"But what about the knee-high socks and the baggy clothes? Why aren't you wearing a dress or a crown or something?"

"You sound like my mother. I may not look it, Noah, but I am the last survivor of a royal bloodline, which means I am the last piece to achieving total foresight. I believe the master of the Chronographers wants that power. It would speed up his quest to learn everything."

"Is that so bad?" I wondered aloud, looking out the window toward the thin sliver of a moon. "If their master learned everything, wouldn't that be it?"

Luna's expression darkened and she turned toward me. "No one has seen the master of the Chronographers since he made his deal with the gods. Many think it is that search for knowledge that keeps him from showing himself. If he gained complete understanding, he would be free to pursue any other goals he desired. Think of someone with the power of five Lojos. He could take over both planes of existence, maybe even overthrow the gods."

I thought about that for a while. Staring up at the ceiling, I imagined the things society had lost because a few deranged historians had decided they had taken everything a place had to offer. What scientific advancements had Lojo stolen? What else did Colere do before I had ended his long life? I imagined the city of Rome burning to the ground as a statuesque, dark-haired man casually waded through the fire and rubble, smiling all the while. Now what if someone like that took over the world? It was hard to fathom.

But I had killed Colere, so didn't that mean I could kill the others? Could I protect Luna? Heck, I could barely save her from an army of vicious teddy bears. How long had she run alone before she came across me? There had to be something I could do to help.

"Luna, does the man who's doing all this have a name?"

Silence weighed down on the room for several minutes. I turned my head and saw raw anger trace an outline over Luna's soft face.

"Prometheus—the man who brought fire from the gods."

"Prometheus." I tested the weight of the name. I rolled over on my pillow, away from her quiet fury. I closed my eyes and tried to let sleep take me. Instead, I found myself lying awake for hours, just on the edge of relief.

A wolf's howl carried over the night air.

Prometheus—the man we had to stop.

TWO

I sat in a worn, steel chair. I tried to move my arms but they were heavy and hollow. I looked about the familiar room full of unfamiliar things. Impossible combinations of architecture sprawled out over the cavernous amphitheater. A few feet away, an ornate fountain spewed water from the hollow sockets of a human skull held in the chubby hands of a stone cherub.

The man with timeless eyes stood in front of me, his hands intertwined behind his back.

This must be Prometheus.

There was no one else who could look so young but harbor so much age under the surface.

Two blue lights pierced the darkness from the silhouette kneeling before him. "I am impressed they eluded your capture, Five." Prometheus watched the groveling figure like a child evaluating a broken toy. He spoke to Five—the one I knew as Lojo—with cold amusement.

"I am sorry, Father. Their actions were unpredictable. For an orphaned seer, she is very resourceful. As for the son of man, he will fall easily. Their breed is an inferior lot."

Anger flushed Prometheus's face.

I tried to turn away to escape the intensity of it, but my body wouldn't comply. Images of crumbling cities flitted through my mind; the wail of an infant—left alone in the woods—rang loudly in my ears. I desperately tried to cover them—anything to keep out the noise—but I couldn't lift my hands. I mentally clawed my insides, trying to tear open the shell of my skin so the pain could be released back into the room. In reality, I watched silently until the unyielding assault faded away.

A new calm surrounded Prometheus.

Out of the corner of my eye, I saw a tiny stream of water flow over the edge of the fountain. It trickled over the multicolored tile, winding its way toward Lojo. When it touched the back of his heel, it began to expand. The Chronographer fell forward—startled—and attempted to swat the offending water away. Slowly, the tide crept over his legs and up his body, enveloping him in its current. Lojo began to spark and thrash about wildly, but it was no use. In a matter of seconds, the killer was floating helplessly in a glassy orb of liquid. He grabbed for his throat beneath the gray hood and let out a wail, but instead of sound, a flurry of bubbles spewed from his mouth as his lungs filled with water.

"Do not forget that I, too, was once a son of man. You should also remember the boy may have killed One, your brother, but I can do much, much worse." He waved his hand and the water unfolded, giving birth to a gasping, drenched Lojo.

"Yes, Father." He spewed water onto the tile.

"You are forgiven. I would not punish one of my own for such a trivial matter. There will be more chances for you and your siblings to accomplish your task. Besides, there will always be five immortals to bring me the world's knowledge, something our young troublemaker will soon find out."

Prometheus glanced over his shoulder.

My heart stopped beating in my chest.

His gaze surged outward and coiled itself around my entire body.

I doubled over in pain.

"Isn't that right, Noah?"

VII

I awoke in a panic, clutching my chest. My sides heaved until, with a shuddering cough, the ache began to subside.

"Noah, are you all right?" My eyes darted around the RV. Luna sat cross-legged in the middle of the floor, stuffing folded clothes into my backpack.

"I'm fine. It was... just a nightmare." But was it? I had paid little attention to the first dream, but both had seemed so real. Was Prometheus really that powerful? To defeat the man who'd almost brought us to the brink of death without so much as batting an eye must have required a huge amount of power.

I remembered everything so clearly: the shrill cry in my ears, the huge sphere of water, Lojo's gurgling breath. I remembered something else, too. What had he meant about there always being five Chronographers? I thought Colere's death looked pretty permanent, and I doubted I could take him in a fight where he wasn't holding back.

The Winnebago swerved and the horn honked. Confused, I peeked out the window and saw other cars passing by.

"We decided to get started while you slept. I figured your kind needs more sleep than the rest of us."

"Oh, thanks." I was unsure whether to take it as an insult or a compliment.

Luna nodded happily and continued stuffing things into my backpack.

I noticed there was a significant lack of pillows on the floor outside of my small hovel. Most had been neatly stacked in corners and around the edges of the vehicle. In fact, it looked like someone had tidied up the whole cabin. The musty smell of damp fur had been replaced with something a tad more pine fresh, and the thin carpet of wolf hair had been swept away.

I began piling the pillows I had used the night before into a free corner next to the couch.

Luna lifted up one of my shirts and examined the squat leprechaun on the front, waving a rainbow that spelled out "Ireland." She shook her head and placed it into the backpack. Her hair was wrapped up in a tight bun and it bounced against her head as she went about her work. She pulled out a bra and wedged it into the side pocket of my bag.

"Hey!" I abandoned my tower of cushions. "That is definitely *not* mine."

She looked at the lace brassiere and began to laugh. "I know, stupid. It is mine. I figured you would not mind if I put some of my things in your pack."

"Oh, yeah. I guess it's fine. Do you need help folding anything?"

Luna passed me a small stack of clothes. She lifted another shirt into the air and examined it. "You have a lot of clothes from different places. Did you used to travel often?"

It was my turn to laugh. "Actually, I've never gone anywhere before all this. Buying the shirts just made me feel like I was part of the world at large. I'm sure you know what I mean. I bet you've traveled all over the place, being a princess and all."

Luna folded a long, striped sock and placed it on top of the stack. "No, my father was pretty insistent I stay near the castle grounds. I did everything I could to defy him, though. Chip was often my accomplice."

"Chip? So you guys have been friends a long time?"

"Oh, yes. Ever since I was young."

The thought of the two of them together was funny. What would it have been like to run around the neighborhood with a werewolf instead of David? Hide-and-seek would have been kind of unfair, but at least bullies wouldn't have been an issue.

"I don't think Chip likes me very much."

"Nonsense. He is just very protective of me. I am sure when he gets to know you like I have, he will loosen up. You should go sit up front with him—talk to him like he is already your friend. Maybe you will find something in common."

I nodded and set the last piece of clothing in the bag. Wobbling to my feet, I pushed forward as the Winnie cruised down the highway. After a few embarrassing stumbles, I finally reached the front. Chip sat in the driver's seat, wearing a worn baseball cap with ear holes cut out of the top and aviator sunglasses.

"These cars move like squirrels," he barked. "We want to rip them apart."

"Whoa there, Chip. You seem a little stressed."

The big wolf glanced at me in the rear-view mirror. "Our head itches but we must keep our eyes on the road."

"Well, I can help you with that." I reached over the old hat and scratched Chip behind the ear.

His leg began to twitch and the mobile home lurched forward suddenly. "Whoops, sorry."

I scratched lower and he thanked me. Proud of my first steps toward friendship, I took up the copilot position. "So... um... where are we headed?"

"To Kansas. That is where our nose tells us." Chip raised his snout into the air and sniffed while pointing to his nose. "We should be in Missouri soon, but many hours remain on our trip."

It was nice to know that, at the very least, the names of states were the same. I leaned back and watched the open road fly by. "So, what's in Kansas?"

"The listener. He hears all that is said and he will help the Lady Luna find what she needs." Chip swerved around an older automobile with no doors. I was a little surprised at how crowded the roads were—an assortment of beaten-up vehicles surrounded us.

"If there are no humans, why are there so many cars?"

Chip scoffed. "Well, first the sons pump them full of dragon's essence, and then they leave them out to rot. What did you think was going to happen?"

I didn't feel like that was a very good answer. I leaned out the window to get a better look at the driver of the doorless clunker we'd just passed. The angle was weird, but it looked like no one was in it.

"Um, I can't see the driver of that car."

"That is because there is no driver."

I did a double take and stared at Chip for a long time. "You mean... the car is alive?"

"Of course. What do you think happens when you pour the blood of great beasts into something?"

"The blood of great beasts? Dragon's essence? What are you talking about?"

Chip gave a gruff laugh. "You man-sons are so simple. You fill your cars with the remains of ancient creatures to make them move and don't expect any repercussions."

"The remains of— do you mean gas? Like fossil fuels?" The thought was almost too ridiculous to say aloud. I knew gasoline contained some biological materials from decayed animals that lived billions of years ago, but I never thought there could be anything magical about dead dinosaurs.

"Call it what you will, little son, but when you give something the blood of ancient beasts then abandon it in some trash heap with a full belly, it eventually becomes magic, and magic things can't live on your side of the world. Instead, they end up here.

"Then what about this one?" I pointed to the center console of the Winnebago.

Chip rubbed a fuzzy paw on the dashboard. "She's special, is she not? We are the only ones she will let drive her." Without so much as touching the steering wheel the car gave two loud honks. I almost jumped out of my seat. "That is right, Thalia. It is you who drives Chip."

Thalia's style of driving was something to witness. I wasn't sure what I'd expected from a half-beast motor vehicle, but it definitely wasn't this. The car followed the speed limit for the most part, but if another car swept past us, Thalia would switch lanes and pursue. It reminded me of a cat chasing bugs. She would swerve between lanes, flashing her brights and honking at anything and everything.

"Why does it keep doing that?" I finally asked as she nearly side-swiped a particularly fast motorcycle.

"What do you mean?"

I looked at Chip, agitated. "This car is a terrible driver. If you took full control of it, we would probably get where we're going in half the time."

Chip furrowed his bushy eyebrows and heavy creases appeared on his forehead. He wrapped both gigantic hands around the steering wheel and stared angrily off into the distance.

"Thalia is not an *it*; she is a she. You may think you're smart, and you may think you're strong, but you still are unpleasant to us. If it weren't for the Lady Luna, we would break your spine and drink your fluids."

"Jeez. Got it. You're big and tough 'til you need your head scratched."

"Be quiet, the both of you." Luna leaned over the two seats. The once tight bun was half undone and she looked pale and a little green. "Chip, pull over. Now." Chip obliged and we pulled onto the side of the road. We all sat, waiting for her to explain what the fuss was about.

Finally, I decided to ask.

"Luna, what are we waiting for?"

"Hush! Just one more moment... There!"

A small creature tumbled out of the woods. We watched the little critter take several steps from the tree line before crumpling face first into the dirt.

VIII

Luna leapt through the door as soon as the creature hit the ground. Chip and I followed behind. She dropped to her knees and cradled the thing's scaly head in her lap. I experienced a moment of joy; the creature resembled one of my favorite childhood cartoons. It looked as though someone had crossed a turtle with a short man. Long limbs gave it an almost human appearance, while the flat face and beaklike mouth reminded me of a snapping turtle. It even seemed to have the beginnings of a shell on its back.

"I had a vision. I saw this kappa stumble out from the woods and die."

"Then we have no business here." Chip turned to go back to the RV.

"Chip, I may have lost my castle, but my duties are still the same. So how about we have a little less negativity and a little more help? Go fetch a bottle of water from Thalia and make sure it is sealed."

Chip shuffled back into Thalia, leaving me alone with Luna and the beaked reptile. As the sun hit its scales, they glinted from green to yellow.

"So, what is this thing?"

"It is a kappa. They guard bodies of water. This one seems to be dehydrated."

Chip appeared behind us, handing Luna a water bottle. She undid the cap and poured it over the kappa's skin. For a while, nothing happened. Then its beak snapped open with a dull clack. The creature in Luna's lap reached its webbed hands up and brought the bottle to its mouth. It drank every drop in a matter of seconds.

"Thank youuuu," the creature croaked. He looked up at the woman who had saved him and gasped. "A celestial! We are savedddd."

"Who is saved, little one?" Luna cooed.

The kappa looked up at her with its big, round eyes then rolled over, crawling to its feet. The stout turtle only reached Luna's waist at full height. "Please, Lady. My name is Kappadowri. My village has fallen to a terrible blight. But if you come, you could fix everythinggg."

"I cannot guarantee results, Kappadowri, but I can try. Please lead us back to your   village."

Kappadowri gave a tiny jump of delight before he straightened his loincloth and waddled back into the woods. Kappadowri assured us that the village wasn't very far from the road. He grasped Luna's hand and led us down a weathered path through the trees.

Chip groaned but it was cut short by Luna's stern look.

I hopped back into the Winnie, grabbed my backpack, and rushed to catch up with the group. We walked in single file for about an hour. Every so often, Chip would smell something and dive off into the woods. I didn't mind, but considering we were being chased by immortal killers, I really wanted to know where the werewolf was.

On a particularly long disappearance, I decided to spark up a conversation with Luna. "So... you had a vision about all this?"

"No, not about us. Only about him. I saw him walking through the forest, half dead. If we do not help him, I am afraid his whole village will share the same fate."

"Do they hurt?"

Luna looked at me, puzzled.

"The visions, do they hurt?"

"Oh, I would not describe them as painful. They are more like being splashed with very cold water while sleeping."

"Less talkingggg," Kappadowri scolded us. "We are hereeee."

Light broke through the treetops, enveloping everything in a bright glow. Large, triangular teepees were scattered about the glade and a dirty, brown river bisected it down the center. We approached a large tree at the edge of the camp. A withered, human-like figure was tied to its trunk with a thick rope. As we passed in front of the skeletal corpse, it opened its blood red eyes. They looked at me—and only me—as we were led by. I felt uneasy as we walked away, knowing that the thing was still staring holes into the back of my head. I hurried to the front of the group as we were led to a particularly large orange tent.

Kappadowri swung the flap open for us and we went inside.

It was surprisingly roomy in the teepee. A fat kappa rested in the corner and a haze of incense lingered above our heads. It gave the whole room the smell of musty, old flowers.

The heavy turtle lifted his head to see who had entered. A necklace of sharp teeth rattled around his throat. He spoke in an ancient, labored voice. "Who have you brought me, Kappadowriiii?"

Our escort dropped to one knee. I noticed that he, too, wore a necklace of sharp teeth. However, his only had two teeth compared to the old one's ten.

"Kappazion, I have brought the young celestial. She can surely end our plagueeee."

The elder squinted hard through the haze. "Indeed, you have. Please, leave me to consult with our guestttt."

Kappadowri bowed low and shuffled out of the tent, leaving Luna and I alone with the elder. The old one reached over and lit a long, wooden pipe. He took several puffs from it and added a new cloud to the already standing fumes.

"Please, Princess, why don't you have a seatttt?" He gestured to an empty spot with a long, webbed finger.

We lowered ourselves to the ground.

The turtle took another long puff from his pipe. He sat in silence, waiting for something. "Excuse me, Son of Man. Do you mind if I have a talk with the princess aloneeee?"

I looked toward Luna who gave a reassuring nod. "Sure, why not? I'll be outside." I dipped through the curtain and stepped back out into the sunlight.

At the edge of the clearing, Chip and several kappas came wandering forward. "Does this mongrel belong to youuuu?" It was a burly kappa that spoke. Large muscles moved under his scales and his shell looked particularly hard. He wore several full-toothed necklaces.

"Yes, he does. Did he do something wrong?"

71

"He's trespassing. Make sure he is well behaved while in our villageeee. We are tired of dealing with all the trash that washes up on the banks of our streammmm."

The agitated kappa walked off, leaving Chip behind.

"They look small, but they gave us a good fight," Chip muttered, rubbing the back of his head with a long paw. I watched the burly warrior walk away.

"Who was that guy anyway?"

"That is Kappadarmaaaa," said Kappadowri, coming over to meet us. "He was the greatest hunter in the villageeee. You can tell by all the necklaces he wears. Most villagers have lost count. Then the outsider came and killed many beasts for the tribeeee."

I looked toward the man tied to the tree and pointed with my thumb. "You mean him?"

"Yes. He came a few weeks ago and joined our clan, but the water spirit became angry and stopped purifying the riverrrr. We kappa need the purest water to survive. Without it, we will all dieeee."

"I see. So that's why you tied him up?"

"Until we can figure out what we must do with him to appease the water spirit, that is where he will remainnnn." Kappadowri bowed and waddled after the rest of the hunting party.

I turned to Chip. "Any thoughts?"

Chip remained still for a moment. "The water has become undrinkable and we can see how a spirit would be upset by a bloodsucker."

"Whoa, the guy on the tree is a vampire? I guess that explains why he's been staring at me. Come on, Chip. Let's go talk to him."

We walked over to the vampire. He looked weak and was missing most of his right ear. His deep-set eyes lifted as we approached. They locked onto mine and stayed there until we stood next to him. He looked away from me before he spoke. "Do you have something you would like to pin on me as well?" The venom in the pale creature's voice was apparent.

"I assume that means you don't think you were responsible for the whole water fiasco?"

"Of course not. I came here to find relief. To escape the... well... to escape certain things. I found these kappas and offered to hunt with them. One second they're praising me for being the best hunter the village has ever had and the next, they're calling me a demon, saying I offended the water spirit."

"Sounds unfair."

"I'm a vampire, wolf. Life is unfair."

Luna emerged from the elder's tent and waved to us.

"Looks like Luna has finished her talk. We should see what's going on." As we turned to walk away, I could hear the vampire struggling against his ropes.

"Wait, Son of Man." I turned back, curious about the pleading tone in his voice. The vampire's eyes had become completely red. His fangs were bared—long and pearl white—exposed to the bright sun. He pushed away hard from the tree and the ropes ground against the bark. When he realized it was futile, his whole body went limp. "Nothing. Forget it."

I walked over to the small group that gathered around Luna and Kappazion.

The old turtle looked over the small congregation and motioned for silence. "It appears fortune has finally smiled on ussss," he croaked to the gathered crowd. "The celestial princess did not come here on accident. It is our final chance to repent for our wicked wayssss." He leaned on his stick and turned toward Luna. "Will you go to the sacred cave of the water spirit when the sun sets and ask him to forgive us and once again let clean water flowwww?"

Luna knelt down on one knee and put her arm on the old kappa's shoulder. "Yes, Kappazion, I will do as you ask. My companions and I will travel to your shrine and bring clean water back to the village."

Only one short warrior complained. When he stepped forward, his many necklaces rattled loudly. "This is absurddd. We were punished for allowing an outsider to taint our camp and now we are allowing three to go into our most sacred placeeee?" Kappadarma shook his head furiously. "We are only asking for more trouble on our headssss."

"NO!" Kappazion's ancient voice boomed throughout the clearing with a strength that contradicted his withered body. "The celestials have always been able to calm the powerful creatures. She will convince the bunyip that we meant no harmmmm." Kappzion glared at the lone dissenter. "And as an offering of penance, our greatest warrior, Kappadarma, will bring the princess to the caveeee."

The burly warrior's jaw dropped and he scowled back at Kappzion. As groups of kappa cheered at the sudden arrival of hope, Kappadarma stomped off into the trees.

* * *

The rest of the afternoon was met with good cheer and mediocre food. The kappa made sure to feed us enough of their strange cuisine to keep our energy up for the task ahead. Most notable was a meal of dried fish and ground berries. It tasted like meaty coffee and had much the same effect. I sat with Luna and Chip as we ate.

The large wolf seemed upset as he turned to Luna and spoke. "Lady Luna, will helping these animals teach us how to stop the unspeakables?"

"I do not believe so." She lowered her eyes.

"Then why do we waste our time? We should be hunting down the listener. We should be finding a way to destroy your family's killers."

Luna sank her head, deep in thought. When she looked up again, she seemed to be full of pride.

"We do this, Chip, because it is what my family would have done if they were still alive. Our visions show us death all too often. If I do not do whatever I can to change the ones I can alter, then the visions are nothing more than a vile curse." Her eyes filled with sadness and conviction. "That is what my father used to say. If we do not help the ones we see, we are the worst of the Plane of God's creatures. So will you please trust me?"

We both nodded.

"Good." She sighed. "We should get ready for our trip. We have a village to save."

* * *

The sun slowly set and before long, we were passing through the forest once again. I was scolded for bringing my backpack on the hike, but it felt funny to leave it alone in the village. With its weight slowing me down, I brought up the rear of the procession.

Meanwhile, Luna led the group alongside the grumpy Kappadarma. Despite the obvious animosity between them, Luna appeared to be getting along with the hot-headed reptile.

As we trekked deeper into the woods toward the water spirit, the absurdity of it all hit me.

"A few days ago, I was nobody. Then I saved a beautiful princess from an immortal killer and now I'm on a quest to bring water back to a starving tribe of ninja turtles with the aid of a werewolf." I shook my head.

Chip smirked, his human eyes betraying his animal face.

"You know," I pressed on, "Luna and I are pretty similar."

Chip snorted, amused.

"No, really. Think about it; she's lost her family, and I've pretty much lost everyone I care about, too."

"That's not true," Chip protested. "The Lady has Chip."

"Yeah, I guess I forgot about that." I leaned over to scratch him behind his shoulder. He buffeted me aside with a swipe of his tail and continued slogging through the thick underbrush.

It was true though; in this whole mess, I had lost everyone. I wondered if they were still looking for me or if they had given up already. As the rhythmic parade continued, I imagined my mother and sister, dressed in all black. If only I could tell them I was fine. Well, not fine—I was stranded in an alternate dimension with a very low life expectancy—but the idea was still the same. Luna and I *were* a lot alike and right now, she was all I had.

I heard the gentle trickle of falling water and looked up from my thoughts. Our group had reached the cave that provided the fresh water for the village. It wasn't so much a cave as it was a drainage pipe. Disgust welled up inside me as I realized what our quest truly entailed.

The kappa got their "purified water" from an old sewer drain and we were going to have to wade through it to find the thing that had stopped cleaning the drinking water. As we gathered around the large, stone opening, the smell of old sewage wafted into the air.

"We have to go in *there*?"

"This is the sacred place where the water spirit dwells. Of course you have to enterrrr." Kappadarma's voice was laced with anger.

"But it's gross." It wasn't my best argument, but I found it very appropriate for the situation.

The squat kappa hefted his thick staff and pointed it at me. "Are you insulting the most sacred place of the kappaaaa? I will not stand for such insolenceeee!"

Luna wedged herself between the potential skirmish. "Noah meant no harm, Kappadarma. Let us proceed with our quest."

The warrior turned aside reluctantly and slunk over to a flat rock. "We kappa are not allowed in the sacred shrineeee. I'm afraid I will have to wait for you here. But we have this torch to aid your search on this dark eveningggg." He handed Luna a small, black pocket flashlight. It looked almost as old as Kappazion and the light it emitted was faint. Luna nodded her thanks and waved us into the stinking cavern.

The pungent smell of sewage was overpowering and I could see Chip struggling with the stench.

"Keep a hand on the wall," Luna called out through the darkness. "It will give you a reference point through this maze."

I agreed at first, but after wiping a thick layer of slime from my hand, I decided to take my chances.

Although a blessing, the old flashlight was unreliable at best. It constantly flickered dim light across the cavern before shutting off completely. Then someone would have to shake it until it decided to wake again. After a few minutes, I looked back and was unable to see the light from the entrance.

A low rumble echoed off the walls of the tunnel. The light danced in front of us in search of a source. Heavy footsteps grew louder in the confined space, and I backed up a few paces while Chip moved forward. He crouched into a low warrior's stance and we waited.

A single glowing eye—the size of a volleyball—emerged from the darkness, framed by an oddly pointed face that cringed as the light blinded it. It looked like a giant horse with the face of a one-eyed bloodhound.

The bunyip wailed as the light played across its face. It lowered its misshapen head and dashed forward in an attempt to trample us, but Chip caught the blow in his strong paws. Luna fell backward into me and the flashlight clattered against the wall, extinguishing the bright beam. Darkness engulfed us. Sounds of fur colliding against flesh echoed from all sides of the cavern.

Luna frantically searched for the tiny light and fumbled with the switch as soon as her hands found the cylinder, but it was dead. "It will not turn on. We have to do something!"

"Wait! Luna, let me see it." I took the flashlight from her and unscrewed the bottom. Two antique AA batteries fell into my palm, just as I'd thought. I rolled over and dove into my bag, scrambling through the scattered contents.

"Hurry, Noah!" Luna pleaded as Chip's shrill whine echoed in the darkness. I felt something gently vibrate in my bag. I pushed my hands through the mass of clothing—struggling to find the source of the movement—until I felt smooth plastic. Pulling the electric toothbrush from the pack, I quickly unscrewed the back and forced the batteries into the flashlight. Light erupted from the end of the torch, bathing everything in rays of white fire.

The bunyip gave a throaty roar and powered past Chip. It galloped toward me, its single eye jostling about as it bounded forward. I felt the firm grip of terror take hold of my body and found myself frozen as the awkward creature charged.

Without warning, Luna lunged in front of me, arms spread wide. The bunyip's eye floated to meet Luna's. At the sight of the princess's gaze, the huge creature slammed all four legs into the floor in an attempt to break its chaotic charge. It slid across the slimy, thick mud and halted barely inches away from her.

I held my breath as she reached out a slender hand and stroked the creature's head. "Good boy. Peace is all we need."

Its gurgled whinny was the only response.

"How did you do that?" I stammered, still recovering from shock.

"A celestial's gaze can calm any beast with a kind heart," Luna whispered with a sideways glance at Chip.

In the bright light, something glimmered on the bunyip's neck. I stood on my toes to get a better angle.

"Luna, look!" I gasped.

Around the water spirit's thick neck hung a necklace of long, sharp teeth. On something small—like a kappa—it would have fit nicely, but around the huge neck of the bunyip, the necklace was cutting into its flesh, puncturing its skin with every movement.

Chip rounded the bunyip and looked at the spot where I was pointing. He grabbed the necklace and tore it away from the injured creature. Several teeth fell from the string, scattering across the stone floor. As soon as the necklace was off, the bunyip sighed, clearly relieved. Beneath its hooves, the murky water shimmered and the purified crystal stream ran fresh through the tunnel.

Chip looked at us through the light and held the ruined necklace up for us to see. "Harm was meant by this." Chip passed the sharp teeth between his paws. "To a kappa warrior, these are a great honor. It would not be given away easily."

"Unless... unless the kappa giving it away already had plenty of them." Luna's eyes flashed, even in the dim light of the tunnel.

"Kappadarma." The thought hit me like a steamroller.

Low splashes sounded behind us. Luna spun around, illuminating the warrior's angry silhouette. He brandished a long spear and stood base-wide, ready to fight. His staff took up most of the empty space and its long, metal tip radiated a fierce light. "I can't believe you did itttt." The angry kappa took a step forward. "It doesn't matter. You were all killed by the water spirit, anyway. It was up to me to charge in and save the villageeee."

"I do not understand." Luna closed the gap between the warrior and herself. I sprang forward and pulled her back by the shoulders. "Your village counted on you. How could you ignore your laws and enter the sacred grounds just to harm this poor creature and poison your brothers?"

"Howwww?" Kappadarma's eyes were ablaze with fury. "I was the greatest warrior in the village until they decided to house that vampire trashhhh! It moves faster and kills with more grace than any kappa ever could. The thing had two full necklaces by the end of the first dayyyy. Everyone started praising him—holding feasts in honor of his accomplishmentssss. I had planned to come back here and free the water spirit as soon as they had disposed of the taint. All would have loved Kappadarma againnnn."

"You are sick," Luna spat.

"Well," he countered. "You're deadddd."

Quick as falling water, Kappadarma lunged forward. It would have been a deadly blow if it wasn't for one simple flaw in his plan: we had a 300 pound werewolf on our side.

Four legs clattered against the rock floor as a brown flash flew past. He came in low and wrapped a massive paw around Kappadarma's neck. With the force of a wrecking ball, Chip slammed the kappa against the ceiling and held the squirming turtle there as he examined him like a bug.

"You attack Chip and you are forgiven. You attack the Lady Luna and we drain the blood from your veins." He snapped his jaws at the terrified creature to emphasize his words.

Luna rested a gentle hand on Chip's furry back. "It is not our place to deal out justice, Chip. We will bring him back to the camp and let the kappas deal with him as they see fit."

We gave our last goodbyes to the gentle bunyip and followed the pure stream back to the camp with our prisoner in tow. Night had overtaken the forest, but bright fires lit up the clearing.

The elder was saddened to hear the entire mess had been caused by Kappadarma, and promised his constituents he would set to work deciding on a punishment for the fallen warrior. He freed the vampire and ordered a celebration in our honor. The night was filled with an array of meat, fresh water, and a whole lot of dancing.

We sat around the bonfire's edge, listening to Kappazion tell stories of great hunts while puffing on his long wooden pipe. The smoke mingled with that of the fire and coiled into impressive shapes. Sometimes, I would catch myself not paying attention to the tale and instead watching the smoke's acrobatics.

During a story of how he took on a whole pack of drop bears with nothing but a stick and a handful of poison ivy, I heard cautious footsteps behind me. Before I could turn, a second set of steps intersected the first. I listened to the fast, quiet conversation.

"No, vampire. Don't push your luck here. We won't allow it." Chip's gruff accent carried on the night air. It was as much of a whisper as he could manage.

"I might yet test my luck, dog," the vampire spat. "You don't understand what the hunger is like. It grinds its teeth into my soul and spits out the remains. It never goes away."

"We think you might have outstayed your welcome here. You should leave. Now."

A labored breath was followed by silence. "You're right. It's foolish of me." The vampire pattered away into the distance.

Chip lowered himself next to me, warming his hands by the fire.

"What was that about?"

"Vampires always think they have it worse than everyone else in this world. We thought he should go somewhere else."

"Where do you think he'll go?"

"It doesn't matter. Enjoy the night, Man-Son. Many would like to see you dead." He stood and walked over to where Luna sat.

"Hey, Chip," I called to him. "What about you? Do you still want to see me dead?"

Chip pondered this for a moment. "We are not sure yet, but we still think you would make better dinner than company."

We celebrated until the sun peered over the trees into the clearing. Kappazion gave us his thanks and assigned Kappadowri to take us back to the road. We once again found ourselves wandering through the forest. Luna's eyes drooped into sleepiness every so often, and Chip stayed close so she could lean on him for support.

I was more surprised at my own condition. I felt very alert—considering I'd slept no more than the others had—and I wasn't sure why.

We reached the final stretch of trees and Kappadowri dropped into a low bow before ducking back into the woods. We all stared at the black asphalt for a few minutes. It wasn't the place from which we had originally left. Chip gave a raucous howl before letting the morning stillness cover us once again.

In the distance, the headlights of a beaten motor home climbed over the horizon. It honked cheerfully as it pulled over onto the side of the road to meet us. We climbed in and Luna collapsed on the sofa, immediately falling asleep.

Chip fell into the driver seat once more and bid Thalia forward.

IX

After a few hours of steady driving, we came upon a rest stop. Chip eased the van into a parking space with surprising grace for someone I'd once watched chase his tail. Thalia's motor went silent and Luna leapt from the top step of the vehicle, rushing toward the bustling complex. Chip stood and stretched his arms. He headed for the woods to "mark some territory," as he put it.

I was left to fend for myself. Hauling my backpack onto my shoulder, I ventured forth into the huge structure.

The traveler's station was large and alarmingly normal. Signs for roadside attractions and advertisements for the delicacies inside adorned the sidewalk as I approached the sliding-glass doors. Luna once explained that, for the most part, the two worlds were identical, and this rest stop seemed to prove it. Everything seemed glaringly ordinary. It wasn't until I walked through those wide, glass doors that my preconceived notions were shattered.

Cool A/C hit my face, bringing with it some of the strangest smells I'd ever experienced. A whiff of old cardboard mixed with strawberries and freshly cut grass hit my nose and assaulted my senses. When I focused on actual objects around me, things got even weirder. The contents of Grimm's Fairy Tales poured out in front of me. A short, fat reptile in fishing waders waddled past, while a group of penguins in capes and aviator goggles casually strolled behind him. An eight-foot-tall ape-creature covered from head to toe in brown fur showed a great amount of interest in a wooden brochure holder. "Speak to the world's smartest krill!" was the current object of his desire and he pocketed the small, folded paper into the fanny pack around his waist. I pushed my way through the hall, dodging the assortment of monsters and myths. A crowd stopped to let a lengthy worm crawl by and the small group of penguins showed great irritation with a multi-colored bird who bragged about his newly pressed wings.

Further in, there was a large cafeteria area with rows of tables. At the edge of the seating area, Luna sat alone with a newspaper laid out over the table. She lifted her head from the tabloid as I approached.

"Not a thing about us," she said, relieved. "We made quite a mess back in that city you lived in. When we saw the vampire at the kappa village, I was worried he might have been part of a larger group. If our chaotic escape from Lojo had created a weak point in the barrier, every vampire group in the southeast would have mobilized."

"You have newspapers here?"

"Of course," she replied, turning her attention back to outstretched pages. "They existed long before the worlds separated. It is mostly information on the movement of dangerous creatures and powerful species."

"Is there anything about the Chronographers?"

"No," her tone became serious. "No one ever reports on the Chronographers." She reached under the table and pulled three gold coins from her sock. Placing the glimmering ovals onto the smooth surface, she pushed them over to me without even looking up from her tabloid. "There is a place here called The Jackalope. They have some of my favorite food. Would you mind going down there and getting us all something to eat?"

I nodded. With money in hand, I headed back into the mob of strange creatures. I stopped along the way to ask a purple, amorphous blob where The Jackalope was, but I couldn't understand its gurgling response and its lack of appendages made it hard to understand which direction I was supposed to go.

After a few more minutes of wandering, I recognized a large, stuffed bunny with antlers. Regardless of how awkward the little rabbit looked, the thing attending the counter was much stranger. It was a huge octopus; each of his eight arms snaked about performing separate tasks. It had a short, stubby beak in the middle of its face—which also was its body—and a stained, white apron hung loosely from its shoulders. Its large, single eye was the size of a dinner plate and it stared at me as I approached the counter.

"A man-son?" Its voice sounded like the words were scraping against the inside of the thick beak. "Not seen your ilk roundabouts. Blood drinkers usually scoop you up. Well then, whatilitbe?"

I glanced over at the stuffed rabbit with the large antlers resting next to the register. "Is that a real Jackalope?"

The octopus-bird let out a few struggled wheezes, his whole body shaking like gelatin. "No, that's a rabbit with antlers glued to its head. You man-sons imagine too much. Next you'll ask about leprechauns."

"How do you guys know what we imagine, anyway?"

"Travel between the worlds is impossible for most, but some find ways, and words always were slippery creatures. 'Sides, where do you think your imaginings come from?" He let out another strangled guffaw.

"Just give me three of whatever it is you serve." I slapped the gold coins in front of one twitching appendage.

"Your money's no good here. The tale of your being will be payment 'nuff." He slid the money back to me with one tentacle, flipped some strange stew into three bowls with another and scooped what looked like rice with a third. Then he moved all three of these onto a tray and handed them to me with a fourth while a fifth maneuvered around his body, bearing a small paper bag.

"This is a token for your travels. In your legends, it's appropriate."

"Thank you." I couldn't help but be warmed by the gesture. I took the three coins from the counter and carried the tray back to the table. Chip had joined Luna, and they were huddled together in quiet conversation. I passed the bowls around and sat in the empty chair. I removed the paper bag from the tray and opened it. A small, white rabbit's foot was inside, a metal chain looped around the back. I placed the bag in the outside pocket of my backpack and turned back to my bowl.

Chip and Luna were already spooning globs of brown goo into their mouths. The sight of a wolf and a princess gorging on the steaming gruel was slightly off-putting, but my stomach was making stranger noises than the purple blob had.

I leaned in close and smelled the liquid. The aroma was so thick and enticing, I could no longer hold back. I collected a spoonful and popped it into my mouth. It was a sweet tasting stew that brought back memories of family meals from somewhere deep in my mind. Before I knew it, I had drained the bowl and sat at the table, full and happy.

It looked as though the others were just as content. Chip had curled up underneath the table and Luna was leaning her chair back on two legs.

"Luna, the thing at The Jackalope stand said that traveling between worlds was impossible for most. Are there any creatures that can go between the Plane of Gods and Man?" She looked at me guardedly, and then her pale features softened.

"Yes, there are a few species that can. Mostly vampires looking for a fix; their hunger draws them to the weak spots and they can pass through for about a minute before being pulled back to our side."

"Weak spots? Didn't you tell me about those before?"

"Yes. When emotions get very high on either side, it creates a weak spot. The spots make it easier for things to pass through. Our side cannot stay on yours for too long, but some species can hop in and out quickly." I looked at her, confused. She sighed. "Remember when Lojo was chasing us? I assume you could make out some figures panicking and running through the streets. Those were sons of man passing between the worlds momentarily. In order for creatures to remain on either side permanently, the trauma has to be much worse. Wars of man have sometimes sent your kind our way. Other than that, only the Chronographers can move as they please."

When she spoke of the Chronographers, her eyes shut tight and her head jerked forward. Red hair fell over her face like a silk curtain. After a few seconds, her whole forehead scrunched up and her eyes opened wide—delicate full moons with a little too much gray. "I think something is wrong."

"What do you mean? Did you just... like... see the future?"

"Yes and no." Her eyes raced back and forth frantically. Chip began to stir under the table. "I had a vision, but there was nothing in it—just thick, black smoke."

"So, you're having a misfire? I'm sure all great moon people have hiccups."

Luna glared at me. "I do not get 'hiccups,' and all of my 'moon people' are dead, which means my visions have been particularly strong as of late."

"I'm sorry, I may not know much about this whole seer thing, but I'm pretty sure a vision about nothing is not a bad thing. You're telling me you've never made a mistake with a vision?"

"I guess they *have* made mistakes before," she shot back, leaning over the table, "because *they* led me to you!" She dropped back into her seat with her hands crossed.

I just stared. "You... you knew you were going to run into me that night?"

It wasn't until then that she realized what she had said. "Well, yes. I had a vision after I escaped from my family's castle. It showed that if I went to Florida, I would find you and you would... well... do something to stop Colere."

My head spun. "So, you're telling me that I'm never going to see my family again and will probably get killed in this stupid world because *you* decided to pull me out of my home to act as a *shield*?" I stood and turned. Chip sprung up next to Luna, letting a low growl escape from between his sharp teeth.

"Noah," she pleaded. "At the time, I did not know what to do. I just saw that you would help me if I found you. I was desperate."

"*You* were desperate?" I whirled back to her. Strange patrons began to stare at us from other tables. "Did you even stop to think what you were going to do to *me*? That you were going to ruin my life?"

"I am sorry, Noah." She reached for me over the table, but I pulled away.

"You're *sorry*? Sorry isn't going to give me my life back, Luna. Sorry isn't going to stop my funeral." I turned and grabbed my bag, elbowing a shaggy, horned monster out of the way as I went.

She knew! She knew what she was doing when she ran down that street. She knew what she was doing when she pulled me from my home. She knew what she was doing when she killed me!

I ducked through the sliding glass doors and stopped in my tracks. A stout man with a pointy, black goatee—like a spear tip—stood impatiently in front of me.

"Oh, there you are, Noah." His acidic voice slithered into my ears. "I've been waiting for you."

X

The sun sat high in the sky and a calm wind blew across the rest stop parking lot but all I could do was curse under my breath. Was I holding up a sign that said, "HERE I AM! PLEASE ATTACK ME AT THE LEAST OPPORTUNE MOMENT?" I'd hoped I could at least recover from the most recent bombshell that had just been dropped on me but instead, my imminent death stared back at me, once again. Couldn't a guy get a break? At least this time death wasn't as frightening.

The Chronographer that stood before me was just a pudgy little man. He was a bit shorter than me and wore a pair of old, stained jeans with a black, short-sleeved shirt. His rosy cheeks puffed out like a chipmunk, and his skin seemed oddly undernourished for someone immortal. He sported a black, trimmed goatee that pointed sharply at the bottom like an arrowhead. His long hair—tied back into a neat ponytail—fell like oil dripping from a high ledge. His eyes were a violet storm that seemed to flow around his pupils like a lava lamp. Overall, he reminded me of my old friend Mitchell, who had spent most of his time playing on-line role-playing games.

The squat man stood firm. I looked back toward the doors and saw various species forcing their way in and out of the rest stop pavilion. Included in that crowd was Luna, and despite what she had done to me, I felt the need to protect her. All I had to do was keep this freak's attention.

"So," I yelled as bravely as I could while slowly moving away from the crowd, "you're the next big bad, eh? What's your shtick? Bad grooming and casual dress?"

He laughed. It was forced—like a mad scientist practicing in front of the mirror. As luck would have it, he moved parallel to me, away from the automatic glass doors.

"I apologize for not introducing myself." His shrill voice was reminiscent of a prepubescent boy. "I'm the third Chronographer, Astrian, and my shtick, as you say, is magic."

"Not much of that around, is there?"

Astrian's smile grew large, filling the whole of his round face. "Thank you for noticing. Now, boy, pleasantries aside, I'm looking for the child you are with. However, I must admit I'm much more interested in mutilating you. You see, I'm not very happy with what you did to my brother."

"I hit him with a pipe. Nothing too special."

"Ah, as much as I abhor such physical demonstrations, sometimes the most barbaric measure is the best. Just look at what I did to Houdini after I finished taking everything he had to offer."

We were almost to the edge of the parking lot. Soon, we would be a safe distance from the shuffling masses entering and leaving the rest stop. Luna was now outside and had moved to the front of the crowd. I wished I could somehow tell her to run. It was while I stood there—futilely wishing—that I noticed the furry, brown dog exit the automatic doors and knew that things were about to get out of hand. I quickened my pace, trying to lead Astrian farther away, but Chip acted too fast. The brown ball of fur burst out of the gathering and barreled toward us. I could always count on Chip to ruin a plan.

Everything happened so fast I was barely able to react. I saw Luna start to move forward and I sprinted toward her to whisk her to safety. As I hurried to her side, Chip ran past me on all fours. I reached out my hand to take Luna's just as Chip leapt into the air. An evil cackle echoed from every direction followed by a deafening crack. Chip's limp body flew though the air above our heads, colliding into a red sports car and crushing it like tin foil. I tried to keep my focus on Luna, but no one could ignore the deep, familiar sound of snapping fingers that erupted behind me.

Instinctively, I turned around to see the danger.

Astrian strolled toward us, obviously taking his time. The familiar black miasma appeared, but it didn't crawl from the cracks around us like it usually did. This time, it fell from Astrian himself, as if trap doors had opened just over his shoulders. The mist fell heavily and whipped across the pavement in every direction—like a bucket of water poured on level ground. As he walked through the apex of the black storm, his clothing changed from stained rags into a black ceremonial robe with blood-red trim on the bottom and over the sleeves. I didn't know too much about how the mist worked, but I knew it was probably bad if it originated from the person calling it.

The Chronographer's violet eyes swirled and flickered as he spoke. "Did you really think a mongrel dog could hold me off for more than a second?"

I turned back to Luna to pull her away, but she couldn't move. She just stood there with an outstretched hand. In fact, everyone was standing still as death. The crowd—which had begun to disperse in a panic—had frozen like statues, stuck in mid-stride. I waved my hand in front of Luna's still, gray eyes, pleading with her.

"Luna, please. Snap out of it."

Astrian chuckled, "I couldn't let her run away, could I? I don't want anyone interfering with our appointment."

Psychedelic colors flowed from his fingertips as he waddled forward. The stream of hues hovered in the air before fading into nothingness once more. "I think it was very rude for you to kill my brother, so I wanted to find a suitable punishment. I was thinking about slowly tearing the skin from your body."

I was gripped with fear, but not from Astrian's cruel taunts. I needed to get Luna out of here. I grabbed her shoulders and tried to shake her free from the frozen stream of time. "Luna, *please* wake up!"

Astrian brushed the ponytail from his shoulder, sending sparks streaming upward. "Maybe I could drown you a few times. Or burn you alive." Serpents writhed from the black smoke at his feet, slithering forward and bearing their pointed fangs toward my heels.

I kept trying to wake Luna. I couldn't lose her now; she was all that I had in this crazy world.

"Perhaps I could slowly rip the limbs from your body and feed you your own entrails."

The group of snakes wormed into a pile and burst apart. From the bloody remains, a large, crimson-winged panther crawled forth. It roared with evil glee as it circled us hungrily. I waved my hand frantically in front of Luna again, doing anything I could think of to wake her. The predator lowered into a crouch, tensing its powerful legs to strike. No matter what I tried, nothing seemed to work. Finally, I did the last thing I could think of to wake someone: I pressed my fingers together and snapped.

The air rippled and shook as my fingers parted. A deep echo poured from the space left behind and the world cowered at the sound. It cut through the sky, leaving deep fissures in its wake. I felt a tight pull from everything around me. A white mist poured from the clefts between the two realities, gliding across the ground like a battalion of smoky soldiers. It ignored everything but me, yearning for my touch as it moved ever closer.

When it reached me, it coiled around my feet and wound itself over my body. Genuine warmth filled my being and I reveled in its embrace. It softly kissed my cheek before diving forth to intertwine itself with the dark brume already settling over the landscape. In it, I could see flickering images—thousands of tiny scenarios playing out before my eyes.

"You filthy heathen! Not only do you murder my family, but you attempt to defile our bloodline!" Astrian marched forward with shock and anger splashed across his face. The black haze curled around his hands as he raised them into the air like a sorcerer about to cast a spell.

For some reason, I felt calm—as though the strength of eons flowed through my veins. It was like some miniscule understanding of the world brought peace into my troubled mind. I looked back into the history that was unwinding itself to my touch and bright colors danced at my feet. Without hesitation, I reached for one.

Immediately, everything changed. My mind slipped from my body and cast itself into one of the memories. It was dark and I was in a jungle—but this wasn't any jungle I'd ever seen before. This jungle was wild and rarely disturbed by anything moving on less than four legs. I turned to look at the bright fire that leapt toward the heavens, piercing the darkness as it licked the sky. All around me, a familiar chant echoed through the night. A small group of dark-skinned men and woman sat around a blazing pyre while two warriors danced around it. Their naked skin—painted in orange runes—trembled against the biting flame. Flitting about wildly, they threw their hands into the air. A cloud of black dust shot into the sky and after a few seconds, it burst into a spectacular display of fire. The crowd cheered and sang louder. The two men cantered back and forth, throwing coarse powder into the air and watching flares erupt into amazing shapes. I was filled with an overwhelming happiness that took me completely by surprise. The whole scene was so alien, and yet it was as commonplace to me as breathing or eating.

Something rustled in the bushes and the festivities immediately stopped. Fear crossed every face as a man—who seemed to be carved from stone—edged his way out of the bushes. I recognized the man who stood before them.

It was me.

But it wasn't actually me; it was the memory's owner, Colere.

Suddenly, I was back in a parking lot outside of some nondescript rest stop. The strange wave of memory had only taken a moment. Astrian was still in the same place he had been when my mind had left. In his raised hands, swirls of clouds and thunder had begun to form. I shifted my weight to defend myself and felt something tucked into my palm that hadn't been there before. I opened it and a mound of black soot spilled through my fingertips.

"I have killed men who had the power of a supernova. I have stared into a black hole and not blinked." Astrian's magic shimmered, mirage-like, bending light as it cleaved through the rays of the sun. "I have devoured beings with the power of gods and yet your death, Noah Lane, will be the one I remember most."

Astrian raised the glittering ball of energy—it cracked with raw power. His crooked teeth spread wide over his inflated maw.

I sank low and threw the handful of dark powder straight into his face.

He stopped in his tracks, releasing the energy back into the nostalgia as he uselessly tried to shield himself. He coughed out a small cloud and looked at me through confused violet eyes. The ash ignited into a searing explosion of fire. Astrian screamed and clawed at his burning face.

I focused on the memory again. The white mist coiled over my fingertips, depositing as much of the dark ash into my hands as I could carry. I took a step forward, leaning in close toward the smell of burning flesh. "I think we're done talking, Astrian. I'd appreciate it if you left my friends and me alone." I thrust my hands into his flabby chest. The resulting explosion would have made a military general froth at the mouth.

Astrian soared across the parking lot in a ball of fire and collided into the pavement in a burning heap. Everything went silent and the mists, both black and white, receded back into the cracks of the world. He dragged himself out of the hole and struggled to his feet. His goatee was singed and his ponytail had been burned away. Deep red welts arched across his skin. When he spoke, it was small and strained. "As long as Prometheus lives, there must be five Chronographers. I was foolish not to heed those words. Next time, the element of surprise will not be on your side. 'Til we meet again, Noah Lane."

What was left of the dark mist circled around Astrian's battered form, enveloping him. It shot into the sky and rose out of sight, leaving nothing but burnt asphalt in its wake. The battle instinct that had carried me through the fight receded away along with the mist and I felt myself relax. I turned to Luna, who was still standing a few feet behind me.

"Did you see that? I just totally showed him who's boss. Whoa, man! I hope somebody filmed that!"

Luna just stared at me.

"Hey, Luna, didja see that? We won!"

"I saw everything." Her voice was small.

"Great! I just beat the hell outta him. We should be celebrating." I reached forward to grab her shoulder but she cringed away.

"Do *not* touch me." Her voice rang with a raw anger. "I saw *everything*."

"Luna," I said hesitantly. "What's wrong?"

"I cannot travel with you, Noah. You are... you are a monster."

"I'm not a monster! What are you talking about?"

"When you killed Colere, you took his place. Did you not feel his power move into you? Did you not see what he has seen? How long do you think it will be before you decide to finish what he started?"

"I would never do that! You can't just leave me!"

"Yes, I can, Noah. I will not travel with one of the monsters that killed my family." She turned and walked toward Chip, who was limping up the steps of the mobile home.

"Luna, you can't do this! After all, *you* did this to me! I'd still be with my family if you hadn't decided I'd make a good shield!"

Luna stopped and looked back. Pity filled her eyes. "The past has happened, Noah, and I am sorry. But I do not regret meeting you, even if this is how our friendship ends."

I tried to hold myself together. "What am I supposed to do?"

"I do not know, but it is best if you stay far away from me."

"Luna, I promise I will never hurt you."

She looked over her shoulder, her red hair sliding over her frame. "I believe you, but I cannot promise that I will not hurt you."

She walked up the remaining steps and closed the door. I stared, dumbfounded, as Thalia's engine rumbled to life. She flashed her headlights at me as she backed out of the parking lot. I stood there as the RV whirled toward the street and took off down the road, a strawberry-red spot visible in the back window as it coasted out of sight. Strange creatures milled around me and the sun gently set in the distance. I stood alone and abandoned in a world I didn't know. A warm breeze carried the scent of lavender on its fringes while darkness settled in around me in oppressive dominance.

I turned toward the woods and began to walk.

XI

Alone.

XII

It had been two days since I'd watched Luna drive out of sight. The woods had been no comfort whatsoever. Every tree was just another painful reminder that the world still existed around me. Here, in this endless forest, I could at least pretend that none of this had ever happened. I could imagine I was still in my own world and all the trouble of the last week had been nothing more than a strange dream. I wanted to get hopelessly lost, but no matter how hard I tried to lose myself in the trees, I always knew exactly where I was. I was here, in a hellish universe, where *I* was the monster who stalked innocent children, lying awake in their beds.

I hadn't slept since I had left the kappa village. I wasn't sure if my new stamina was a side effect of the filthy disease that had taken hold of my body or of my abated desire to live. I wanted to be lost, but no matter how many turns I took, the memories still found me. The things I'd left behind haunted me at every turn. I'd never amounted to much in my past life; my mother was as proud of me as any mother could be for their son. My sister, Shelly, was the one who was the popular cheerleader. Now, it seemed like I couldn't do much better here. Would I rather be forgotten or hated? The answer seemed easy. Let the ground open up and take me; let me be lost to history; let me be the one well of knowledge that Prometheus never finds.

The steady pace allowed my mind to address a few things: like all these animals that kept dashing from tree to tree—where did they poop? I'd been walking non-stop through the forest for two days and I'd yet to see a single animal go number two. So where did it all go? What about food? All I'd eaten so far were a few clumps of berries. Where were all these animals getting their share? And if everyone I'd ever loved thought I was dead, and the one person who still knew I was alive was afraid of me because I could turn into a brutal killing machine at any moment, what should I do next? I'd been unsuccessful at answering any of the questions.

I continued my hike over unearthed mounds of tangled roots and through thick clumps of underbrush for another few hours. Eventually, the sun began pulling its rays out through the top of the canopy for a night's rest. I made a few adjustments to my course, trying to avoid the inevitable towns and highways I knew I'd run into if I went in one direction for too long. Once the moon took its usual place in the night sky, I started my newest tradition: I found a small clearing where the trees had grown apart and stood alone. I stared at the light coming from the pale orb.

I'd heard that people who stared at the moon for too long went crazy. I was starting to think those people had just met a celestial like Luna who had slipped through their fingers like the waxen moonbeams that beat down on the grass.

No matter how many times I examined what had occurred, it never made any sense. She had known what she was doing when she had run into me that night. For all intents and purposes, she had killed me. And even though she had left me to die a second death, I still missed her. I missed the smell of her hair when the wind would catch it just right and the way her eyes changed color, depending on her mood. I missed the strength she carried when defending her friends. I missed the grace with which she fought and the way she always spoke with a refined poise. Hell, I even missed Chip and his gung-ho way of dealing with problems.

I turned my attention back to the expansive woods and resumed my desperate attempt to fall off the face of the planet, but in the distance—where there should have been nothing—there was a light. It flickered enthusiastically beneath the blanket of night. I crouched low and crept close to the forest floor. The light slowly took on an animated form. It was a lone fire, crackling blissfully alongside the other musicians of the forest.

Peering around an old evergreen, I saw two men. One wore an old pair of worn jeans with the knees torn out, and the other wore khakis, loosely tied about his waist with a rope. The pair sat about five feet away from the fire in opposite directions. I didn't really understand the point of making such a large fire if they were going to sit so far away from it, but the two men seemed comfortable enough.

The first looked up as I moved into the light. He wore a beaten leather jacket over his thick frame and had a bald head with a bushy beard sprouting from a pair of feathery sideburns. It was like the hair had slowly fallen down the sides of his face. The fire cast a fleeting light and he appeared to be nothing more than a dirty panhandler. But when he smiled, his teeth were a stunning white.

The second man was much thinner than the first and his hair was cut short, like an army recruit. He sported a stained wife beater and seemed prone to violent twitching fits. He was obviously coming down from some kind of drug. It was uncomfortable to look at him for too long.

"Well hello thar," the heavy one called in a curious southern accent while waving a large, meaty hand. "Figured if'n we built this fire, you'd come hither when you's done starin' at that sky. Ain't nothin' but bright lights up thar. 'Sn't that right, Leeroy?"

Leeroy flinched and looked up. Dark shadows played across his sunken cheeks. "T-t-t-t-that's r-r-right, Hosef."

"You were waiting for me? How did you know I was coming?"

The large man chuckled loudly. I noticed that his brown eyes were sunk in, like some of the homeless men I'd seen back home. "The sons of man never did hide their stink well, boy."

"Oh," I said surprised. "You know I'm human, then."

"Yessun. We've known a man was about for quite some time now."

Hosef was very animated for a vagabond. He reminded me of a preacher I'd once had when my mom used to take us to church. The preacher would march around the chapel as he talked—captivating even my restless, childlike attention. This man had that kind of power in spades. He waved his hands about as he talked, withdrawing them if they ever pointed too close to the fire.

"Awlthough, I would never call yer kind humane. 'Tis ya'll's fault we've been locked in this closet of reality."

"You mean it was the hu—I mean, 'the sons of man' that caused everything to split?"

Hosef rolled a long arm out toward an empty stump adjacent to his. I fell into place, ready to listen to his story. Once I was seated, he coughed into a balled-up fist, clearing his throat.

"Why, yes. 'Twas the sons of man that caused this here great rift. Yer kind's so pliable it made it easy fo' others to use them against the gods. An' those gods had quite a soft spot fo' yer kind. Hell, ole' Prometheus got his fire and even went back fo' more. Ya' see, lots o' the higher beings decided they din't wanna be puppets o' the gods if'n they were always gonna side with you lesser creatures. So, they began to amass armies of sons, since you pro'crate so fast an' all. An' once the magical bein's wrangled up enough o' yer kind, they unleashed hell upon the gods. 'Sunt that right, Leeroy?"

Leeroy unburied his head from his folded arms. "Y-y-y-yessir, Hosef. Unle-le-le-leashed hell."

"Then what?" I leaned in close to the round man as he continued to pontificate.

Hosef threw a rock into the fire and cowered back when if flared up. "Well, them gods got pretty upset. Their favorite toys were creatin' quite a mess and sumthin' had to be done. The gods split the world betwix the magical creatures and the sons. The sons kept on fightin' for a while, but once they was done and settled, they had their freedom to enjoy. They moved on without any o' the gods breathin' down their backs. Meanwhile, we remained puppets and suffered whatever cruel jokes those holier-than-thou blue bloods decided to amuse themselves with. 'N that's what bothers me, even though ya'll are the pathetic scum that was so easily moved, they favored you." His voice became an angry, hungry sneer. His bright, white teeth glinted in the moonlight.

I couldn't help but notice how sharp they were. I looked over at Leeroy, but he was gone. I heard the whistle of an object sailing through the air just before pain rattled through my skull. I fell to the grass and everything went blurry.

The vampire handed his bat to the lumbering Hosef. He hefted the object over his shoulder and leaned down over me. A double-image made it hard to pinpoint which was real and which was the illusion. The last thing I remembered before the bat was brought on me a second time, was a deep southern voice and hot breath on my forehead.

"Nighty-night, puppet."

XIII

Something stank of dried blood and mildew. It permeated from every direction, rousing me to my senses like a foul-smelling salt. When I tried to open my eyes, pain blazed through my face. The place where Hosef had hit me was swollen and tender. The slightest movements caused violent eruptions of distress to race through my temples. I reached over to feel the lump covering most of my face but was unable to move my arm. An attempt at moving the other proved futile as well. I bit down hard and forced my eyes open as wide as they would go. I was chained to a huge, flat wooden plank propped up at about a forty-five degree angle.

It reminded me of one of those classic, wooden torture tables from medieval times. The victim would be laid across it and chained down. As he was interrogated, the torturer would pull a large crank that stretched his arms and legs in opposite directions.

I tried to examine this new room. It looked like an old, abandoned saw mill from the 1800s—like the kind you see in the cartoons where the damsel in distress is tied to a log heading for a giant buzz saw as the mustachioed antagonist cackles maniacally. Above me were long, wooden tubes that must have once carried water around the mill. Now, they were the dried out arteries of something long dead. The roof of the chamber was absurdly high—the rotting wood exposed long, crooked fissures. I could see stars through some of them. Moss ran down the sides of the walls along with old stains of undetermined origins. The floor was covered with the remains of furniture and foundation—shattered bits of a once prosperous facility. To my right was a rickety staircase that led to an exit barred by a sturdy-looking iron door. To my left was a pile of corpses, dropped haphazardly in the corner. It took all I had to push the bile back down into my throat.

"You're awake," a familiar voice gasped. "But it's only been an hour."

A phantom drifted into view from somewhere behind my tabular prison. A gaunt vampire examined the bruises covering my face. I recognized him immediately. His torn ear was a dead giveaway, but most of my memories of him also involved ropes and a particularly sturdy tree.

"You." Disgust poured from my mouth like vomit. "What are you doing here?"

"This is where I live, Son of Man. Well... lived. I tried to leave once but was only met with hostility from those damn kappas."

"But I saved your life!" Anger boiled under my skin at the treacherous junkie.

"And I thank you for that. But death would have been a welcomed trade for this hunger." He took a step back, his red eyes sizing up a meal. "I really am sorry. I had to let him know about you. Hosef was the only one I knew who could get you away from that girl and the wolf and still give me a fair share of the meal. Although, it looks like you got rid of them yourself. No hard feelings, right?"

"If I get out of here, you're going to wish I had left you on that tree."

"Don't be so dramatic. What's the cow going to do to the butcher, anyway?"

"You have no idea what I'm capable of."

"Look, you helped a vampire. It's a rookie mistake. I really do appreciate you getting me off that tree, but just like that wolf, you don't understand what it's like to spend every waking moment starving; what it feels like to live in a constant state of death. We were forsaken by the gods and if it weren't for leaders like Hosef, we would be less than the nothing we already are."

The large iron door slammed open. It bounced off the ruined banister, sending splinters and dust cascading over the floorboards. The vampire was startled by the sudden noise and he jumped back.

I wasn't going to waste this opportunity. Maybe a little history lesson will teach these bastards how to treat a guest.

I extended my hand as far as I could into the rusty metal clasp, putting my thumb and middle finger together. A rippling pressure began to build around me but before I could summon the fog of memories, a solid object sailed from the opening at the top of the stairs and struck my hand with a crack. Agony ripped through my nervous system—like a lightning strike—as bones fractured apart.

"Nuh-uh, my special little treat. We'll have none o' dat silly magic in my house." Hosef's voice was loud and commanding.

The large vampire stood at the top of the staircase like some grand dictator. Several scrawny followers slunk in through the open door, their thin frames grossly contorted as they crawled over the rotting walls. Sunken faces stared hungrily toward my shackled, mortal form.

Hosef descended the old staircase, clapping his massive hands together as he went. "Whooooowheee! I thought I smelled sumthin' special off you, boy. I had hurd about a son removin' one o' da five from our midst, but I never woulduv' guessed he took his powers, too." All the vampires laughed in unison except for the one from the kappa's camp, who gaped with shock.

"What the hell do you want from me?" My hand had gone completely numb. I wondered if I had time to snap with my other.

"Got powers but still no brains. You so much as flex yer fingers, an' I'll break both yer arms." He circled me while the emaciated followers twitched and cackled in the corners. "We're vampires, boy. The blood o' yer kind is the only thing we can eat. Why else would we track a worthless son of man all over Missouri? Usually, we wait at the soft spots betwix worlds and drag yer kind out, but we apparently missed yer entrance. Wasn't 'til a few days ago that our ole' friend came back home to let us know some food was travelin' with a wolf an' a celestial. Must admit, I was surprised when we found you wanderin' through our woods by yer lonesome. But I didn't know how big a find it was."

A thought suddenly occurred to me. If these vampires could find the soft spots between the two planes, maybe they knew how to get through. "You said you wait near weak points in the world. Do you know how to pass through to the Plane of Man?"

Hosef let out a bellowing guffaw. "I told you, boy. Them gods closed the door and left our primary food source on the other side. Our kind starves for the taste o' the sons' blood—it tears us apart. If we could've gotten through, we'd a done it by now."

Now that he mentioned it, all the other vampires where thin and shaky—like addicts stuck in permanent withdrawal. Their skin lacked any sign of health and deep shadows highlighted all of their features. Their eyes were bright red and darted about the room, and their loose, hanging flesh draped sickeningly over old bones. All of them were nothing but deprived addicts—except for the round Hosef.

"You look pretty well fed, Hosef. It's your followers who look like they might need a bite."

"Now, now, boy. Don't judge. I always get the first taste. That won't matter no more, though. I was gonna just bleed you dry, but I bet we can round up quite a few more snacks with your powers. The Chronographers are the only creatures who can pass through the barrier, an' with yer unfortunate malady, we'll take that power. We're gonna walk through that wall and drink from every one o' the gods' favorite toys. We'll show 'em they can't take our food away. 'Zat right, fellas?"

Hosef's lackeys hooted and hollered in the crumbling mill. I felt a strange anger well up in me, something primal and powerful. I pulled hard with my left hand and ripped the chain out of the decayed wood. Screams echoed off the stained walls as the pawns scrambled for cover, but Hosef was on me almost immediately.

Stars burst across my vision as his thick head powered into mine. A huge fist broke my arm and the other hand wrapped a long length of chain around the table, making sure to weave a line of it between each of my fingers. The other vampires crept back into view, emerging from their hiding places.

"Can't let you do that, boy. I got big plans for you. Need to check some facts an' find out a way to use that there power you got. Not sure what it'll do to one of us, so sit tight and shut up."

"If I get out, I'm gonna rip your throat out and you'll never be able to drink anything ever again!" I was surprised by the hostility in my voice.

"Stay quiet, now." Hosef calmly walked back up the steps, followed by his menagerie of cohorts. "You'll make a demon blush with words like that. We'll have plenty o' time to talk when I'm good 'n ready." As he leaned over the railing at the top of the stairs, he turned to address the vampire who had been in the room at the beginning.

"Son, I want you to tie up this one's hands real tight. We don't want any o' that voodoo in here. An' when yer done with that," Hosef's eyes narrowed and his voice grew deadly serious, "get outta my house."

"What?" the vampire with the torn ear stammered.

"You abandoned dis house once already. I ain't gonna let you fall back in so easily. Secure the prisoner an' git out."

"But... but where will I go?"

"That din't bother you too much the first time you left." Hosef walked through the giant doorway. "Oh, and if I so much as see a bite mark on him, I'm gonna track you down and burn you to ashes. Capiche?"

"Yes, sir."

And so I was left alone with the pathetic outcast.

He picked up some chains and bound me to the board. "That bandersnatch. Thinks he can cut me out of my take. Just like the gods, he is. I don't know how, but I'll show him."

Something warm dripped down my cheek. The vampire's crimson eyes darted toward the spot. Hosef's monstrous headbutt had opened one of the welts on my forehead.

"He said I couldn't bite, not that I couldn't taste." He caressed the path of the dripping blood with a clawed finger. He smiled as he held it to the light, admiring its plasmic sheen. "He said you were his special catch. Well, you don't look too special to me, and I bet you taste the same as all the rest." He placed the stained digit into his mouth. His knees went weak as he tasted the rare delicacy and he returned for two more samples. Then, with a joyous inhale, he turned toward the door.

"Hey," I called, barely conscious. "What's your name?"

"Why does it matter? You'll never see me again."

"I have to know what to call you when I kill you."

The vampire laughed, a tiny bit of color had returned to his anemic cheeks. "If it helps you sleep at night, the name's Therin."

"Thanks, Therin, for giving me a reason to get out of here alive."

The last noise I heard was the steel door shutting and the sound of something heavy being dragged in front of it. Then, silence. I was alone again, or at least I thought I was. That strange feeling—that anger—still sat boiling under the surface. Maybe Luna was right; I might be losing control. At least if I transformed into a killing machine, it would be here and I would be able to keep that promise I made to Hosef and Therin.

My arms and face stung from the damage that had been inflicted to them. I'd be pretty useless in a fight until I managed to heal. I remembered someone once telling me that in war scenarios, it's always best to eat and sleep whenever you could because the chance might not come again. Actually, I didn't remember anyone I ever knew telling me that, but in the depths of my memory, I was sure I'd heard it somewhere. Maybe Colere was the one who'd heard it. It didn't matter; it seemed like the long, sleepless days prior to arriving in the mill had caught up with me. Soreness put a new weight on my muscles and I soon let the soft embrace of sleep take me away.

THREE

The dripping water stirred me. There was no light in the subway tunnel, but everything seemed clear as day. I glanced back and saw a large opening. Outside the smooth cavern walls was a large chamber. Stone tiles led outward, slowly changing material and shape as they led away from the grotto.

I began to walk, my legs working on autopilot. I tried to read the graffiti etched over the rock, but the long, arching curves spelled no words that I knew. Slowly, the markings faded and the mosaic walls became rocky and decrepit. The subway morphed into an old, subterranean tunnel.

Finally, my legs found wherever it was they wanted to go and ceased their movement. A person of my height stood facing a particularly smooth wall. A familiar air of authority exuded from his body.

Prometheus's head lifted slightly, as if realizing someone had just entered the room.

"It wasn't my fault, Father. It was a trap." The plump Astrian waddled past me, huffing loudly. "One minute I'm about to destroy the princess's bodyguard, the next he's summoning the nostalgia and setting me on fire."

"I know. I was watching as it happened."

Astrian's face grew dour. "Then you know it was all a set up. The moon girl and the son planned it from the beginning. They wanted to take Colere's power and now they're using it against us."

"I believe you are reading too far into things, Astrian. You will not be punished for your failure. Just be prepared for next time."

"Thank you for your mercy, Father." Astrian backpedaled out of the cave, bowing as he went. "You will not be sorry. They won't catch me off guard again." He whirled toward the entrance of the stone tunnel and dashed from sight.

Several moments passed in silence. I once again felt trapped inside of my body, but somewhere deep down, I felt as though I didn't want to leave.

Prometheus continued to stare at the tall, smooth cavern wall. He flicked his wrist and a small flame appeared. It hovered midair—like a leaf stuck in a strong wind—casting a bright light over the whole of the cavern. "Hello again, Noah. I assume you are adjusting well to your new gift?"

It was a strange question to ask. I had no words to share, but that seemed of little importance to the immortal. He brushed soot from the stone rock face, revealing crude caricatures of large horses and bison. Thin, dark lines flowed from the stone, revealing a strange life residing in each of the drawings. A memory flickered behind his old eyes and he seemed to become warmer. Distant happiness filled his features as he slowly traced the designs with his fingertips.

"I remember painting these. France was a much different place back then; it wasn't even called France yet. One day, floods ran through the valley where we lived and everyone found themselves fearing disaster. As they huddled close, water rising outside, I mixed some herbs and minerals together and began painting on the cave wall. The others soon gathered and we worked together to create beautiful murals over every inch of our home. It was one of the first things I had my children take." He turned toward me and those piercing blue eyes met mine. "Do you know why I started painting on that night?"

For the first time in this strange place, my voice was my own. But even though I could speak freely, I chose to simply shake my head.

"There was no reason. And the reason I felt it necessary to tell you this story? There is none for that either. You see, Noah, a conclusion is simply the rationalization for telling a story. Sometimes things just happen and there is no moral. How a person perceives an action is irrelevant to the action itself."

I continued to stare at him. The rambling seemed that of a mad man.

"I guess I didn't expect you to understand. I just figured somebody who has gone through as much as you could use the advice. Just take it as knowledge from someone who's been in your shoes."

He turned back to the painting and pressed a palm against the cool stone. When he lifted it, the images were gone. "I am impressed with your performance thus far. You made interesting work of

Three—I think you've been calling him Astrian. They change their names so often I've grown weary of trying to remember them all. Maybe if he wasn't so caught up in his theatrics, he wouldn't have fallen so easily. Alas, I cannot begrudge you for another's faults. You will eventually make a fine addition to my ranks, even if it is for the little time I allow the world to exist."

Anger welled up inside me. I would never join him. I wanted to reach out and strangle him, but I simply remained still.

"Save it. You've got more interesting troubles. I will see you again soon, Noah." Prometheus turned toward the darkness of the old tunnel and walked away, fading into the shadowy corners of the room.

The small flame gently fell to the floor until it licked the coarse soil, coming to rest in a small pile of ash. It burned low and surrounded me with an acrid smell. The smoke began to make my eyes water.

Then, I woke.

XIV

A yell from somewhere in the mill roused me. The smell of smoke lingered in my nostrils. The room where I was being kept was empty. A dim sunlight broke through the cracks in the ceiling. *It must be early morning.*

The yelling grew louder, moving closer to my cell. An explosion sounded to my right and the heavy steel door flew off its hinges and sailed over my head, followed closely by a sturdy oak bookshelf.

And Hosef.

They slammed against the far wall, erupting into shrapnel and splinters, and clattered into a pile on the floor. A dark mist crept over the edge of the steps and a man walked out onto the overhang.

He was short and thin, and he wore a pair of gray, paint-stained, woven pants and sandals. Multi-colored acrylic streaks covered his shirt and skin, like he had been painting haphazardly all day long. Over his shoulders rested a thick, brown overcoat, which barely hovered above the floor. His skin was a deep tan—as if he'd been standing in the sun for too long—and his brown hair fell to his shoulders in a band of loosely tangled curls. He smiled through his bushy beard and his white teeth stood in deep contrast to his darkened features.

Hosef rose from the pile of rubble, brushing large chunks of wood from his leather jacket. "You damn puppets," he yelled. "We ain't never get no credit. Yer masters left us to die, and now yer gonna contin'ya interferin' in our lives? If'n a mongrel son of man can kill the scum o' the gods, then so can the king of the vampires." Hosef didn't get a chance to find out if he could take on the Chronographer.

The man in the brown duster simply lifted a finger to his lips, an inky mist curling around it. A twitch of smoke danced across the room and Hosef's top half tumbled to the floor followed shortly by his legs, the top half of the bookcase, and the remains of the thick metal door.

"Shhhh," the man whispered. "Not in front of the guest."

He stood at the head of the wooden table, eying me with interest.

I was better off with the vampires. I was pretty sure they couldn't cut people in half with their minds. I really didn't want it to end here by Prometheus's resident hippie. There was no running this time; I had to figure out a way to fight now or die on the table. My fingers felt a lot better. If I could wriggle them from the chains, I might be able to summon my own mist.

"No, my friend, I wouldn't do that. Sleep may heal your injuries, but your spirit may still be damaged." The man with the long, curly hair twirled his finger in the air. The length of the chain began to shake and every link that bound me split, sliding to the floor in a rattling cacophony. I slid off the table and crumpled onto the damp wood.

As soon as I was free, I patted myself down, looking for the wounds—but there were none.

A hand dropped from above my head. The paint-stained man glanced down at me. "Well, c'mon, Noah. We don't have all day."

I reached up and took his hand. What else could I do? "Who are you?" I grunted as he lifted me to my feet.

"I am Four, Chronographer of Art."

"Okay, so what do I call you?"

"Hmmm." Four pondered. "I guess you can just call me Art."

"Simple enough," I replied, stepping over a piece of Hosef. "So, Art, why aren't you trying to kill me?"

Art laughed—a charming, pleasant laugh. It didn't hold as much bravado as the others I'd heard in this strange world. In a way, it was very close to human.

"I'm not as narrow-minded as my siblings. However, this is neither the time nor the place. We have some ground to cover, Noah, and there is much to explain."

Art turned to the door and climbed up the ramshackle steps. I followed close behind.

The main room of the mill was worse off than the one in which I had been kept. The roof had been broken apart and beaten furniture littered every square inch of the floor. Where there weren't old, stained sofas, there were scattered scraps of past meals. I knew those victims could rest easy now. Littered between the bones and blood were the severed remains of Hosef's vampire coterie. Many were still moving, crawling about in search of whatever lost limb they had suffered. Others did their best to drag themselves away from the large fires burning in the corners of the building.

I hurried forward to keep up with Art's pace. I didn't know why I was following him—I should have run in the other direction or attacked while his back was turned—but for some reason, I just trusted this guy. He wasn't like the others. There was no malice in his eyes and I didn't feel that heavy air of danger around him. It really was as if I was talking to something human.

"If you've been keeping track of art all these years, where did you learn to cut people in half?"

"Not all art is paint and canvas, Noah," Art countered. "Connoisseurs would say surgery is an art." He looked back and winked. "Grab your bag. You'll need it."

I picked up my bag from a table at the end of the room and we stepped through the large, open doors of the mill. Dawn was rising over the trees and a cool wind swept across the forest floor. Art glanced about quickly and located the path he wanted. He quickly waved me on and headed through the dew-covered glade.

"So, really, why aren't we fighting?"

"Not all of us are killers. We just have a job to do."

"But you're still killing. You destroy people and ideas just to gather whatever knowledge they have."

Art stopped and looked at me. His brown eyes hid a powerful anguish. "You know, I have... taken millions of artists. I used to have Leonardo Da Vinci show me who he thought were the most adept painters of the time. I have been the only person to see some of the greatest inventions never created, and I've pinched the flames of the most talented musicians from whom no one else had heard a note. But I've never played a guitar, and I've never painted a picture. I can't even read a blueprint. Still, I admire these things that I see—these things that I take. They are beauty and grace, and are the only joy I get in life. Yet, I still must be the one to destroy them." Art turned and shuffled through the brush again.

I stood for a moment, thinking about what he had said. I'd viewed the Chronographers as mindless creatures of destruction, but here I was hearing remorse. "Then why?" I shouted at his back, hustling to keep up. "Why don't you stop?"

"We're not too different than you—humans, I mean. We were carved from the same mold, but our souls were burned away to make room for the memories. That's what the nostalgia—the dark mist—is made of. It contains the remnants of a human soul."

He ducked under a low branch and continued. "Because of this, we are left without some key components. We cannot love or hate. We aren't supposed to be able to die, and we cannot create life. Those gifts are reserved for other species."

I hurried to get next to him.

"So many stories are untold or misrepresented. For instance, most of the creatures on this side believe the worlds were separated because your race was too malleable."

"It wasn't?" It was my only winded contribution as I somehow rediscovered my mortal clumsiness.

"No, it was because you were too valuable. Your species were the creators. You made monuments and wrote sonatas. You had the most diverse range of emotions. Have you ever seen a Cyclops cry? Have you ever seen a werewolf paint a picture? If our task were to simply collect the knowledge from this side, we would have finished eons ago. The gods wanted to preserve your kind."

"I still don't understand. Why can't you just stop the killing?"

"Don't you?" Art glanced at me and his coat caught the morning wind. A blue smudge across his face reflected a deep hue of sunlight. "Every story has its pertinent details, even Prometheus's. He was punished, and we are a part of his punishment. As I said, key traits were removed from our being. I am obsessed with art, but I do not love it... nor can I. The gods saw fit to keep that from us, and so we live to serve the only purpose one can have without hate or love to guide him. We try to learn from those around us."

"I thought the gods gave Prometheus a gift?"

Art laughed again and a flake of blue paint chipped and fell from his cheek. When I looked again, the smudge on his face was as solid as it had ever been. "That is a complicated story and our time grows short. You will learn many things as you continue your journey, but there are a few you must know now. Prometheus has larger plans than you can imagine and your involvement is the key for every outcome. Your friends are in danger. They are close to the one who hears all, but so is my brother."

I wondered if I was even welcome with them anymore. Luna had warned me not to come back, but I knew Chip wouldn't be able to hold off one of the five. Even if she no longer wanted to see me, I had to help. "I have to go find her."

"I agree, but I don't believe my siblings will hold back against you any longer. You have our power, but you are still mortal. It may take a lot more to kill you, but you *can* die."

I tried not to let him see the shiver that ran down my spine at the thought.

If Art saw it, he didn't show it, and instead continued faster through the forest. "Just remember that a mouse living among lions will eventually learn to roar, but it will never hold the same meaning. The emotions we have are learned, not real—just farces gained from a life of mingling among other species. This gives you—as a human—the edge. Think outside the box. Use that creative mind the gods gave you."

"I will. I promise. But how am I going to get all the way to Kansas in time to do anything? I've walked miles in the other direction."

Art stopped and placed his hand on an overhanging clump of moss and ivy. He pushed it away, revealing a derelict overpass looming over a beaten, overgrown road.

I stepped forward, amazed.

"I believe Luna misplaced something of hers the last time she was in your bag."

I dropped my backpack to the grass and knelt down. Tossing my clothes aside, I dug all the way to the bottom and felt the smooth length of a polished bone. It was the wishbone that had saved us in the city. I turned to show Art, but he was no longer there—just the trees and the morning dew. "Thanks, Art," I muttered to nothing. "I guess I owe you one."

I pushed all of my stuff back into the bag, swung it over my shoulder, closed my eyes, and ran toward the overpass.

XV

The calming sounds of the woods faded into the darkness. I concentrated hard on Luna and a small glow appeared behind my eyelids. I reached out toward it and felt a strange warmth enter my hand. I closed my fist around the warmth and pulled with all my might. It was oddly familiar—like this was the natural purpose for a common wishbone and it was telling me exactly what I needed to do.

Heat from a high sun beat down on my face. When I opened my eyes, I saw lush, green fields all around me. A car passed on my right side, buffeting me with loose gravel. I stepped off the road and inspected the wishbone. I looked at the deep cleft down the center and felt it shiver in my hand. With a crack, the left side chipped off and fell to the dirt.

"Guess you're all out of juice." I dropped the smooth bone next to its broken companion.

It looked as though it were midday and there was no sign of Luna. I wasn't really sure where I was, either. I squinted hard and looked into the distance. The sun burned my eyes, but I could barely see the outline of some sort of farmhouse. If Luna were anywhere nearby, she'd have to be there. I took a deep breath and started jogging toward the old house on the horizon. I knew the wishbone had put me several hours later than when I'd started. I bit down and hoped I wasn't too late.

As I got closer, I saw a white, beaten-up RV. Hope welled up in my throat and I choked on it. Somewhere in the sky, a thunderclap broke through the stormless clouds. Fumbling to a halt, I looked up and saw a single, blue lightning bolt careening toward earth. When it struck, the shockwave sent a cloud of dust swirling in all directions. I raised a hand to divert the approaching wave of soil. When the storm passed, a figure stood on the dirt path leading to the house. It wore a gray, hooded jacket and jeans, and began walking—barefoot—toward the parked vehicle.

I broke into a full run. I could just make out the faded, red paint and the large, lone oak tree in the front yard. The howl of a wolf rose over the field. I lowered my head and raced next to the white fence. My heart pounded in my chest but I pushed on.

I veered around the edge of the worn picket fence and hurried down the long dirt driveway. My feet thumped loudly, and clay-colored dust sprang from the earth with every heavy footstep.

I could see Chip striking swiftly in the distance—like a hairy boxer. Lojo skillfully dodged each blow and through these quick feints I saw Luna, her red hair dancing about her white eyes. I ran faster. I was so close I could hear Lojo's mechanical voice spouting nonsense on the futility of fighting back.

Chip swiped at him with a heavy claw and Lojo parried with a powerful blow to the chest. The wolf collapsed to the ground, winded. The Chronographer raised a pale fist, sparks crackling thunderously through the air.

I pushed myself as hard as my mortal body could handle, lowered my shoulder, and plowed into Lojo's back. We rolled across the dirt in a tangle of limbs.

Chip sprang backward into a defensive position and Lojo staggered back to his feet. His hood had fallen, revealing his face. It wasn't an improvement. He was completely bald, which included a sickly lack of eyebrows and lashes. His skin was translucent—blue veins traced a heinous outline that flashed with surges, like electricity. Pointed ears sat to the sides and sinister fangs slept between icy, blue lips. When he raised his head, our eyes met. The sockets were empty chasms except for eerie, blue LED lights that shone from somewhere deep within those black holes.

"Noah?" A shocked expression flashed across Luna's face.

"The scum returns? At least it is good timing," Chip addressed me politely.

"How did you find us?" Luna interrupted. "I told you not to follow."

"A friend told me you were in trouble. Looks like he was right."

Lojo had gathered his wits about him. "I was not sure if I would see you again, Noah Lane," he droned. "Your petty tricks will not save you this time."

"We'll see whose petty tricks trick who." I cursed myself for such a lame opening. I was kind of a super hero now, so the least I could do was come up with better quips.

"I heard you have stolen our bloodline. I will remedy this error."

We raised our hands at the same time and a boundless sound rang from our fingertips. The echo sent ripples tearing through reality. The effect was much more intense than I had remembered. Two sets of mist—his black and mine white—ruptured from the deep lacerations.

I concentrated and pulled it toward me, scanning the cloud of memories for something useful. Each dewy drop flashed with bright images of triumph and despair. As I poured through Colere's nostalgia, I wished I had taken one of the other Chronographer's powers. All I could find were religious rituals and architecture, but I knew there was one culture that prided itself on its fighting ability. I could only hope Colere had found it interesting enough to visit.

I raised my hand and cast a line into the swirl of recollection. Bright bursts of sparring men and lines of warriors marched through my head. I was pulled into a hectic world of battle and death. The rise and fall of an entire civilization played in front of my eyes. The mist wrapped around my hands and hardened into solid objects. In my left, the damp cloud became cold and round. Twenty pounds of wood and bronze attached to my forearm. The smoke curled around my right hand and sprang outward as a seven-foot Spartan war spear sprouted from the abyss. I hefted the two objects and faced my opponent who was standing—hands crossed—examining me with empty eyes.

"Crude weapons. I see you do not fully understand the power you have taken. Allow me to demonstrate."

Lojo stretched his arms to his sides and the black mist surrounded them. Azure sparks crackled and jumped from his body. The nostalgia spun violently—like two livid tornadoes. They grew and slithered outward, his sleeves tearing under the fierce winds.

Large cylinders materialized from his shoulders. The smoke continued to twirl outward as long, snake-like cables—the width of tree trunks—came to rest against the ground. They continued to grow until they spanned half the length of the beaten driveway. Lojo had turned his arms into two huge, severed wires—sparks flashing dangerously at the tips.

I heard Luna gasp from somewhere behind Lojo and saw Chip's mouth hanging open, eyes wide.

With no effort, Lojo raised one large, gray tentacle. A long shadow sprawled across the dirt as the thick coil blotted out the sun.

I stumbled backward as it whipped toward me. Raising my shield in defense, I attempted to deflect the blow but the titanic impact sent me tumbling across the ground.

"You are now witnessing the power of technology. There is no hope, Son of Man." He assaulted me with both tentacles, moving them independently—like it was normal to have two thirty-foot cables exploding with electricity for arms. They crashed to my left and right, uprooting large chunks of earth into the air as I dodged between strikes.

Using my shield, I parried a whip snap on my left and struck out with my spear, slowly gaining ground until I could hit something vital. I blocked a sweep on my right and lunged, pinning down a slithering tentacle with my spear.

Blue sparks erupted from the wound, but Lojo looked unfazed. His other wire collided into my back, sending me tumbling over the one already down.

Pain surged up my spine as I lay on the ground. The spear clattered against the earth nearby and another dark shadow fell overhead. I saw the two large arms coiling around one another and rising high above. I pulled my shield closer, preparing for the full force of the impact as the tentacles fell toward me. A howl pierced the sky and the deadly wires smashed into the empty dirt at my sides. I looked up and saw Chip riding Lojo's back.

He had him in a disarming hold with both hands strung under Lojo's armpits and wrapped behind his neck. "We'll hold him," Chip called in his gruff accent. "Wash the ground with his blood!"

His savage words fueled my fighting spirit and I sprung to my feet, hauling the spear up as I ran. Lojo struggled but remained calm as I sprinted toward him, weapon raised. This was it. I heard Luna's voice cry out.

"Noah, stop!"

I ignored her words as I struck downward with all my strength. Before I could land the hit, Lojo let out a high pitch scream. It sounded just like the noise that had come from the phone in my old apartment. An explosion of blue sparks collided into me like a wrecking ball and threw Chip and I away from the deadly creature.

I hung in the air as a black flash crossed my vision. The cold slap of a heavy tentacle colliding into my side sent me rocketing back to earth. I slammed into the ground, digging a trench with my body as I skidded through the dirt. I felt my ribs crack when the lone oak tree brought me to a complete stop. I could see Chip coughing up blood into the grass behind Lojo who, for the first time since I'd seen him, was smiling.

"You creatures are pathetic. Your very existence is a blight to the world." His usually calculated voice was now passionate and unfettered. His eyes grew brighter, flickering with every word. "Nature has never created anything worthy of living, and in time, technology will be all that remains."

I had to think of something fast. Obviously, direct attacks weren't going to work; not if he could create a shockwave every time we came close. But there was something Art had said that echoed in my memory. The Chronographers may have power, but they lacked creativity. If I could just find a way to trick him I could take him out. But how? I pushed myself up using the butt of my spear, bracing myself against the tree.

"Yes, get up. You organics and your fantasies will never match technology's exact logic."

That was it! The Chronographers were like actors stuck in a role. The fake emotions they portrayed were nothing more than predictable stereotypes. Lojo was the same as the evil supercomputer in every science fiction movie I'd ever seen. All I had to do was play the opposing role and goad him into attacking. If I could do it right, I just might have a chance.

"Please, Lojo." I tried to sneer at him through the sting of my broken ribs. "If it weren't for us 'organics' and our fantasies, technology wouldn't even exist."

Lojo's face remained stone cold. "Elaborate."

"It's not really complicated." I stood in front of the oak tree the best I could manage, using the worn spear as a cane. My side ached and blood was pooling at the bottom of my "Bonjour France" shirt. "Without us to imagine all the crazy, high-tech gadgets, they never would've been made. So... without the sons of man, your existence would be impossible."

"Incorrect. Nothing is impossible." Lojo's LED eyes faded a little. His shoulders shrank and his tentacles twitched a little less.

"Oh really? Nothing's impossible? Well then, isn't it impossible to find something impossible? Logic your way out of that one, Mr. Silicon."

Lojo dropped his gaze and began to shake. His usual poise fell from his body like sparks from a severed wire. He looked at Chip, who was beginning to stand, and Luna, still poised in the backfield. Then, he turned back to me and spoke quietly and concisely. "Your assumptions are erroneous. We are superior to the sons of man in every way. I will not have such filth be spoken by a bag of meat. As of now, this battle is over."

Both of his rubbery arms shot out directly toward my chest. I said a quick prayer that my plan would work and dropped down into a low crouch, lifting the shield above my head. Both tentacles slid over the polished bronze, colliding into the large tree. As soon as I heard cracking wood giving in to this new opposing force, I spun around and jammed the spear through both Lojo's arms and as deep into the tree trunk as I could. The tentacles sparked and flailed but couldn't break free. The huge impact sent the tree toppling over, pulling on the cables and lifting Lojo off his feet.

As he stumbled wildly in my direction, I stepped to one side and watched him rocket toward the spot I had been previously standing in. When he drifted past, I raised my shield into the air and slammed the blunt edge into the back of his neck. With an awful crack, he crumpled to the ground. I lifted the shield and, with a yell, slammed it into Lojo's body again. I thought of all the pain he and his brothers had caused me as I dropped the heavy bronze shield onto his soft flesh again and again and again.

"Noah, that is enough!" Luna's voice rang in my ears and a hand came to rest on my shoulder.

Lojo's thick, wire arms had turned back into a black mist and were dissipating into the air. When the receding smoke reached his broken body, it began to glow a bright blue. With a thunderclap, he soared into the sky and out of sight.

I lifted my arms and let my weapons dematerialize back into memories. I felt the heavy weight of the nostalgia lessen. I was breathing hard and my side ached. A deep cut across my face burned through the impacted soil. I looked up into Luna's eyes, which had turned back into a comforting grayish-yellow.

"So," I wheezed, still kneeling in the dirt. "How've you guys been?"

Chip covered the distance between us in two long strides. He scooped me up by the shoulder with his huge, furry paws.

"You were very impressive. We commend your fighting spirit, but we could have done better."

"I bet," I choked out, turning a unique shade of blue.

"Sadly, you're still a vermin and are not fit to be near the Lady." Chip let forth a low snarl. His hot breath stung my eyes and I felt blood streaming down my leg. "We will crush your skull between our jaws."

"Chip!" Luna shouted authoritatively. "Put him down."

"But Lady Luna, he is one of them. We should finish this right now."

"He saved us and he is our friend."

Chip looked at me and then at Luna. He let out a high whimper.

"Down, boy," Luna ordered again, like he was a puppy that had just taken her slipper. He looked at me one last time and let go.

I crumpled to the ground and felt my insides shift. I had thought that since I had the power of a god, getting my ass kicked wouldn't hurt so badly. Guess I was wrong.

"I- I am glad to see you again." She reached a hand out to me.

"Me too."

She took my hand and slung it over her shoulder. Chip folded his arms and put his back to us, his tail curling between his legs.

I looked back at Luna and saw her staring at the smoking crater where Lojo had been moments ago.

"Did you kill him?"

"No, but I think he'll be gone for a while."

"So you and they *are* immortal."

The words stung, for some reason. "No, I'm still mortal. I'm just a little more durable than average."

Chip let out a cheerful bark. "Good! That means you're still crushable." He swung around and patted me on the back. I almost fell over. "Still, we do thank you for your help."

I hoped I was right about Lojo. I figured that if I had to sleep for a few hours to work off a head wound, a broken spine would take at least a day. With any luck, Prometheus would punish him, too. At the very least, I took solace in knowing I was back with my friends. Sure, Chip was more dog than man, but Luna always seemed to make me feel more comfortable. I looked into her twin-moon eyes and instantly felt more relaxed.

Just as I had begun to appreciate being near her again, Chip walked over and took me from Luna. He slung me over his shoulder with one burly arm and I was suddenly assaulted by the smell of unwashed dog fur. He spun me around, facing me forward, and I winced.

"Looks like the big hero didn't get away without his own wounds," Chip mused.

"I'll be fine, I just need to rest."

Together, we went up to the big farmhouse. It stood two stories tall and was painted a dull red, which was chipping away from lack of care. A worn, stone sidewalk started from nowhere in particular and led up to the old-timey deck, complete with wooden bench swing.

We traveled up the two steps to the front door. Luna pulled aside the first door—which was screened in—and looked toward the second, which was painted with streaks of white. She raised a hand to knock on the sturdy frame but before she could, it flung open.

A tall, lanky man in a white robe stood in front of us. He had a long, gray beard that flowed all the way to his rope belt and his skin was fiercely tanned. He squinted hard, eying the three of us with caution. Then, he looked directly at me. "You're late."

XVI

The ceiling fan spun rhythmically overhead in the dark room. It was the first time I'd laid in a real bed since I'd left my apartment. The quiet pull of sleep tugged at my eyelids, but my mind was aflutter with the events of the day. That, and I felt that if I let my weariness take me, I'd find myself in that familiar theater with those demanding eyes breaking though my defenses.

I rolled onto my side and felt a twinge of pain. My rib still ached from the fight and I knew the only relief would come with rest. The clock on the nightstand read 2:11 a.m. I could barely make out the thick, vertical lines decorating the white walls surrounding me. An ancient wooden dresser sat lonely in the corner of the room with a large mirror mounted on top. From what I'd seen of the house, all the bedrooms were just like this one. In fact, I had noticed that the old building seemed much larger on the inside than it looked from yard. I suspected this was one of the many magical charms this side of the world had to offer. From the moment we walked through the door, things had got increasingly stranger.

The tall man in the white robe had beckoned us in, shifting from one foot to the other. "Please, please come in. I grew tired of waiting for you and minded some distractions. I'll reheat the meal and have you full of food in no time." The man spun around, his white beard arching slowly with his movement, and jaunted into another room.

The three of us exchanged perplexed looks, shrugged, and walked in.

The main room was large and friendly. A round, green carpet rested in the center of the floor, and wooden floorboards extended outward from it like the petals of a strange flower. The varnished boards continued up the walls and over the slanted ceiling where a glowing chandelier watched from its high perch. In the center of the cozy den, a navy blue leather sofa sat facing the door. A matching recliner sat caddy-corner from it, and a coffee table nuzzled in front of both. All of these faced an antique television with a dial channel changer on the front and a silver, bent antenna on top.

Luna gasped and danced gracefully about the room, looking at the golden trout statues and crystal snow globes with tiny boats inside that sat on the mantle of the fireplace and on the many other shelves that littered the room. Even Chip drifted in with a conservative awe.

The walls were littered with all sorts of memorabilia from the sea. On one wall, a pegged ship's wheel rested above an assortment of freeze-dried sea creatures. Urchins, seahorses, and blowfish all sat still, as if the frozen in time.

Chip set me on the recliner and gazed longingly at an enormous blue marlin mounted on the wall near the door where the old man had entered. "We didn't know they made fish this big." For the first time in a long while, I heard more human than animal in his voice.

"You've never been to the ocean, Chip?" I asked skeptically.

"No, we can't swim."

I sank into the comfy chair while Chip and Luna explored. The first pangs of weariness sidled into my joints. There was too much happening to succumb to it now so I tried to focus on something to keep my mind aware. There were several old *Field and Stream* magazines resting on the coffee table, and sand dollar coasters glistened white underneath the chandelier's glow. In the center of the table was a medium-sized fishbowl with a medium-sized goldfish inside. I leaned forward to get a better look at the creature.

It circled the bowl above a collection of multicolored gravel. A tiny treasure chest opened and closed every few seconds, allowing an army of bubbles to march toward the surface of the water. I reached out and tapped the glass. The hefty goldfish spun around in surprise. The reaction seemed odd to me, but the fish swam up to where my finger was placed. First, he examined the spot where my finger had made the noise. Then, he looked up at me and shook his little fish head and smiled with his little fish lips.

I blinked the confusion from my eyes and looked about the room. Everyone else was still wandering around, looking at trinkets. I turned back toward the bowl and leaned in close. I pointed at myself and the fish nodded in reply. I was about call Luna over to see for herself when the old man in the robe reentered the room.

"My guests, please come with me. Dinner is served."

Chip lifted me from the recliner and followed the old man behind Luna. I looked back at the bowl and could have sworn the goldfish waved me goodbye with a medium-sized fin. Chip plopped me into another chair and we all gawked in amazement. The steady pat of Chip's tail against the back of his seat was the only thing that assured me I wasn't dreaming.

The dining room was impossibly large for the size of the house. The ceiling was adorned with an old fishing net, complete with fake sea creatures tangled within. But the table—oh, the table!—was the best thing I'd seen in days. An enormous turkey sat glistening in the center. Chocolate and vanilla swirled pudding and light, fluffy biscuits, buttered to perfection, called my name.

The color in Luna's eyes glowed pale yellow as she savagely eyed a bowl of simmering crab chowder. Chip seemed to be doing everything in his power to hold himself back from the juicy leg of ham that rested just a few inches from his salivating tongue, which bobbed restlessly from between his lips.

The man in the white robe pressed his hair back and beckoned us to eat.

The explosive flavors that attacked my senses was nothing short of divine.

The sound of Chip's ravenous chomping played steadily, and even Luna would let out an exuberant sigh after tasting particular items for the first time.

The dinner seemed to last forever and I wished it would never end, but eventually, I set down the end half of a chocolate-chip cookie and slumped back into my chair, so full I could barely move.

The kindly man smiled wide beneath his bushy beard.

Luna wiped her lips with a napkin and politely addressed him. "I give you my greatest thanks. We have been traveling long and have not eaten such a meal as this for quite some time. Is there any way we can repay you... um... I do not believe you have given us a name?"

"Oh my." The old man laughed, leaning forward in his seat. "I can't believe I forgot. My name is James."

"Well, James, we thank you for your hospitality and this fine meal. Your reputation truly precedes you. We have come very far to tap into your unique ability."

James rubbed his fuzzy chin, obviously confused. "And what 'unique ability' would that be, my dear? If it's my cooking, you have already partaken in all I can accomplish."

"Your knowledge," Luna persisted. "I have heard there is a man who lives in this area—in a house just like this—who hears all the goings-on in the world. A terrible grievance has been done to my family and I wish to know where I must go for retribution."

The old man looked at Luna for a long time, and then he laughed a boisterous, cheerful laugh. His beard leaped about as his chest inflated and fell.

"My dear, I've heard what has happened to the children of the moon, but I believe you're in search of my master, not me."

"Your master? But you seem to know so much and you dress in the humble attire of a sage."

James fell into another giggling fit.

Annoyed, Chip looked up from the bone he was gnawing on and let loose a low snarl.

"Calm down, pup," James wheezed as he recovered his composure. "The situation is merely amusing. As I said, you were late. I was informed of your arrival days ago and prepared the house. Then you got into that little altercation outside and I figured I had time for a quick shower. Whence you finished the disagreement, I had no time to change and had to greet you in my bath robe."

All of us stared at the old man, stupefied.

"If you'd like, I could take you to see the master of the house. Although, I must warn you, those who come to hear his knowledge rarely leave with what they came for."

Luna closed her eyes, gathering her thoughts. "Please, if you would not mind, I wish to speak to him as soon as possible. It is of utmost importance."

"Well then, Princess, please follow me. Don't worry about the dishes, young Noah. I will tend to them once you are settled with the master."

We pushed our chairs from the table and moved back into the den. I waved Chip off when he tried to carry me. My rib was still a splitting reminder of my own mortality, but the meal had given me new strength and I felt I could move without having to nuzzle up to his fur.

James led us to the couches and bid us to sit. Luna and Chip took the long sofa and I resumed my original position on the recliner. James stood between the two couches and remained motionless. We sat in silence for some time. I began to wonder if we had all been frozen along with the dried up fish. I fidgeted in my seat to remind myself that I still could, but it was Chip who lost his patience first.

"Well, are you going to bring your master in or do we sit here for the rest of the day?"

"My bipolar, canine friend," James retorted, amused but obviously irritated. "I didn't know you were so ill-informed. You currently sit with the master of the house and I beg you show to him more manners than you have shown me."

I looked around the room for some other living creature before my eyes landed squarely on the husky goldfish at the center of the table. He did a small circle around his bowl, halted, and pressed his face against the glass.

"The fish?" I asked, pointing down into the top of the bowl.

"Beg your pardon, sir. The master is no mere fish. He is the Elderfish—the fabled fish from the thousand-year-old legend. He is the fish who granted the fisherman who caught him one wish in exchange for release. He has heard all and knows everything that is spoken in the world."

"How does a fish know what people are saying around the world?" The question seemed silly. How could a fish know what anyone was saying even right next to it?

"Son, haven't you heard that sound travels better in water?"

I looked at him dumbly.

"Well, it's true. Everything said aloud in the world resonates through every drop of moisture in the air. It travels millions of miles though sky and sea until it reaches here... and the Elderfish hears it. From this, he has learned many things that will come to pass and the deepest secrets of those too afraid to utter words to anyone but themselves. Go on, ask him a question."

I leaned forward and peered through the glass bowl. The orange fish darted about, growing in size as the bowl magnified and shrunk him, depending on his position. I voiced my request loudly and slowly, as if speaking into a drive-through microphone. "Um, oh great Elderfish, I... uh... wish to know what Chip had for breakfast yesterday."

The fish swam close to the glass and moved its tiny mouth. Small bubbles floated to the surface and whenever one popped, a posh British accent exploded into the air.

"I'm not deaf, you bipedal oaf." The bubbles spilled out. "He ate some socks you left in the automobile. He chewed on them for days prior. I dare say, he could have washed them first. Speaking of wash, my bowl could use a good scrubbing. Have you any jam?"

I looked up at Chip and saw him turn away in shame, a small whimper of embarrassment escaping his lips.

"Well, it works."

"Indeed it does," James replied. "I'll leave you to speak with the master while I tidy up the kitchen." He shuffled back toward the dining room, his footsteps falling silently on the hardwood floor. I looked down and saw he was wearing fluffy, white bunny slippers with comically small, brown antlers jutting from each side.

We sat in silence, once again. The goldfish quickly swam laps around his tank, stopping frequently to examine the sunken treasure chest over and over.

Finally, Luna cautiously leaned over the lip of the bowl. "Elderfish, my family was recently... killed... by one of the Chronographers. Since then, I have traveled through many hardships to find you. I wish to know why they came to our peaceful lands."

The magical fish darted about the bowl, leaving bubbles in its wake. "My dear girl, you have already spoken this answer aloud. Your gift is powerful in their hands and was well used in their goals. Can I have some of those flakes?"

Luna reached out, taking a small tube of food and shook it into the tank.

"I knew Prometheus wanted my family's sight. He will not have it completely until he takes mine. We must stop him before he gets the chance." She turned and addressed the goldfish again, who was snatching the food from the water's surface. "Elderfish, where is Prometheus? How can we stop him?"

"Did you know that monofilament fishing lines account for two-thirds of the retail market?" The fish's bubbles broke against the surface in quick bursts. Luna closed her eyes for a moment, rubbing her temples with her thumb and forefinger.

"No, I did not know that. Could you tell me what we must do to stop Prometheus's plan?"

"Well, first you could—Hey, did that seahorse just move? Did you know that there are over fifty varieties of seahorses? I think the hippocampus is the most beautiful species of horse on the planet. Then again, it is the only one I've actually seen. Is it Tuesday?"

"Why will you not answer me squarely? I must know how to avenge my mother and father." Luna was on her feet now, yelling down into the water.

The Elderfish fled behind the small, sunken chest. James entered the room again and set his old hand on Luna's shoulder. "I'm sorry. I told you—many who come here do not get the answers they seek. My dear, many say fish have short memories, but that's incorrect. You see, they just have very low attention spans."

"But he answered my first question!" Luna's usual composure shattered. Waves of emotion flowed from her body like a torrent rushing from a broken dam. "He told you that we were coming. Why will he not answer me?"

"I've been in this house for many years," James replied calmly. "His information comes in waves, much like the waters he was once accustomed to. I only knew of your arrival because he spoke it aloud late one night."

Luna closed her eyes and tried to calm herself. "Then how am I supposed to find Prometheus?"

"Although the Elderfish doesn't often give information readily, he does give information. You may safely stay in this house for as long as you deem necessary."

"I could use a night to recover," I chimed in.

"Then we will stay for a while, since I do not know what to do without his help."

James smiled. "Good! I'll prepare your bedrooms." He moved swiftly from the room with a hop in his step, obviously glad to have company.

The three of us sat around the glass bowl while the Elderfish swam cheerfully in circles, occasionally informing us of weather patterns and reciting the alphabet in different languages. Before long, James returned and bade us into our new rooms. We stomped up the stairs and through the narrow hallway. Chip's bulky shoulders brushed against the high walls, casting dark shadows as he maneuvered around the lamps that illuminated the corridor.

James waved Chip and then Luna through the first two doors we passed. As we continued on, he favored me with a few cursory glances. Before I could ask him what was the matter, he bowed low and opened the last door. Ushering me in, he turned for a final word. "You are much younger than I anticipated. The follies of elders are truly heaped upon the shoulders of babes. Good night, Noah."

And here I lay, wondering what we were going to do now. How long would Luna wait for this fish to spill some vital piece of information? There had to be something I could do to help. But how could I help her if I couldn't even help myself? I was too afraid to even sleep.

It seemed like every time I rested, I moved a little closer to Prometheus, losing some speck of control over myself. So I sat there in the bed, fretting the very thought of sleeping, wishing I could excavate some long lost piece of my life. Everyone, whether it was vampire or seer, had some kind of use for me, but I remained an unsolved puzzle to myself.

I wondered if I still truly wanted to return home, even if I could. Would my family accept me for what I had become? Could I fall back into the regular swing of things, now that I knew the truth about the world? Could I leave Luna behind? Strange questions tumbled through my mind beneath the slow turning of the ceiling fan. The steady sway blew such quandaries from my cluttered mind and I drifted into restfulness.

XVII

I awoke to the morning sun edging through the curtains covering my window. Dust motes danced on the beams as if to celebrate the new day. A dreamless sleep had blessed me that night, bringing with it nothing but healing rest. It's something people frequently take for granted. My joints popped as I stretched under the beams of sunlight. I rolled out of bed and felt no pain in the broken rib that had plagued me the day before. Looking at my stomach and sides, I confirmed that all my injuries had faded into pink obscurity.

Lifting up my backpack, I dumped the contents onto the old dresser. I pulled on a pair of jeans and took stock of my supplies. I still had a pack of beef jerky, a no-longer-electric toothbrush, floss, three gold coins, and the rabbit's foot the octopus had given me. All my T-shirts were covered in dirt or blood or other mysterious stains I couldn't identify. I chose from the two that were in the best shape and pulled one over my head. It was the green Ireland shirt that Luna had shown interest in on the trip up. The color was dark enough that most of the obvious markings had faded into the dyed threads. I made a mental note to ask James if there was a functional washing machine in the house.

I threw the food and toiletries back into the bag and raised the rabbit's foot into the light, twirling it between my fingers. The white fur caught the dust from the air and hid it somewhere deep inside. I tested the weight in my hand, holding it by the chain and inspecting it with a squinted eye. Satisfied with its mediocrity, I dropped it back into the outer pouch and set the pack on the floor.

I moved out into the dim hallway and down the stairs into the main room. On the couch, I could see the vibrant hue of Luna's red mane. She was asleep, sitting up in front of the Elderfish's bowl.

"Luna," I whispered, shaking her awake. "C'mon. It's morning."

She stirred and pushed the matted hair from her face. "Morning?" she whispered drowsily. "I must have dozed off. I was afraid this stupid fish might say something important while we all slept so I came down here." She flicked the bowl, sending the Elderfish darting into the corner. A few swears broke the water's surface. "A lot of good that did me."

"Well, did you learn anything?"

"No." She yawned. "Just that some vampires pulled a girl from a weak spot somewhere in Maine... and a great recipe for pecan pie."

"The fish isn't going to say anything without someone hearing it. Why not go up and take a shower? Enjoy the peace and quiet while you can. I'm sure it won't be long before we're fighting for our lives again."

"But then you will come running to my rescue, right?" She smiled that perfect smile and headed upstairs.

"She thinks you have a cute bum," the Elderfish chimed.

"Shut it, you. Stop spouting all your nonsense."

I went into the kitchen, peering over my shoulder to get a better view of my backside. A pile of bagels had been laid out to greet me at the table. The enticing aroma of freshly baked bread pulled me forward like a moth caught in a delicious flame. I picked up one with sesame seeds and buttered it. The savory taste sent shivers down my spine. After indulging in seconds, I headed outside.

The warmth of the sun's spring rays wrapped me in their pleasant embrace. The smell of new grass and budding flowers unfurled over my senses as a placid wind swept through the field. James knelt in front of the fallen tree I had used to trick Lojo. He wore a pair of jean overalls and a red shirt. His beard was neatly braided and his hair was combed back, flattened over his scalp. When he saw me step off the porch, he beckoned me over with a quick wave.

"Ah, lad," he crooned. "I was hoping you'd show yourself after a while." He patted the grass with his withered hand and I knelt down next to him. "This was the only tree we had out here. I liked it quite a bit, actually." He saw the distress on my face and shooed it away. "No, no, don't get bent up about it. I understand it was necessary, but I would like you to bring it back."

I stared at him incredulously. "I don't think we can just stick it back into the ground, James."

"My boy, don't think me so foolish. I want you to use your powers to put my tree back."

"Wait. Colere's memories are easy, but I've never tried to make one of my own." I looked hard at the tree and tried to imagine what it would take. The magnitude of the task seemed impossible.

"You're like a writer without a pen, Noah. You can read what has been put down for you, but you can't create anything of your own. This," he said rubbing the scarred trunk of the beaten tree, "will be your task while you are here. Learning to use your power is the only way to protect your friends from those who wish them harm. You're not like them, Noah; you have a human soul. This will make it more difficult for you, but I believe you are up to the task. Give it a try. See if you can pull this tree into your memories."

I was shocked at how knowledgeable the old man was. Then again, I was sure he knew more than I could imagine from being near the fabled fish.

Squinting my eyes, I glared at the fallen oak. I looked at its simple ridges, trying to memorize the small indentations left by Lojo's thick tendrils. I focused on the particular shades of green each leaf still held, but felt no great draw to any of it. "I don't know what I'm supposed to be doing."

"Well, boy, from the stupid look on your face I'd say you're trying too hard. You need to understand the thing—know what it is on the inside. It's harder than just recalling what you ate for breakfast. Keep trying and you'll learn."

My frustration boiled over. "Why can't you just tell me what to do?"

"Well, knowledge is a dangerous thing when it's freely given. There's more to be gained from finding it out for yourself."

I was going to reply, but I heard the front door clatter shut. I turned and saw Luna. She was wearing a sky blue sundress and it flowed over her body like water cascading down ice. Suddenly, the sun wasn't the brightest thing outside today. James clapped me on the back and I realized I wasn't breathing.

"What do you think, Noah?" Luna did a little twirl. "I found it in my closet."

I saw James's subtle wink out of the corner of my eye. "It's beautiful," I managed to choke out.

Her pale cheeks flushed pink.

James cleared his throat. "Well, I'll leave you to your studying. Remember, I want this tree up before you leave." The old man stood, cracked his back, and shambled into the house.

Luna sashayed through the windswept field and lowered herself next me. We sat quietly while the cool breeze whipped around us. The tall grass ebbed like the ocean waves and I thought that if I could make a memory of this, I would live in it forever.

Finally, Luna broke the silence. "Noah, I am sorry we left you at the rest stop—"

"It's fine. Don't worry about it."

"No, it is not fine. After you used Colere's power, I became afraid. When I looked at you, all I could see was the face that had murdered my people. I should have known you would not be like him."

"You did what you thought was right. I can't fault you for that."

Luna moved closer and placed her hands on top of mine. "It was cowardice. Just like it was cowardice for me to take you away from your old life. At the time, I was desperate and my vision showed me you could help, but that is no excuse. It was incredibly selfish of me to sacrifice you so willingly."

I was speechless. In that instant, I realized I didn't care that she had pulled me from my home. Looking at her hair pirouette in the breeze and staring into her dream-filled eyes, I could forget about everything I'd lost—what I'd gained meant so much more.

"If it means anything, I missed you after we left. Chip is not the conversationalist that you are."

"I'm sure I smell better, too."

She nudged me with her elbow. "That is debatable. I am going to see if there are any chores I can do in the house. At least that way I can be useful while staying near that scatterbrained fish." She leaned over and gave me a kiss on the forehead then turned toward the house, the hem of her dress elegantly turning with her, and walked up the steps, out of sight.

I could see how people might have looked forward to her becoming queen. It made me wish I could have met her family. If they had half her power and grace, they would have been amazing. I thought about what it must have been like for a lonely girl to trust a simple vision and run while her whole life burned to cinders. I wondered what those days were like as she tried—with all her strength—to find me, and how much courage it took to be willing to confront the man who had condemned her kingdom. I pressed my fingers against the warm spot left on my forehead. I'd ask her what her home had been like the next time I got the chance, but for now, I turned my attention back to the upturned tree.

I spent the rest of the afternoon alone, studying the tree and trying to "understand" it. My attempts bore little results. I moved down the wide trunk and found new things to observe. I studied the small nests of animals that had once called this their home and counted how many branches still remained on the furrowed tresses. Still, there was nothing earth-shattering. All I had to show from the experience was a brief moment where I felt a tug in my gut and was able to call a single torn leaf from the mist. Every time I thought I was making progress, a great pressure would surge through my head and I'd lose whatever it was I might have gained. As the sun fell behind the horizon, I felt like I had gotten nowhere.

Luna called me inside for dinner and I abandoned my study spot, heading for the dining room. As I passed the Elderfish's bowl, he whipped around and let a single bubble float to the surface. When it popped, the fish's stern voice addressed me.

"It has nothing to do with how well you can remember the tree. What's important is how it remembers you."

I whirled around and dropped to eye level with the bowl. "What did you say?"

Another bubble rose to the surface. "There is a dragon in New Zealand who is being tormented by an invisible man. The dragon is very perturbed and is afraid the man will do something to his tail. Have you ever seen the Hoover Dam?"

I shook this nonsense from my head. Whatever point the fish was making was gone now.

Dinner was less extravagant than the previous night, but still delicious. James had cooked a huge pot roast with mashed potatoes and gravy. It reminded me of the meals my dad used to cook. Not so much the taste, but the fact that pot roast was the only thing he could make without needing a fire extinguisher on hand. I helped myself to three plates of the tender meat before my bulging midsection brought me to a halt.

After dinner, Luna resumed her station on the couch to monitor the all-hearing, all-knowing goldfish. Having no desire to spend any more time with it, I went up to take a shower.

I had forgotten how wonderful warm water felt. So many feelings came rushing back as the stream blanketed my bare skin. The sweet smell of shampoo, the soothing of worn muscles, and the odd sense of total privacy were all sensations I had sorely missed. They were things I would never take for granted again.

I threw my towel on the bed and lay back. For an hour, I stared at the ceiling fan and recalled the day as I had the night before. I rolled over on the plush covers, still feeling no desire to sleep. It seemed that rest was now more of a quick fix for injuries than something I needed to do every night.

After shifting restlessly on the bed, I rose and paced about the room. I went through all the drawers of the dresser and found nothing of interest. I scanned the room and looked under the bed like I used to do as a child when my family would go on vacation. Peering out the window, I could see the moon high in the air at its first quarter. It called out over the lonely field and I felt compelled to answer.

I opened the closet and found a pair of flannel pants and a plain cotton shirt. James must have left fresh clothes in all the rooms. I pulled them on and tip-toed through the hallway—past the two doors preceding mine—and headed down stairs. The lights were out and it seemed as though Luna had decided not to spend the night with the talkative fish. I pushed the screen door open and walked out onto the steps.

"Hello, Man-Son." Chip's baritone voice drifted on the breeze. He sounded different. I could usually hear a rough animal side to his tongue, but ever since we'd reached the house, I only heard the man. "This place has a strange effect on us," Chip continued, sensing my question. "The moon drifts toward full and we do not hear the beast as much. It's when we have a clear head that we appreciate the night the most."

I wondered what it must be like to constantly share your mind with another creature.

"Up late, Man-Son? Couldn't sleep?"

"No, I couldn't." I looked up at the bright stars spread across the night sky. "Actually, I can't," I corrected. "One of the side effects of having this power is I only need to rest when I'm hurt."

"You may not need to, but that doesn't mean you shouldn't."

"Well, I've also been having these bad dreams. Hey, let me ask you something, Chip. Do you remember your family?"

"Our family..." Chip stared into the moon's glow. "We are an orphan. Our family was of a tribe of warriors, living in a village to the east of Surgut. We were feared throughout Russia.

"One day, an unspeakable came to our village. We believed ourselves to be invincible, and our arrogance was our downfall. She murdered every creature, laughing the whole time. I can still remember that laugh." He kicked a clump of dirt into the air. "We fled into the woods and were picked up by a passing carriage two days later. That is where we met the king and queen of the moon children. They were well known among the werewolf clans. They brought us to the castle and let us protect the Lady Luna until we left to learn more about ourselves. We wish we would have been there when the unspeakable attacked the palace, but we were cowards."

I stared in awe as Chip told his story. I had never heard him speak so clearly and passionately. Despite a slight grimace at the mention of Luna's parents, he was quite civil.

"Chip, can you teach me how to protect Luna? Can you teach me to fight?"

He growled and his tail began to wag. "Come, Man-Son! During the day, the old man trains your mind. At night, Chip will train your muscles."

XVIII

I was sore the next day. I think Chip had taken my inability to sleep without first being hurt into full account. Not once during our sparring did he hold back. He stalked around my advances and leapt about the field, knocking me from my feet several times. He forbade the use of magic, saying I wouldn't always have power to fall back on. His heavy swipes were hard to dodge and felt like a truck when they made contact. During the few hours we trained, I only managed to get in one good hit.

Each day went much like the last. Luna moved about the house, helping with chores and staying as close to the Elderfish as she could. She even stopped by my room to get my clothes for the laundry. I spent much of my days trying to absorb whatever I was supposed to from the fallen tree. Sometimes, James would appear from the old farmhouse and pass on some cryptic advice. Regardless, no matter how hard I studied the tree, I was never able to recall more than a torn leaf or a broken branch.

Meals were different each night and always delicious. James would tell us stories of his time in the old farmhouse and some of the more interesting things the Elderfish had told him. We laughed and ate sour fruit and strange dishes comprised of meats I'd never tasted before. Seeing all the smiling faces around the table reminded me of what it was like to be part of a family again.

Nights brought cool weather and allowed for intense training matches. Chip spent most of the time beating me senseless, but by the third day, I began to hold my own. Swift dodges and ripostes led to stalemates. I was able to slide under his guard and disrupt his advances while crafting an offense of my own. Chip praised me for being such a quick study and his human side provided interesting conversations, sometimes even proving insightful.

"Too often we fear losing control," he preached one night after dislocating my arm. "It is this fear which causes all others. The wolf fears the danger he can't see, and the man fears the moon he can't stop. Once we abandon those fears, only then will we be free." Then he punched me in the stomach. It didn't diminish the importance of his words, but it did hurt like hell.

On the morning of the fifth day, Luna approached me, her blue dress trailing like a fair brook. "We are leaving tomorrow." Sadness struck me like Chip's stealthy paw. I was just getting accustomed to this quiet life. I wasn't happy we would soon be leaving it behind. "Did the goldfish tell you what you wanted?"

"No, I do not think we can rely on the Elderfish. I had a vision. It will lead us north toward a snow-covered mountain, and we know Prometheus is somewhere inside the boundaries of North America. With a little luck, I think we can get Chip to sniff out a trail." I started to interrupt but she stopped me with a raised hand. "Noah, I am tired of waiting. We are losing our edge staying around here, and the trail is growing cold. I would rather continue to follow our friend's nose than sit by idly. I will not abide peace while my family's killer is still out there."

I decided not to argue. Luna was dead-set on this course of action and, with or without me, she would carry on.

I passed the rest of the afternoon in a dour mood. James seemed upset that his only company was leaving, but worked to make our last day on the farm as nice as possible. He cooked a steak dinner for us and promised he would make sure our RV was well cared for and ready to go by morning.

Everyone decided to turn in early and Chip announced we should skip our lesson in order to get a good night's rest. Nonetheless, I lay awake on my final night at the farmhouse. I rolled out of bed and looked through the polished glass of the lone window. I still hadn't replanted James's tree. The mirror on the dresser reflected a moon beam through the room. Luna had folded all my clothes and had set them out on top of my sheets, clean and ready to be packed. On the top of the stack was my "I Heart the Sunshine State" shirt with a little picture of the ocean and a palm tree. I smiled at the sandy shores and tugged it over my head.

I stepped out onto the dewy grass and felt its coolness seep into my skin. I stared out at the sad oak, lying alone in the dirt. After shuffling up, I sat on the tree. The clear sky and bright stars pushed the troubles of the day out of my head.

I would truly miss this place.

I rubbed my hand against the bark of the tree and felt a deep crack in its side I hadn't noticed before. The crack was where the tip of my spear had pierced the trunk. A pang of guilt washed over me;

if it weren't for my actions, this great oak would still be alive. Birds would have continued to nest in its leaves, and squirrels would have harvested their acorns here for long winters. As I thought about these things, something tugged at my fingers. It was uncomfortable, but I found myself unable to pull away. Numbness ran up the length of my arm and heat spread through my body. It crawled its way up my spine and pulled at the back of my eyes.

* * *

I was no longer a man; I was a seed. I reveled in the comfort of the warm dirt surrounding me until a gentle call told me to rise from the ground. It was very bright outside the cocoon of soil, but it made me happy. I watched a thousand sunsets and a thousand sun rises. I saw springs and winters and creatures playing. I watched animals grow and have babies and die and I watched their offspring do the same. I saw a man come with only a rickety boat and bucket of water. I watched as he brought large planks and built a shelter. Many a nighttime he slept outside under my branches. I enjoyed the company.

Eventually, he finished his shelter and moved inside, along with his bucket. He left his small boat with me. I didn't see him as much after that, but occasionally he would sit under me. I made sure to shade him every time he visited. Summer breezes rattled my branches and a bolt of lightning once burned half my leaves away. After a long while, the boat turned to nothing, but the man continued to visit.

Sometimes, other visitors would come and enter the tanned man's house, bringing odd trinkets with them. One day, a group of loud, unpleasant visitors began running around my field. They tore me from the earth and left me on the soil to die. Hurt and lonely, I lay there as the familiar warmth I had shared with the earth faded. Still, one of the men came and sat with me every day. I enjoyed his company.

The end of some distant string plucked from the tree and ran up my arm. It settled somewhere in the recesses of my mind. I was breathing hard and sweating from the unknown strain. I had seen what it was to be the tree—the tree that now felt hollow and dead. It was just as the Elderfish had said—it wasn't what I could remember about the tree. No matter how hard I examined it, I would never be able to commit it to my memory. I needed to know what the tree had been, not what color its bark was or how many leaves it had.

I summoned the mist from the cracks in the world and focused in on what I had seen through the tree's spirit. The ground shook and an identical oak erupted from the soil next to the old, fallen one. I walked around the new tree—standing tall in the earth—surveying my work, and smiled.

* * *

I sat in the dark living room. The magazines on the coffee table had been neatly stacked and the Ederfish's tank was freshly cleaned. The goldfish did a small lap around the bowl.

"I guess I should have listened to you earlier, little guy."

The fish spun around to look at me. Slowly, he swam toward the glass and his fishy eyes grew wide. Bubbles flowed rapidly from his mouth and exploded on the surface in excited sentences.

"What is that on your chest? Is that... is that the ocean? I've always wanted to see the ocean!" I glanced down at my shirt and pulled it taut. "Florida!" the fish exclaimed. "That's right near the ocean. Growing up, I always wanted to see it."

"Really? I was raised near there, but on land, of course."

"Is it true what they say? Does the sun shine bright during the day and make the water warm?"

"Yes," I replied, reflecting some of his lightheartedness in my voice, "and at night the waves can be heard over all the other noises. The cool breezes soothe anyone who sits near the water."

"Ah, lad. It is so nice to talk to someone about the ocean. There is so much there I want to see. This bowl offers very little comfort."

A thought popped into my head—this was the first time since we had arrived that the Elderfish had said more than one related sentence. I sat up straight so the whole picture on my shirt could be easily seen.

The Elderfish moved so close he bumped into the glass. A deep awe frolicked in his wide eyes.

"So... would you happen to know where we could find Prometheus? He did something kind of nasty to one of my friends and we'd like to talk to him about it."

"Yes, yes." His eyes were locked on the beach on my shirt. "The young moon girl. I have heard many talkings of her. What you seek lies in your state of Washington. If you climb Mount Rainier toward its tallest peak, you will find the Lake of Gold. It is a last resort for travelers and adventure seekers. There you will find the end of your journey."

"Thank you, Elderfish." I rose and started to my room. His voice stopped me in mid-stride.

"However," the fish roared through a particularly large bubble, "I think you should be more concerned with yourself than her aspirations, Noah Lane. You are to be the lynchpin separating life from the end of the all things. You are a bastard mutation of the plans set by the gods, and your decisions will hold more gravity than even the highest beings."

I stared blankly at the bowl as the Elderfish hovered in the water. Light from the moon caused the surface to sparkle ominously.

"Would you mind leaving the shirt on the couch when you leave? I would like to look at it for a while longer."

"Sure." I draped it on the back of the couch and maneuvered toward the stairs. A strange, empty feeling had enveloped me. I stopped at the foot of the steps and turned back. "Do we have any chance of beating Prometheus?"

"Hmmm." The fish pondered this, still staring at the shirt. "No idea, lad. I just hear things."

* * *

The following morning, everyone gathered at the table for breakfast. I threw myself into the chair opposite Luna as she picked apart her pancakes.

"So... did anyone else have trouble sleeping last night?" No one looked up from their meal so I continued. "Yeah. Me, too. I decided to go for a little walk and had a really nice talk with the goldfish."

Luna's fork clattered to her plate. She looked up at me with moonlit eyes. "No," she whispered in disbelief.

"Yup." A smirk touched my lips. I leaned back in my chair and folded my arms behind my head. "We're real good friends now, he and I. We talked about our younger days and past loves and—"

"Get on with it, Noah!" Luna yelled, on her feet now.

"He might have told me where we can find Prometheus."

Luna jumped over the table and hugged me.

I felt heat rise up my neck and into my face. She let herself slide back into her seat and begged me to tell her what I had learned. I told her that her vision had been correct: we needed to travel north, toward Washington. From there, we had to climb Mount Rainier until we reached the "Lake of Gold." I left out the whole part about the end of the world.

She threw her chair away and danced about the room. She leapt onto Chip's back and rode him toward the den—his tail wagging furiously behind him—so she could wash and be ready to leave as soon as possible.

I was left alone with James and breakfast.

After a minute of silence James stood. "I'm glad you got through to the old fish, Noah." The old man spoke gruffly. "I noticed you got my tree back up, too."

"Yeah. Last night it all just kind of came to me."

"Good. Then your new task is to keep it there."

"What do you mean?" I asked, perplexed.

"You haven't noticed the pestering feeling in the back of your mind? As soon as you let your concentration fall, that tree will disappear into mist again. In order for it to stay, you will have to leave a small part of yourself here. In exchange, you will always be able to find your way back to this house."

I closed my eyes and felt the gentle tug of a cloudy string leading out into the yard. A piece of me circulated between the tree and I. "Thank you, James. I'll make sure it stays up. What are you going to do with the old tree?"

"Oh, I don't know. I'm sure I can use it for something." He rose from the table and stalked toward the door.

"James," I called to him. "While I was taking the tree's memory, I saw the fisherman who caught the Elderfish." He turned slowly as I spoke. "The fisherman in the legend... it's you, isn't it?"

James came back to the table and sat down. "Aye, it was." His eyes grew distant and I could hear the smallest trace of the sea in his voice. "It has been so long since the day I pulled the little guy out of the water."

"I don't understand. The legend says the fisherman made his wish and set the fish free."

"It also paints the fisherman as a fool. I was human once, too, and I understood what I had in my hands. I wasn't even that much of a fisherman. It was more of a hobby on a lake near my small village than a profession. Why throw a magic fish back when I could keep it? Then, I found out he knew things—amazing things—that no one else could know. Think of what a man could learn from such a creature! It could have made me rich.

"But when I brought him back to shore, the world was a much different place than when I'd left—I had slipped between the two planes. He promised to bring me home if I threw him back into the lake, but the temptation of knowledge told me to keep him. After a few years, I noticed I aged slower as long as he was with me." Sadness radiated from the fisherman and for an instant, he looked as old as he really was.

He turned toward me and our eyes locked. "The temptation of power and knowledge are strong, boy, but both roads are paved with loneliness and end in the loss of your humanity. You've been given a dangerous gift, Noah. I pray you use it well."

We continued to look into each other's eyes. I imagined James as a young, ambitious fisherman, stumbling upon great fortune, and then spending the rest of his life with a rambling fish. How long had it been since he'd had people stay in his home?

Luna broke the silence when she poked her fiery head around the corner. "Let us hurry, Noah. We do not want to keep destiny waiting."

I glanced toward James, who nodded to me that our discussion was over, and went upstairs to pack my things.

I surveyed the room I had stayed in and wondered how long it would be before I saw a comfortable bed again. Collecting my bag, I hurried down the stairs and into the main room where everyone was waiting.

Luna had acquired a pair of jeans and black tank top. Her pale skin contrasted with the dark colors and I found myself struck by her beauty, once again.

We said our goodbyes to the Elderfish and he said his with information on the weather in Taiwan and how to store venison in the snow. Together, we went outside and piled into Thalia. She let out a rumbling yawn as Chip fell into the driver's seat. I paused to run one hand down the length of the new oak tree and say farewell to James. As Thalia pulled away from the farmhouse, James continued to watch us from the porch. Eventually, the small, red building that had been such a comfort over the last few days faded to nothing more than a speck on the horizon. I sat back from the rear window and looked forward.

XIX

Chip shoved me to the floor. It wasn't the first time since we'd left the peaceful farmhouse that his temper had flared like this. With each passing mile, he seemed to get less and less forgiving. Whatever had grounded him for the past few days was long gone now.

I kicked a couple pillows out of my way before standing. "Jeez, I just said you should watch out for that sports car."

"No," he snarled. "We drive Thalia as we see fit."

"If you keep driving 'as you see fit,' you're gonna get us all killed." I stared him down and his lip curled back.

Luna appeared behind me. As soon as Chip saw her, his fiery demeanor cooled.

"We are sorry. The moon is too close to full and it's getting harder to control ourselves."

"Maybe you should teach Noah to drive, Chip. You know how hard it is to divide your concentration when you are like this."

He nodded his huge, furry head. I followed the lumbering giant toward the front of the vehicle. As he lowered a paw to signal the

169

driver's seat was now mine, I thought it might be important to let him know that I was completely capable of driving a car.

That was until I touched the wheel.

Thalia honked defiantly. She swerved between lanes, cutting off an angry, driverless motorcycle.

"Calm her down," Chip ordered. "She does not like being handled by strangers."

Feeling extremely stupid, I rubbed my palm against the leather steering wheel. The dome lights in the cabin flickered furiously.

"It's all right, Thalia. It's just your good ole' pal, Noah. You remember me, right? I squeegeed your window that one time."

The blinking stopped and the RV began to slow.

"That's a good girl. I'm just going to sit right here with you now." I'd never driven anything as big as Thalia before, but I'm not even sure you could call what one does with her driving. It was more like mindfully watching a child in a playground. I'd push the steering wheel to the right to let her know we could pass the three-wheeled station wagon hogging the center lane. I'd tap the gas when the road was clear and she would happily accelerate. I'd bear down hard when a small creature on the other side of the road would get her attention and she would dart toward the median. Overall, riding this living mobile home was a cathartic experience.

Chip sat with me as I tried to convince Thalia she didn't need to blink her high beams at everything we passed. He watched me tweak the headlight knob and whisper to her. Soon, the night's darkness was illuminated by a steady beam from the headlights. Chip patted me on the back; it felt like someone had hit me with a hammer.

"You handle her well. She's taken a liking to you."

"C'mon, I beat Lojo to a pulp. Steering a thousand-pound-dinosaur-injected RV is child's play."

"You know, we may have misjudged you."

I turned to see if he was making some kind of joke.

"You're strong, fast, and brave. It is an honor for us to fight beside you."

"Thanks." I was genuinely touched, especially knowing the state he was in. I guess seeing me work so well with Thalia was the final confirmation he needed to accept me as one of the team.

"Yes, we're glad you will be the one taking care of her. She means very much to us."

"It's okay, Chip. I'm sure once the full moon passes, you'll be able to drive Thalia again."

Chip rose from the passenger's seat and lumbered toward the back compartment.

"We were not talking about Thalia, although we can see that look in her eyes as well." He laughed, circling a spot next to Luna and finally lowered to rest. She immediately cuddled closer to his soft fur.

I continued to drive through the night. I held some minor amount of pride that my talent for sleeplessness was yielding some kind of fruit. The dark sky settled onto the black asphalt. I glanced from the road to check on my passengers.

Chip lay curled in a ball, sleeping soundly. His snores created a reassuring melody to the ambiance of the night. Luna rested her head on his fur—her red hair aflame against his brown.

Looking back to the road, I noticed a thick fog rolling in. At first, it seemed to be a freak obstruction. Then, I felt the weighty pull of the nostalgia on the wind. I convinced Thalia to slow her pace until we came to a complete stop on the side of the road.

A figure moved through the cloud. Black mist curled away from his steps and a cloak of similar hue trailed behind him.

Astrian.

I silently pushed open the door. Maybe I could get rid of him without waking everyone else. Thalia blinked her lights and I brushed a comforting hand across her dashboard. I walked out into the mist, feeling the gentle pull of memories long past.

Astrian stood—plump and patient—in the middle of the road. His angular features twisted into a sneer of superiority.

"What do you want, Astrian?" I put as much venom in my voice as I could.

"Is that any way to greet a brother?"

"I'll never be what you are—some petty murderer with no soul."

"That hurts, Noah. It really does." He raised his hand to his forehead in mock despair. "You know we lost track of the girl and her merry band of rogues when she walked into that farm house. Your little troupe is quite the contradiction. Do you know the history of the celestials and the werewolves?"

I wanted to pull his tongue out. I wanted to beat him until he needed to sleep for a year to recover, but my curiosity somehow conquered my anger. I was compelled to listen. "Enlighten me."

A sickening smile formed on his lips. "It started a long time ago, before the worlds were separated.

Images sparkled in my vision. A clear recollection of history coiled in the mist and sprang to life in front of my eyes.

"That little witch you've been protecting comes from a long line of seers. The earliest of her family were called insane for their moon-like eyes and strange predictions. The common folk called them Loonies for those very reasons and sought to get rid of them."

In the mist, several celestials dashed out into the street. They pulled cowls over their glowing eyes as a mob hurled rocks at them.

"It was the right move if you ask me."

"Stick to the facts, Astrian," I cautioned, angry but still intrigued. "I don't need a commentary."

Astrian's smile grew wider. "Likewise, the werewolves were hunted across the countryside. Some might say they were misunderstood. They retained the personality of both human and animal, but the moon's phases picked which side was most dominant. However, it was what they did when the animal took over that justified the hunt."

Around me, the simple highway faded completely into the fog, leaving behind some strange, new environment. I found myself wrapped up in Astrian's words. They ruptured and spilled forth, leaving in their wake an accurate picture of some history long passed. I watched wolf-men larger than Chip storm villages with the full moon at their backs. They tore through houses and pulled women and children from their beds, tearing them apart in the streets with their razor-sharp teeth and claws.

Men came forth to repel the attackers but were struck down like so many leaves in the wind. The monsters had no goal; the animal hunting spirit was tainted by the human lust for destruction. Families tried to find sanctuary in cellars and closets, but the wolves' senses led them to these hiding places. These people were toyed with, some living long enough to watch their sons and brothers mangled and devoured. The wolves harbored the smallest spark of man and took twisted pleasure in torturing the more unlucky of their victims, not allowing them to die until their fun was over.

I closed my eyes but couldn't escape the images of these villages, burned to the ground over blood-soaked soil. And when the slaughter was done and the moon's phase had shifted, the wolves with men's minds curled into tight balls and wept over the bodies of murdered children.

If I hadn't seen it for myself, I wouldn't have believed it. This was no trick; I could feel the truth of the nostalgia deep within myself. Tears streamed down my face. I wanted it to stop but could find no words.

"Conveniently enough, the celestials have the power to calm beasts with good in their hearts. It was only a matter of time before they met the werewolves and in exchange for their loyalty, the celestials used their magic to suppress the rage they felt during the full moon. But that's not where this story ends."

More images bloomed to life. Celestials marched into battle with hordes of werewolves at their backs. "The celestials used the werewolves to reclaim freedom from their persecutors and take their place in history. When the battlefield would begin to shift away from their favor, these gentle fortunetellers would change the moon's phase in the eyes of their warriors to turn the tide. They treated the wolves as slaves by holding sanity above their heads and built a vast kingdom on a mound of blood and sins."

As the visions popped and faded back into simple words, I could feel the pain of those forced to fight for their mortality.

"That is what you travel with, Brother." Astrian sneered. "A slave driver and her unwitting slave."

I shook my head, trying to push the images of war and death from my mind. I wanted to tell myself it was all lies. I needed to believe that the Chronographer of Magic was playing some elaborate trick on me, but no matter how hard I tried, it still remained true.

"Luna and Chip are good friends. They're nothing like what you've shown me."

His violet eyes swirled with mischief. "Are you sure?" His lips curled back from his teeth in a disgusting grin. "Well, then. Let's see how good of 'friends' they really are." He flicked his wrist and a ball of light the size of a quarter flew through the air, casting a trail of sparks behind it. The tiny comet phased through Thalia's windshield and settled somewhere inside. Her transmission popped nervously, and a bright flash of light illuminated the whole of her inside.

"What did you do?" I yelled at Astrian, his putrid smile bringing the heat in my body to a boil.

He simply waved a finger about in front of his arrowhead goatee. "I simply appealed to the beast's better nature."

A wolf's howl cut through the night like a blade and I whirled around to its source. It had come from the RV. I turned back to Astrian but he was already gone. I knew he couldn't be far because his thick mist of memories still hung in the air. A woman's scream demanded my attention and I sprinted toward the Winnebago.

I flung the door aside and leaped into the van. Even the visions I had seen couldn't have prepared me for what Chip had become. His fur stood straight up, making him seem twice his usual size. His bristled back now pressed against the roof. He licked his chops hungrily with an enormous tongue and a fire in his eyes flickered with the desire to kill. Every one of his muscles throbbed under the weight of the pure hatred that flowed from his body.

Luna defended herself, huddling in the corner between the sofa and a stack of pillows, kicking at Chip's swift advances. Her black tank-top bore three deep cuts and hung loosely from her frame. Something soaked into the fabric making it several shades darker than the rest.

I reached out and felt the cool mist pull in around me.

Immediately, Chip raised his head. Realizing the danger I posed, he stalked toward me with murder dancing behind his wild eyes. Before I could muster a defense, he was upon me. His hot breath stung my eyes as his snapping teeth threatened to tear flesh from bone.

A low growl escaped his lips. "You have no chance of escaping us, prey." He smiled from chin to ears—revealing a row of fangs that seemed to stretch into infinity—and warm drool splashed against my cheek. His teeth bit hard into the flesh between my shoulder and neck. Blood sprayed from the wound like a punctured hose and I let out a tortured scream. Chip's fur shivered with joy at my pain and he clenched his jaws harder.

The pop of a gun rang out and Chip let go of his vise grip. Relief flooded over me while the pile of fur and teeth let loose a howl into the sky. He leaped through the door and barreled into the woods.

Luna lay on her back with a rifle braced against her legs. An open box of red and yellow tranquilizer darts sat scattered on the floor next to her. "He keeps a pack under the bed, just in case." Her words were forced, tinged with disbelief.

I rolled over clutching at the deep, dripping wound. I felt sick, and I gasped hard through the ripping fire that enveloped my shoulder. "Well, at least he's out there now. Damn near tore my neck out!"

"We have to go find him." Her look changed from fear to desperate determination. I looked at her, confused, and she read my expression. "He is our friend, Noah, and he is a danger to everything around him. The beast has control of his mind and wishes nothing but evil."

"There's no one out there he can hurt, Luna. Even if he runs into a town, there's a barrier to prevent him from killing anyone."

Luna crawled over to me, looking down into my eyes. "You know the barrier between worlds is weakened when there is heightened emotion or destruction. What do you think a creature with no desire but to annihilate everything he comes in contact with will do to it? How do you think the vampires breach the gap? Chip will find a place where your kind lives and will pull them through the barrier like it was made of tissue paper. Then he will murder until he comes down from his affliction." Her eyes swirled a dark, pleading gray.

I thought of the friend who'd trained me and acted so humbly at the farmhouse and how we had sat under the stars at night sharing his take on the world. Then, I thought of him kneeling over a pile of corpses.

I nodded, wincing as I found my feet.

XX

We crept through the trees, following the trail of uprooted bushes and broken branches—a blood-raged werewolf apparently wasn't very hard to track. The thick cloud of mist still hung like a blanket over the forest. Although I could no longer sense Astrian's web of memories, his fingerprints were all over the phenomenon. He'd made sure to make this task as challenging as possible. Every rustle of branches and stirring of wind sent Luna and I jumping.

She carried the rifle close to her chest. We had torn apart some of Chip's spare bed sheets to make bandages for our wounds. The once-white linens were now damp and stained with blood. The constant movement was keeping Luna's scratches from healing and she limped as she walked, which slowed our progress. I was doing a little better, but winced every time I had to turn my head. I hadn't thought Chip capable of turning on his friends so easily, but after what Astrian had shown me, it didn't seem so unlikely.

"Luna, is it true your people made slaves of the werewolves?"

She stopped and shot me a dirty look. "Who told you that?"

"Astrian did... before he put the whammy on Chip. He showed me visions of your people gathering up the werewolves. They used them as warriors in exchange for their minds during the full moons."

Her features softened and we marched on, "My people..." Luna started softly, as if grasping onto a distant thought, "...before the great rift between worlds was created, my people were persecuted. Greedy kings collected us for our visions, and religious zealots murdered us in droves, claiming us abominations. We were a broken people who had never experienced peace."

There was conviction in her voice. I could see her standing in full regal dress, speaking to a stadium of subjects. I could see her as a princess. "When we discovered our power over the werewolves, we held it in our hand like a diamond. We used them to free our own and build a kingdom where all could be safe. After that, we gave the wolves as much freedom as possible."

She glanced over and saw her speech hadn't won me over.

"Do not look at me as though we have done something so wrong. The celestials are not so far descended from the sons of man; many were placed on the other side of the barrier. I have heard tales of the prisoner of Delphi and the fate of those in Salem. Do not pretend the sight we carry is not a curse as much as a blessing, for it is this very curse that places us on this quest against the Chronographers!" Her face was flushed with outrage.

For a moment, I thought she might hit me.

A rustle in the bushes called us back to the task at hand. We both jumped back, attempting to distance ourselves from the sound. Luna raised her gun and I brought a cloud of nostalgia to the ready just as a small rabbit-like creature with a beaver's tail hopped into the clearing in front of us. We both let out a sigh of relief.

Luna laughed was tinged with hysteria. "I do not know why I allowed such an animal to startle me. If that was Chip coming to claim us, we would scarcely hear him coming before he broke our necks."

I took no comfort in her words and knelt down in front of the timid creature. Claws flashed in front of my eyes and the animal disappeared from sight. I stumbled back into the dirt. Seven feet of fur and rippling muscle stood in our path.

Indifferently, he took a large bite from the struggling animal. "You track well for prey," he grumbled, letting meat and blood fall from his jaws. "Now, whose entrails should we eat first?"

Luna fired a shot, but Chip swatted it away with blinding speed. With two great steps, he wrapped his paw around Luna's throat and began slowly crushing her neck, reveling in her struggle.

I reached into the mist and pulled snaking chains from its depths. I launched them forward, binding the werewolf's arms to his sides. Luna fell to the earth, clutching her throat and pushing herself away from his massive frame. I pulled taught the length of the steel and attempted to hold him steady while Luna re-loaded the rifle.

Chip doubled back toward me and with a giant foot, sent me skidding across the rocky earth. He sank his teeth into the linked chain and shredded it like dry branches. A leap put him on top of me again, pinning me to the dirt. As jaws snapped menacingly, I heard two dry thuds. Darts hit their mark in the back of Chip's neck. With a howl, he spun to face Luna, whipping a stone into the air as he moved. It hit her squarely between the eyes, and she collapsed into the dirt. He roared in triumph and lumbered toward her with slow, deliberate steps and death playing behind twisted eyes.

I tried not to panic, concentrating harder than I ever had before. I reached into the haze and found something I hoped would hold him. Padded walls and concrete took shape as the asylum cell emerged from the abyss. It sprang from the earth like a crocodile, jaws closing around the murderous beast. The thick dust hardened into reinforced steel, padded and inescapable.

With a roar, Chip attempted to spring from its clutches, but it engulfed him wholly. He threw himself at the cell door, barking threats through the small viewing slot at its center. Slowly, the tranquilizers took effect. Chip stumbled about the cell like a drunkard. "Let- let us... out! We'll kill you! We'll... we will... rip... your throat..." He spun to the left and fell face first into the wall.

I pulled myself up the best I could through fatigued muscles and the reopened wound in my shoulder. I staggered over to where Luna lay motionless. Cradling her in my arms, I stared down at her pale face as a thin stream of blood traced the outline of her features. I begged her to wake, shaking her gently in my arms. Panic wracked my brain and the beating of my heart drowned out the night's sounds. I held her to my chest and rocked her slowly.

"You have to get up, Luna. I can't lose you again—not after I just got you back."

Her eyelids fluttered then finally opened. Pale moons stared up at me.

"Hey, Noah," she whispered. "Is Chip okay?"

"Yeah," I chuckled at her as relief washed over me. "He's just peachy, Luna." I pressed my forehead to hers and breathed in her lavender scent.

She was okay.

* * *

Traveling back to the RV was slow going. We both had suffered serious injuries that hampered the speed with which we could travel. Our makeshift bandages were no longer keeping pressure on our wounds and a dizzying lightheadedness was settling in.

Despite how difficult it was for her to speak, Luna explained that Chip was afflicted with a simple spell her people used to instill the fighting spirit into their wolven warriors. At their strongest, the spells could only carry until the end of the lunar cycle. Until then, he had to remain alone and fettered. I nodded—processing the information—and we wandered the rest of the way in silence.

Wearily, we pushed through the last line of trees into the open air. A cool mist rose off of the dark asphalt, but not a single memory lingered in it—nothing but the gentle tugging of the one I had left in the forest. We crossed the road and climbed back into the RV, stopping briefly to straighten the door back onto its hinges before closing it.

Luna staggered into the back and slumped onto a pile of pillows. I lowered myself into the front seat and gripped the wheel. The first sound that broke the silence was the whining rev of Thalia's engine. She refused to move without her lost owner. With some quiet determination and calm words, she veered back into the winding black stream. The headlights cast a beam that cut through the night, gently flickering with sadness.

I found it strange how—when I had so much to think about—my mind retreated into itself. I barely remembered driving that dark night and had no recollection of how I aided Thalia down that winding highway road.

After staring into the unyielding darkness for some indeterminate amount of time, I heard quiet sobbing coming from the rear of the RV. I asked Thalia to move to the shoulder of the road, once again, and set her in park. Rising from the driver's seat, I looked back and saw Luna lying on her side, clutching her knees to her chest. Her back arched violently with heart-wrenching sobs.

I went to her side and sat down behind her, pulling her into my embrace. She had seen her best friend at his worst and now, at least for the time being, he was gone. I could only imagine the pillar of strength Chip had provided her, and now she was powerless to help him. I held her tighter, feeling her lithe muscles strain with anguish.

I didn't know if what I did next was because of my desire to fill the deep void in my chest or if it was simply a loss of restraint spurred by grief, but I leaned forward and pressed my lips against the small of her neck. Her skin was cool under my touch. I hesitated a moment, savoring the feel. When I pulled away, I noticed she no longer shook with tears. I could barely feel her breathing at all. Slowly, she turned herself in my arms and looked at me—through me—piercing my soul with those luminescent eyes. I was a fool. Why had I chosen now to kiss her? Now, after she had lost a childhood friend and companion?

I waited for her reprimand—for her to scold me and shoo me away—but instead, faster than I could comprehend, she leaned in and kissed me back. Her lips pressed hard against mine and the coolness of her soft skin contrasted sharply to the heat I felt, infiltrating my body and surging through my veins. The ground disappeared and I found myself wrapped in radial bliss. It could have lasted a second or a thousand years—it didn't matter. A decisive energy flowed through her lips and sent sparks through every nerve in my body.

She delicately pulled away and I gasped air into my lungs. Despite the puffy redness that lingered on her face, she looked more beautiful than I had ever seen her.

She smiled at the play of emotions that crossed my face.

I lost myself in that perfect smile and was only brought back when her hair fell in front of her face, like a crimson snowfall.

With a shudder, tears fell down the contours of her pale cheeks. She buried her head in my chest and continued to weep.

I held her until the chaotic tremors of her sorrow were replaced with a steadier breathing. I pulled in her sleeping body and bathed in her natural perfume. As I sat in her embrace, I gently lowered my guard, sending myself into deep sleep as well.

FOUR

The four of us watched as Prometheus paced between two large archways—one made of steel and one made of stone. Astrian was next to me—squat and grinning—followed by Lojo, who slouched lower than normal. It looked as though he had seen better days; the glow in his eyes was decidedly subdued. I couldn't make out the person on the end. It seemed like a dark shadow was blocking my view. After another moment, Prometheus stopped and sat. Although there was no chair, he crossed his legs and leaned an elbow on a non-existent arm rest, setting his chin on a clenched fist. "Well?"

Astrian stood straighter, not realizing at first that Prometheus was waiting on his report. "I've done what you asked, Father," he muttered quickly, unsure if his words were what his master wanted to hear. "I've separated the chaff from those desired by you. Only the princess and the boy remain." A drop of sweat beaded down his forehead.

"Well done, Number Three. The pieces on the board are falling into their correct positions. Soon, freedom shall be mine and with it, an end to this suffering." He stood swiftly and strode about the congregation. "I wonder what they would do if they only knew the futility of their intentions, as well as the repercussions. Would you not wish the same, Number One?"

"Yes, Father. I would," I heard my voice say.

Prometheus turned toward me, the rest of the congregation changing their attention, as well. It was the first time I had felt as if all could see me. I wanted to shrink away from their stares, but as usual, I could not make my body do anything it was not willed to do.

"I as well," Prometheus finally replied with dark satisfaction. "I as well."

XXI

As the sun rose, I found myself still tangled in Luna's embrace. The morning warmth filled the cabin, beckoning me to rise and start the new day. Luna shifted slightly in my arms and it took all the strength I could gather to break the bond between us. I stood above her and watched her sleep for a moment longer. This peaceful being at my feet had suffered so much. I longed to see her as she was before the Chronographers had stolen her happiness. I wanted to watch her stand with the people who revered her and have her smile at me with a clear mind and joy in her heart.

I woke Thalia with a pump of the gas and she lumbered back onto the road. As I sat in the driver's seat—steering a car that needed very little guidance—I examined my thoughts and the events of the past few days. We had lost Chip for the moment, and if all happened as Luna predicted, he would return to us after the full moon passed. The downside, however, was that he would be no use to us in the trials to come. We would be victorious or dead by the time his human consciousness could once again deliver him peace.

Unless, of course, the Elderfish's words proved to be true and I ended up bringing about the apocalypse. Heck, I found choosing clothes that matched difficult, and now I was supposed to be entrusted with the task of changing the world as we knew it forever? The sheer absurdity had me laughing hysterically as Thalia flew down the road at eighty miles per hour.

Luna appeared behind me and draped her arms over my shoulders like a soft scarf. "What is so funny, mon capitaine?" A quick peck on the cheek almost caused me to drive off the road.

"Nothing. I just had a funny thought."

"Fine, then. Be that way." She spun around and leaned against the back of the passenger seat, looking at me intently. "Thank you. I do not know if I would have made it through last night if you had not been there for me." Her praise caused my spirits to lift five stories and suddenly, I was filled with confidence.

"It was my pleasure." Color rose in my cheeks. "Uh... how are the cuts healing?"

She lifted her shirt to look at the three, dark scars on her pallid torso.

I found my eyes fluttering from the road to the rear-view mirror, attempting to steal a glance at her midriff. Strange how the smallest allowance of perversion leads to bolder acts of depravity.

The scars were still red and irritated, but a fine pink was forming around the edges. She was healing better than most humans would. Her eyes rose up and caught me staring. She pulled her shirt back down over her stomach. "Keep your eyes on the road, you peeper."

"I'm sorry," I stuttered, flustered by the accusation. "It looks like it's healing really well."

She raised her chin and spun around nimbly.

I noticed a particular sway in her hips that I hadn't seen before. Despite her swagger, I could see twinges of pain in her strides.

"You are not the only person in this world who heals fast," she quipped as she turned into the bathroom. "In fact, it is a common evolutionary trait among most species." She slipped through the doorway, pausing momentarily to stick her head out one last time. "Except for yours, of course." And with that, she shut the door and left me to my devices.

The following days moved almost like a dream. As darkness fell and the sun retired each day, Luna would beckon me to the back of the bus. She would say she couldn't sleep without me there and would go so far as to tug me from the driver seat to sit with her.

I would take her into my arms when called and listen to her breathing slow, watching her twitch like a dreaming animal. I'd lie awake, stroking her strawberry hair as she rested dreamily in my arms. I felt incredibly lucky on these nights, especially if I could steal a kiss from those cool lips that always sent me spiraling off into blissfulness.

We tried to keep our diversions to a minimum and the green roadside forests quickly morphed into rocky cliffs with white tops. Our stops were limited to eating and occasionally visiting a gas station for supplies. The RV, as well as the other vehicles on this side of the barrier, no longer needed to be filled with gasoline. The fossil fuels ran through them like blood. Instead, the skeletal remains of human gas stations had become hubs for roadside bazaars.

At one of these attractions, we found a familiar fast food chain that I used to visit in my world. We bought some burgers from the kindly reptilian folk who managed the store. Luna explained that, although we inhabited separate planes, we shared the same world. Sometimes, the inhabitants from the Plane of Gods would take to operating an already furnished venue that existed in the Plane of Man, much like these lizards had chosen to run the burger joint. Exceptions to the rule lay in the use of magic. For instance, her castle had been charmed to keep it hidden and since all magic had been stripped from the Plane of Man, it rendered the location nonexistent on that side of the divide.

Finally, after a few long days and nights that were not long enough, we stopped at a gas station just outside of what would have been Seattle, Washington to prepare for the final push to Mount Rainer and the Lake of Gold near its snowy summit.

Luna went inside to see if she could buy some provisions from the vampire behind the counter.

As I cleaned the dirt and dust off of Thalia with an old car wash hose, I watched a large ape participate in a verbal altercation with one of the reptilian creatures I'd seen from the fast food restaurant. Then again, they all kind of looked the same.

The ape was complaining that the reptile had gotten into his wares and had stolen some of his dried meat, and the reptile was aghast at the accusation and found the character defamation a most grievous insult. As words evolved into a shoving match, I began to notice the ghostly flicker of human specters going about their uneventful day on the other side of the world. It had been ages since another human had crossed my path in any form and suddenly, I was accosted with memories of those I had once loved.

I looked through the gas station window, trying to catch a glimpse of the one thing that made everything I'd lost bearable—the poison that had brought me to this fate and the ambrosia that kept me alive. Instead of finding her, my eyes fell upon the vampiric owner.

Compared to the tribe I'd encountered in the woods, he seemed well fed and round. The shimmering phantom of a human blinked in and out of existence and I saw the vampire's red gaze dart toward it. Rage boiled in my veins as the association solidified in my head. How many innocent people had this predator murdered for his own benefit? How many families had lost their children to unexplained disappearances? I ran through the multitude of child abductions at gas stations and diners in my head. How many had been torn from their reality and murdered before even realizing what had happened? I raised my hand instinctively—ready to call forth my own brand of justice—when a familiar voice beckoned to me.

"Probably not the best course of action, Noah."

I turned and saw Art's multi-colored appearance calmly coming toward me—a large duffel bag draped over his shoulder. He reminded me of one of those vagabonds you hear about, jumping from train to train to cross the country.

"Why not?" I spat, forgoing all pleasantries. "How many humans do you think that monster has pulled out and murdered? How many sons and daughters have gone missing at this gas station so this junkie vampire could have a full belly?" I took a step forward and felt Art's hand rest on my shoulder.

"You speak of them as if they chose this path. What would you do if you were confronted with everlasting life but forever deprived of the essence of living? Wasting away for eternity, never able to satisfy that single, most basic craving? The vampires are a victim of their environment. In fact, I believe that could be said about many of us."

Hurt flickered across his eyes, like a wound reopened after a long time of healing.

I stared hard at the monster behind the counter, his dark-rimmed eyes darting back and forth from his customer to the blinking morsels surrounding the arguing pair.

"If I were you," Art began again, "I would be more worried about why a hungry vampire doesn't notice the human standing not twenty feet away from him in broad daylight."

He was right. In the woods, the vampires had apparently tracked me for days, predicting my movements and setting up a trap. Yet here, this one barely knew I was around.

"Why can't he see me?" I asked, my voice seemingly coming from some great distance.

"Oh, he can still see you; he just doesn't perceive you as you once were. I believe you're now more Chronographer than man. With each passing moment, you burn away a bit of your humanity."

I looked around at the creatures milling about the station. I had been feeling stronger and recalling the memories had been more natural the last time I'd done it. Would I soon be just another monster?

"Don't fret too much, Noah. You needn't go changing your name just yet. I believe you won't move much further away from you current state. You still harbor some key traits that will keep you grounded. For instance, you still have your soul and your mortality." He leaned up against Thalia.

"It doesn't matter, I guess. Luna and I are going to stop Prometheus from escaping. I won't let him claim either of these worlds."

"Yes, yes." Art rolled his eyes. A green streak chipped and flaked away as his brow furrowed. "It is the prerogative of ants to nip at the heels of giants. I can promise you it won't be easy. My father plays a game in which he holds all the cards and makes up the rules as he sees fit."

I felt a twinge of despair. I had seen how Prometheus had punished Lojo after his failure. I couldn't imagine what he would do to someone he perceived as his enemy.

"So, do you think it's hopeless to try?"

"No, Noah, it's never hopeless to try. One hand of cards can change the outcome of the entire game as long as the stakes are high enough, and not even the game master can recant the rules once they are set. Here, take this." He handed me the large duffel bag draped over his shoulder.

I opened it and peered inside. There was a lamp, a folded tent, some pots, and various other camping supplies.

"If you plan on hiking up a mountain, you might as well have the correct equipment. You are weakened by the constant upkeep of your dog's cage, and I figured you would inevitably lack the foresight to equip yourself."

It wasn't until then that I truly felt the weight of the string I had been holding taught for the past few nights. Compared to the oak tree I still kept in my mind, Chip's cage was like a leaden anchor.

"Why are you doing this for me?" I asked as I looked into the bag of supplies.

Art looked lost in thought for a moment. "I've spent much of my existence ending the lives of those I admired. I remember watching Elvis's last show and wishing for a reprieve from my duty. I too feel like I have let myself become a victim of my environment and with you, I am trying to break the cycle the best I am able."

Looking at Art and listening to his confession sent a shiver down my spine. This man seemed to love something in a way his kind never could, and yet he had spent his life destroying everything he held dear. Possibly, through me, he saw some kind of freedom.

Art looked at me again and became very serious. "When you return to the road, head north about fifty miles. You will see a large, upturned stone. Pull into the woods. The rest of the way, you will have to hike. Just keep heading toward the summit."

"What about the Lake of Gold?" I asked.

He thought about this for a few moments. Eventually he gave a brisk nod, his dark curls springing about with the effort. "Yes, I believe that would make a good landmark to shoot for. The light that shines from it at night will guide you to your destination."

I took a mental note of that.

Art backed away. "As for the girl, keep her close to you. In her, you will find your greatest strength and possibly the card that will win the hand."

A thud sounded from behind. I whirled around to see Luna slurping from a large cherry slushie. She had placed a second one along with a bag of pretzels on the hood of the car.

"These have to be the best inventions your species has ever created. Our kind could never create magic such as this." She attacked the straw again, making slurping noises as she drank the icy beverage.

I turned back to Art but he was no longer there. I still had his duffel bag in my hand.

Luna looked at it incredulously. "What is *that*?"

"Some supplies for the climb. It's a tent and some other stuff."

"Great! I got the snacks covered." She thrust a large bag of candy, chips, and bottled water in my face.

"Well then," I started, unable to hide my amusement, "looks like we're ready for a camping trip."

She pushed the second cherry slushie into my hand and stepped through the door.

I looked at the pavement and noticed green flakes floating in a small pool of water. Not only would I free Luna, but I would free Art as well.

I climbed into Thalia and closed the door.

XXII

We careened down the icy road toward Mount Rainier. I spent a majority of the trip trying to think of a way to explain to Luna how I knew exactly where our destination was. I figured now wasn't the best time to tell her that one of the bloodthirsty murderers we were fighting was kind of my pal and was kind enough to draw me a map. Needless to say, I was relieved when Luna gasped excitedly about the large rock that had moved into view. It apparently was exactly like the one she had seen in her vision while at James's house.

It was larger than I had thought it would be—at least ten feet high and as thick around as a small car. Moss grew up one side despite the snow blanketing down the other like a white cape. I didn't even have to pretend I was surprised as I pulled off the road into a little clearing where the snow wasn't deep enough to keep the RV from traveling.

We stopped for a moment to gather everything we thought we would need for the hike ahead, spreading the contents out on the thick rug in the van. We had stopped at a small merchant's stand as we drove into Washington and had purchased some warmer clothes for the hike using the last of Luna's money. She was wearing brown boots with white fur on top, the pair of jeans she had kept with her, and a thick, brown, feather-down coat with similar white fur protruding from the collar. It was the most stylish clothing I had ever seen on her and I liked the way she looked in it. I wore a pair of black hiking boots, jeans, and a heavy, green jacket with the inscription "R'lyeh, The Last Paradise" embroidered in black stitching. I wasn't sure where the place was, but as I piled most of my treasured tourist shirts onto the floor to make room for supplies in my backpack, it gave me some comfort to still hold on to one.

Luna filled a satchel with some personal belongings. I finally had to ask her where she had been keeping them all this time. Apparently, she had been storing the things she felt inclined to carry in the knee-high socks she constantly wore and in small pockets she had sewn into all of her clothing. "You can *never* have too many pockets, especially in places where people do not often look," she told me with a wink.

When I took catalog of the things in Art's duffel bag, Luna shot a confused glance in my direction. She didn't ask any questions, but I could tell she knew I was hiding something. I told her I had found them in the back of the supply bin inside the Winnebago. Something Chip must have prepared for the journey. Her features drooped as she nodded at his wisdom. I hated myself for the lie.

Finally, we gave our loving goodbyes to Thalia. She rumbled in sullen disagreement, but we assured her she couldn't come with us. Instead, we told her to go back for Chip. When the lunar cycle ended, she would have to whisk him north as fast as her wheels could carry them. It was the only way he was going to join us in time.

Waving goodbye, we braced ourselves and trudged out into the cold weather. An icy wind bit at my nose and clawed at my cheeks. I looked back and saw dabs of color appear on Luna's face. Once we were behind the tree line, we wouldn't have to worry as much about the wind. I hopped in place to get my pack into a better position and turned myself toward the peak. Together, Luna and I began our trek up the mountainside.

* * *

"That wasn't so bad." Luna hugged her shoulders in the fading dusk light. She sat in the back of the tent with the zipper door ajar while I cooked a can of purple, sprout-looking things in the small pan just outside. When she had pulled the can of food out for me to cook, I had thought it would be something I'd recognize. Apparently, even though buildings were a shared commodity between worlds, much of food still remained exclusive.

"It's barely been one day," I called back to her, adjusting the pan while the fire licked about its sides.

The climb had been steep and the trail non-existent. For the middle of the spring months, I was surprised at how much snow was still about the lower reaches of the mountainside.

Luna had followed behind me for the most of the hike. She walked with her hands stuffed deep within her pockets and her red hair dangling around her face like weaves of licorice.

I had stopped and offered to help her, but she had simply lifted her chin and had taken my place in the leading position until we'd made camp. I felt guilty for misjudging her.

She climbed through the opening of the tent with a blanket wrapped around her shoulders. "That is enough, Noah," she reproached me as she peeked into the pot of lumpy purple and brown spheres. "You are going to burn them."

I removed the gruel from the flame and poured it into two bowls. Luna lifted hers up and blew on it to cool it.

I stared in awe as she scooped up a purple globule the size of a fist and shoved the whole thing into her mouth. She smiled like a simpleton as she chewed the oversized lump.

"I thought princesses were supposed to have manners?"

"Oh, be quiet." At least I thought that was what she said; it was hard to tell between her full mouth and the shower of food that sprayed when she tried to talk. She swallowed the mouthful and with an approving sigh, continued. "My father used to say the same thing. 'If you are going to eat like a wolf, Luna, then maybe you should eat with them'," she said, dropping her voice two octaves.

"So, what did you do?"

She smiled and laughed, "I pushed my plate aside and went down to the barracks to eat with the werewolves. They had better food anyway, and better conversation, too."

I thought of a tiny Luna eating amongst a league of monstrous wolf-men. I could see a little girl with red locks and a small frame sharing a greasy sheep's leg with a six-foot, hairy beast as he spun tales of war and battle. She'd been strong and rebellious, even then. She would have been a queen of action—one who would fight alongside her bestial warriors. She may never have that life now. I added "see Luna atop a throne in front of her people" to my growing list of goals. It felt strange that most of my recent plans had nothing to do with going home. I guess it was because here, I had something to stay for.

Luna saw me staring at her and a new blush appeared on her cheeks. "What? Do I have something on my face?"

"No, I was just thinking."

"Well think with your head, not with your eyes... and eat your jamplé before it gets cold. That would defeat its purpose."

I spooned a helping of muddy ooze to my face. It smelt like onions... and mud. Hesitantly, I stuck the lump into my mouth. My tongue was attacked by the sweet taste of juicy honeydew but with the characteristics of a meaty stew. When I swallowed, a warm sensation settled in my stomach. I made short work of the rest of the bowl and by the time I had finished, the feeling had spread all the way to my fingertips. A blanket had been cast over my body from the inside out and with that comforting warmth, a sense of ease.

Luna and I sat outside until it was dark enough to see the stars. We huddled together in front of the fire with the blanket draped over our shoulders. While looking at the bright specks in the sky, I found my mind wandering. "What was it like where you came from, Luna?"

She continued staring at the stars as she spoke, looking for the words in the shining lights. "My people found refuge in the space that flutters between dreaming and consciousness. It was there that our visions held the most power. The physical location of the castle varies by account, and many believe it constantly changes its locale." She smiled at the night's sky. I could see the pride shining in her eyes. "The randomness of its location makes it difficult for large armies to invade—those who tried to attack the castle would often find it was no longer there when they tried to plan their siege."

"Did it actually move around the world?" I asked in awe.

"No, it was the world that moved. The castle always remained right where it was supposed to be. But no matter where it was, it brought beauty to the location. Snow would gleam with a shade of white that made one think the clouds had come to rest on earth. And when the castle made its home in a grassy field, it would look as though the greenery had been shaped for years to compliment the large gardens that adorned every corner within the walls. Travelers would come from all over to see its magnificence and would seek council with the king and queen. Court was often held in the great alabaster halls to settle small disputes, and although these decisions were not enforced by any law, they were almost always agreed upon as such."

I waited to hear more about this place, but Luna simply stopped talking. I studied the wide-eyed, distant look and followed her gaze back to the stars. But it wasn't the stars she was looking at; there was something new sharing the sky. A bright light shone forth from the mountain, splitting the sky and carrying on into the distance.

"It's the Lake of Gold," I whispered to no one in particular. We jumped to our feet and hugged each other, dancing about and cheering at our good fortune.

Looking back at the beacon, Luna spoke softly. "We should get some rest. I think we have a long hike tomorrow."

I marked the direction of the landmark with a few sticks and crawled into the tent after Luna. As I nestled up next to her under the covers, I didn't think to remind her that I couldn't sleep so easily anymore. I merely pulled her close under the comfort of the blanket and breathed in her scent until the sun rose.

XXIII

The days on that mountain were separated only by the nights I lay awake beside Luna. We trudged through the cold and snow with a determined resilience to reach the Lake of Gold. We stopped briefly to eat and rest every so often, but soon our desire to prove our strength to each other began to wane.

Luna started walking closer to me, burying herself in my side as we dragged our feet up the white trail. Our pace may have slowed, but I cherished the little warmth I could steal during these instances. No matter how strong my body had become, it still succumbed to the natural elements. Was it like this for the rest of the Chronographers, or was it a sign of my leftover mortality? Despite my discomfort, I put the thought away—deep inside myself—and kept it safe. I wasn't ready to be a monster yet.

We talked very little on our hikes. Sometimes I would ask about her life, and others she would ask me about mine. Our casual conversation somehow seemed to make the cold and weariness less daunting. On one evening, I told her it had been my birthday the day she had pulled me into her world.

She stopped in the knee-high snow and refused to move. I did my best to comfort her, but she just kept apologizing. I felt oddly guilty for causing the reaction in her, so I just held her until she agreed to continue.

That night, when we sat down to make camp and cook dinner, she surprised me with a gift. She split a Twinkie with me that she had been saving since we had left the rest stop so long ago. According to her, it was one of the few foods that held magical properties.

As night fell, we ate what provisions we had saved. When we had the strength to fight out the night, we ate small portions of the dried meats Luna had bought from the gas-station bazaar and pressed on toward the shining beacon. When a day's hike and foul weather drained too much from us, we brewed the purplish stew and restored the warmth to our bones. On these nights, we sat outside until the bright light from the Lake of Gold instilled some kind of hope in our hearts.

My mind wandered as I lay awake next to Luna. I played countless scenarios in my head of what it would be like to face Prometheus—the man given eternal life to acquire all the knowledge in the world. I had stood before him and had watched what he could do. I still vividly remembered the trapped feeling that gripped me every time I entered his enormous halls; he was a man who seemed powerful enough to destroy anyone without remorse and with barely any effort. Yet everyone continued to say that I was the stone that would tip the scale in either direction. That had to mean that I had a chance, right?

On the fourth night, we sat around our campfire until the stars were high and bright in the night sky... but the light from the Lake of Gold never shone. After patiently waiting with no results, we retired, feeling defeated. There was something very painful about not knowing whether we had lost our path or if perhaps the light wasn't hitting our destination just right to warrant a reflection. It was especially cold outside, and even sharing warmth under the covers wasn't enough to completely stave off the frigid air outside. Regardless, Luna's slow, even breathing sent my mind aflutter.

The smell of lavender coiled around me and my mind skipped again. The slight tugging of a memory carried my mind miles away. I saw Chip huddled in the corner of a padded cell—at least what was left of it. Most of the padding had been torn from the walls and lay strewn about the cage. It looked as if he had stopped defacing the room once he tore away some of the concrete and had reached the reinforced steel walls. Since then, he had spent most of his time sleeping and searching for another way out—all of these efforts in the noble pursuit of following our trail, ripping out my throat, and forcing the she-pup I was with to watch.

Now, he lifted his massive frame and peered out the small viewing slot in the door. Somewhere deep inside him, a man sat locked away, waiting for the time when he would have control once again. Part of me wished he would be released in time to help us in the coming days. The other part knew he was better off as far away as possible.

I shivered—not from the cold—and pressed myself closer to Luna. She stirred awake and rolled over to face me, her eyes showing a weary dreaminess. When I looked at her, the fears I had been supporting since we started this climb ebbed away. I leaned forward and slowly brushed my lips against hers, which parted at my gentle touch. Warm breath passed between us and I found my arms coiling around her waist—flowing up her strong back. I pulled her closer and she hummed her satisfaction.

We separated for a moment and I found myself once again staring into her cosmic gray irises, flickering with the light and intensity of the moon. A desire welled up inside me and I attacked her neck with an unfounded ferociousness. I delighted in the taste of her chilled skin, like one savors water after being lost in a desert for days. A soft hand ran through my hair, pressing my head firmly against her sweet skin. Our bodies twined together—like two liquids poured into a single glass—and we shared with each other all the aches and anxiety we had been hoarding, releasing them into the cold night air.

* * *

The following morning was the most difficult by far. The night had left a fresh coat of snow on the ground for us, and the loose powder made walking an arduous task. In addition, the beacon of light that had guided our way for so long was completely lost. We spent the early morning hours trying to point ourselves on a bearing that would lead us toward the summit, but with the thick canopy of trees and overcast skies, all we could determine was that we were somewhere on a very large mountain in Washington.

The day dragged on endlessly and our stops became more frequent. By mid-afternoon we were tired, disoriented, and emotionally beaten. We veered off our non-existent trail and found an evergreen tree that had somehow managed to keep the night's snow away from its base. We made a small camp in the rough patch of dirt underneath.

Luna reached into her satchel and passed me half of a piece of dried meat. Our food supplies were dwindling fast and the water I had been carrying in my backpack was all but spent. We refilled our empty bottles with snow. After about an hour's rest, we repacked our supplies and once again pressed on toward the highest point we could see.

We moved deeper into the high canopy of the mountain forest. It was under these towering umbrellas that held the snow at bay when I got my first inkling that we were being watched.

"Luna," I whispered, "I think we're being followed."

She nodded. "I agree. I think we should give whoever it is a surprise."

We hastened up the hillside toward a thick outcropping of tangled undergrowth. As soon as we pushed our way through the congested brambles, we split up, darting into adjacent bushes. From our hiding places, we waited. If anyone was following us, he would have to take the same trail—and once he crossed into the clearing, we'd capture him.

The thick outcropping of trees drowned out most of the afternoon sun, and an unnatural dusk settled on the forest floor. Despite the fact our plan relied heavily on our ability to blend in with the surroundings, I found my inability to see Luna unnerving.

The lack of light rendered my sense of time useless. What could have been minutes seemed like hours, and after some indeterminate amount of time, I began to wonder if there had been anyone following us in the first place. I started to get up—my knees begging for mercy as the cold-wrought stiffness splintered away—but before

I could completely rise, the greenery shuffled and a figure passed into the clearing.

I sprinted from my hiding spot, but Luna moved more swiftly. She sprang from the bushes and lowered a shoulder into the surprised creature's chest. The shock from the attack sent the stalker tumbling backwards.

It crashed into me and I quickly tangled my elbows underneath its arms, pushing on the back of its neck with my palms in an old-fashioned defensive hold I'd learned from Chip. The creature thrashed inside my tight grip, wailing pleas of forgiveness.

"Hey, now. I'm sorry! I really am! Don't kill me, please!" His voice was low—like a soft whisper—with a warbling pitch. His enunciation and carriage had a strange quality to it, like someone who might rarely use words to express himself. It created an air of eerie calmness, despite the obvious terror the creature was feeling.

I was briefly caught off guard and loosened my hold. The monster slipped from my grip and sat up, rubbing the back of his neck while cowering away from us.

"Th-thank you. I really am sorry. I meant no harm." He lifted himself off the ground, but Luna shoved him back into the dirt and shattered branches.

"Do not get up yet. Why are you following us?" Her eyes narrowed as she examined him.

I rounded the defeated beast to get a better look.

He was covered from head to toe in thick, white fur. His face reminded me a lot of a fox, only much flatter. He had two short, pointed ears and his frame was incredibly lean. His arms stretched all the way to his knees and were topped with gnarled, thin fingers. His legs shared a similar litheness. I guessed from his build that he was accustomed to fast travel and a carnivore diet, but he wasn't built to fight. Most startling was how this information compiled itself in my head. It was as if my brain simply reached into a catalog of human and animal traits and very simply drew the obvious conclusion. Art had said I was more Chronographer than man now—that the power was burning away the human part of me. How much longer would my thoughts be my own?

Luna's authoritative tone shattered the ramblings of my wandering mind. "I asked you why you were following us."

The strange creature cowered away from her. "I- I was told to find out who had been setting the fires every night. If they needed it, I was supposed to help bring them back."

Luna knelt down and looked into the groveling creature's eyes. She studied him intently, looking for some sign that his words held lies. She leaned back, satisfied with his response.

"Who sent you?" Luna demanded, calmer but still imposing.

"My brother."

"From where?"

He looked confused for a moment, as if he thought we might be playing some strange joke. "Why, from the Lake of Gold, Miss," he replied abashedly. "The only magical place for miles."

Luna and I looked at each other, surprised by our good fortune. We immediately apologized and offered him a hand. He was hesitant, but once we briefly explained we had thought he'd been sent to kill us, he clapped his forehead with one long arm as if so many others had fallen prey to this assumption.

Once we helped him up, I was unsure why he had been so scared of us. His slim, furry body was no less than seven feet tall. He dusted the snow and dirt from his wintery coat, cleared his throat, and dipped into a low bow. "My name is Quel'ren, of the Liath tribe."

"The Fear Liath?" Luna exclaimed in shock. "I did not think there were any left, at least not on this continent."

"We are few and far between. Our kind tends to make those around us feel uneasy. But my brother and I have resided at the Lake of Gold for quite some time. It is the last resort for those walking the winding trail that leads to the end of all things." His voice carried a distant mystery as he spoke.

"Quel'ren," Luna started, moving closer to the liath, "would you please lead us to the Lake of Gold? We would be ever so grateful if you could."

Quel'ren looked Luna over with his large eyes and unleashed a broad smile.

"Of course, Madam. This is my duty." He gave another low bow and spun on his heel, facing northeast. He beckoned us forward with his long, spindly arm.

He moved more nimbly than I'd imagined. He leaped and danced between thick underbrush, grasping low hanging branches in his wide hands and swinging himself forward to gain momentum.

Following the large, nimble creature was hard work, but the path he cut through the forest offered a much easier hike. As long as we stayed behind Quel'ren, we never found ourselves wading through deep snow or tripping over exposed roots. It was as if the white liath could see some invisible trail buried deep below the powdery surface.

Our pace carried us much farther in an hour than we had traveled in an afternoon. Still, I could see that Luna was beginning to tire and I could feel my heart thundering in my chest. I mustered up air from my gasping lungs to call for a break, but before I could, Quel'ren rounded on us.

"Oh, my. I'm dreadfully sorry."

Luna and I stared at him, breathing in large gulps of air before we were forced to run again. With two quick movements, Quel'ren maneuvered the packs from our shoulders and swung the camping supplies over his. "What would my brother say if I made guests carry their luggage all the way up this cursed mountain?"

It was strange to be referred to as a guest, but it brought some comfort that our reception upon arriving might be a pleasant one.

"Come, now. We're almost there. We must hasten lest we be late for supper." Quel'ren galloped off again—this time at a slightly slower speed—with all our bags draped over his back. For a moment, he looked like a large, abominable bell-hop.

I tried not to laugh.

It was much easier to move with the heavy burden lifted. However, after about thirty more minutes of traveling, I was seriously considering a plea to stop for the day to make camp. I looked ahead to flag Quel'ren down, but I couldn't see him any longer. I glanced over at Luna and saw that she, too, had lost sight of him. We hurried ahead to try to catch up and stumbled out of the tree line into a clearing. There was our guide, standing tall with a huge smile on his face. With one outstretched arm, he made a sweeping motion to our surroundings.

My jaw dropped to my knees.

In front of us was an open expanse, about fifty yards wide. In the center stood a three-story building. I was reminded of the old Lincoln Log cabins my dad had bought me when I was younger, except these logs looked as if they were made of diamonds. Every one of them sparkled when the sun hit them, and their bark was the color of polished glass. The roof resting on top of this curious structure was bright yellow. It created the appearance that the sun itself had been set atop the walls to shelter it. Combined, these two elements created a dazzling monolith that suffused the sky with its ethereal beauty.

Just inches from where we stood, the snow had melted as if it had been forbidden to tread on the green grass that budded from the earth. Suburban homeowners would have killed for whatever seeds had been used.

The emerald shine of the turf was only rivaled by what quite possibly was one of the most ornate gardens I had ever seen. Flowers of every color and size mingled together among a variety of pristine statuary. Pink tulips framed a small stone dragon, and roses nestled together in a bed in front. They created the illusion of a blazing, aromatic fire bursting forth from the lizard's jaws. Similar sculptures nestled between a variety of floral splendor and at its center, a fountain sprayed water into the air—which misted in a pleasant breeze—and set about a rainbow that framed the whole scene.

The air itself was warmer in this strange place. Wind that should have been chill and bitter was, instead, warm and welcoming. A small, cobblestone path snaked toward the building's entrance and diamond-like trees lined its edges all the way up to the large front door. Their crystalline branches twined together at the top, creating an archway of lush greenery. Strange fruits flaunted their floral bouquet well out of arms' reach, and birdsong chimed out over the clearing.

I had forgotten how pleasant the sound of scurrying animals could be. It was as if the whole area were set in a protective bubble and cared for meticulously. Seeing this place made me certain that Astrian had not stolen all the magic from the world. My gaze looped around every shape and sprout until it finally rested on the large, golden, etched sign above the front door. My eyes widened at its inscription.

"Welcome," Quel'ren sang confidently, "to the Lake of Gold, the Last Resort."

XXIV

Quel'ren led us under the natural overhang and up to the front door. I was still stuttering shocked syllables from somewhere between awe and confusion when Luna saved me the trouble of trying to put a coherent thought together.

"I do not understand. Where is the lake?" The liath looked down at her as one would look at small child asking why the sky was blue.

"Why, you're standing on it, my dear. I realize that our resort is not on an actual lake, but is a drop bear actually a bear? No, it is simply a name. Now, if you would kindly proceed to the front desk for check-in..." Quel'ren whisked us through the large, ornate door and into the structure.

The inside of the building was that of a snow lodge, but with an elegant twist. Stately red carpet painted the floor, and the interior of the diamond logs were a spectacular white marble. We were pushed past the expensive-looking velvet sitting chairs set in front of a large hearth in the sitting room and into the main lobby. Behind the stained oak reception desk was another liath, presumably Quel'ren's brother. He looked very much the same as Quel'ren, but taller and with mottled brown patches in his fur. He was arguing with a blonde woman in a full-length fur coat. She leaned over the counter seductively and whispered something into the tall fox's ear, allowing her curls to tumble over her shoulders.

"I'm sorry, ma'am," the liath replied. "I will not grant your request and, as you know, there can be no violence in this sanctuary. With that said, I must ask you to leave at once."

The woman went rigid, seemingly growing several inches taller. She slammed her fist on the desk, sending a rattling quake through the entire building.

Quel'ren loudly cleared his throat.

Both the woman and the liath looked back at him. The blonde woman scowled at the source of the interruption then her glare landed on me. Her gold-rimmed eyes gave me a quick once over, and then she smiled a pearly white smile. She turned back to Quel'ren's brother and muttered something under her breath then she turned away and made for the door to our right, stopping briefly to afford me a second look. I felt a strange draw toward the woman's beauty, at least until Luna gave me a hard elbow in the ribs.

With the obstacle removed, Quel'ren led us into the lobby and presented us to the liath behind the counter.

"Luna, Noah. This is my older brother, and the owner of this fine establishment, Dom'roqe."

"Hello." Dom'roqe extended his long hand in greeting. "Welcome to my hotel. Will you be staying with us?"

"I still do not understand." Luna looked from one liath to the other. "We were told to follow the light from the Lake of Gold and that would lead us to Prometheus. Why, then, is our destination some mountain hotel?"

An awkward silence filled the room until Dom'roqe spoke again. "Adventurers, you are indeed at the crossroads of your journey. We liath were given the task of guarding the end of the world, the land sequestered by the gods to house the Unspeakables and the Seeker of Knowledge. This resort is simply the last stop on the way."

"As well as a great tourist attraction!" Quel'ren chimed in.

Dom'roqe glared at his younger brother.

"And the beacon of light we observed at night? Did that not come from somewhere?"

Amusement spread across the hotelier's face. "That is, as you put it, simply our beacon—a spotlight to lead travelers to our resort. When they come close, we turn it off to determine their intentions before allowing them to proceed."

Luna looked embarrassed. She wrinkled her pale nose and made no reply.

Dom'roqe pressed on. "If you truly wish to continue your foolish quest, we will direct you on your way, as the gods have dictated. However, we bid you partake in supper and stay the night."

"I guess we have no choice in that matter," Luna muttered, "but we have no money to pay you with."

Dom'roqe frowned.

"Actually..." I spoke for the first time since we had arrived at the lodge. Everyone turned toward me as I plucked my backpack from Quel'ren's high shoulder. Unzipping the outer compartment, I dug to the bottom for the money Luna had given me to buy lunch at The

Jackalope. "I have three gold pieces. I'm not sure what that will get us, but it's all I have."

Dom'roqe rubbed his temple with one long finger. "I suppose it will have to do. We cannot afford to turn away patrons this far away from civilization, and I won't throw you out into the cold."

"Didn't you just do that to the blonde lady who was in here?" I asked incredulously.

A touch of anger fluttered across the older liath's face, but it was gone as soon as it had appeared. "That," he stated matter-of-factly, "is quite another matter and one I will not discuss with you. As I mentioned, we prefer to turn away certain riff-raff. Now, if you will follow me to the dining room, we shall eat supper. I suggest you bed yourself early this night."

* * *

I sat in the garden, mingling with the multicolored landscape while the fountain sprayed its cool haze over my aching body. I found it impossible to heed Dom'roqe's suggestion of a good night's rest.

Dinner had been held in the Lake of Gold's luxurious kitchen, which seemed to be a terribly boring description considering every wall seemed to be fashioned from marble and the tables constructed out of the diamondesque trees that littered the grounds. The meal seemed fair for the price we had paid for the room. We ate multicolored fruit from sparkling wooden bowls... well, Luna and I did, at least. The two brothers ate lean slabs of grilled meat that smelled much better than our sparse fruit. Our meal did taste good, though. The fruit had been freshly picked from the trees outside, and all were juicy and satisfying.

During the meal, Dom'roqe told us about how his tribe had come to the Americas. Apparently, the liath were accustomed to living in high places. Their ancestors had come from Europe's highest peaks and had lived there for many generations prior. Dom'roqe and Quel'ren's father had lived on the Cairngorms in Northern Scotland and had protected a sacred ground there. In these hazardous climates, their tribes had come to be known as the Fear Liath. This, ironically, was because they always tried to screen visitors before allowing them into their mountain oases, which often led to the travelers being scared away by the large creatures. Then, poachers searched for the sacred places, stealing their treasures—most notably the specially cured diamond trees the liath were able to grow. As these sacred grounds were pillaged, the liath were destroyed with them—save for the brother's father, who had traveled to North America to take care of the newly-discovered sacred ground on which we now sat.

When their father died, his two children had converted the whole thing into a tourist attraction. Taking something as important as this and turning it into some off-the-beaten-path attraction seemed incredibly reckless from where I stood, but if I had been forced to live my whole life in a single spot—unable to see the world around me—wouldn't I try to make the best of it? Thinking back, that had been exactly how I'd lived. I was just some nobody in a small town outside of Orlando until I'd bumped into Luna and had found myself killing an immortal creature of destruction.

Another gust blew through the garden and I could smell the familiar scent of... lavender?

Luna crept around the fountain and grabbed both my shoulders, whispering "boo" into my ear. She scowled when I wasn't surprised. "Well, I am sorry if the *brave hero* does not get spooked anymore." She plopped down beside me and followed my gaze into the night.

We sat in silence for a while, just enjoying the splendor and sights of this hidden glade. After a while, Luna gave a small jump. "Noah, look at the moon!"

I glanced up and saw the clouds part, revealing a glowing orb with a dark crescent edge.

Yeah, it's... uh, pretty." Apparently my lack of enthusiasm carried in my voice.

She rapped me on the skull, turning back to the hovering sphere. "No, stupid, it is waning. That means the full moon has passed. With the snow storms and the bright light this place was emitting, I did not notice. Chip should be free of his curse!"

She was right. I reached out across the thin strand of memory I'd been holding onto since that night. I ventured across miles of countryside and into a forest, overcast with midnight haze rising from the wet grass. I didn't feel the immense hatred or fear I had sensed when I usually tugged on this line. Peering in through the hole in the cell door, I saw Chip, sitting patiently against the wall. As if noticing my presence, he rose and walked forward. I looked at him there for a moment and then—with mental shears—cut the taut string. I felt it dissolve back into the cracks of the world.

"He's fine. I let him out."

"Do you think we should wait for him before we continue?"

I shook my head. "No, we only have enough money to stay here for one night. Besides, Dom'roqe said he would tell us where to go in the morning."

"Oh." Luna sulked. "I guess if we shall be traveling again in the morning, I should rest tonight." She got up and took a step forward before turning back. She was wearing a long, white nightgown. There had been matching sets hanging in the closet of our room. Although I neglected to do anything with mine, hers frolicked delicately about her frame in the brisk night wind. I watched as the light from the garden reflected off her fair skin, exuding a strange aura of life. "Should I leave the door open for you?"

"I'd like to stay out here a little longer. You go on without me."

She nodded and walked up the porch and into the inn. I almost went after her, but decided this night would be my own. I leaned farther back and watched the placid sky until the sun began to rise.

XXV

In the early morning, we met Dom'roqe in the lobby.

Quel'ren met us at the bottom of the stairs and presented us our newly washed clothes, and as a gift, had added thermal gloves to Luna's wardrobe and a black knit cap to mine.

His brother waited by the resort's side exit and told us where to go next. "We aren't allowed to let anyone travel farther up the mountainside until they prove they are worthy."

I felt the breath flow out of me. Hadn't we been challenged enough? I yearned for the days where an algebra test was the most frightening prospect of my day.

"What do you want us to do?" Luna asked with obvious annoyance.

The older liath made note of her tone and pressed on. "East of here is a cave with an ancient artifact inside. If you can brave the storms, return the item to us, and solve its mystery, we will allow you proceed to the end of worlds."

"Fine. But you must promise to leave the beacon up for as long as we are gone."

"Agreed. We will leave the light on. I recommend you leave at once. It would be unfortunate if you were impeded by the storms so early in your journey."

We went back to our room and gathered all that could easily be carried. Once again, we donned our camping supplies and knapsack. Downstairs, we passed through a door on the right side of the lobby and out of the resort. The difference between the front side of the building and this one was extreme.

I felt Luna snuggle in closer to me. Cold wind tore at my face and neck and blew ferociously across the colorless landscape. All I could see in front of us was white.

"Oh, good," Dom'roqe spoke, leaning around the door's frame. "You made it before the storm settled in."

I wasn't sure if he was kidding or not. Luna and I pulled our hoods as low as we could over our faces and began trekking through the deep snowdrift.

* * *

Traveling on this side of the mountain was much worse than when we had walked up toward the Lake of Gold. Within hours of starting our journey, the heavy storm had slowed our pace to a crawl. Visibility was a definite zero in the battering gale. I extended my hand in front of me and was unable to see my fingers through the blizzard. If it wasn't for the sheer rock wall that towered over our left side, we would have become horribly lost in a matter of minutes. It wasn't long before we were forced to make camp.

I zipped the tent shut, segregating ourselves from the painful snow that had assaulted us from the sky. Luna passed me half of one of the purple fruits that Quel'ren had offered us before we had left. As we did our best to regain some speck of the strength that had been stripped from us on this first day, the spotlight from the lodge shone brightly outside the tent. Despite the heavy winds and snow, it instilled some vestige of hope in me.

After an uncomfortable night, we woke up early to try and get as far down the trail as we could before the snow picked up again. As we opened the tent's flap, we were greeted to an almost clear mountainside. Quickly, we packed up the tent and supplies and began anew. I wanted to talk to Luna during this peaceful morning, but the remaining cold crept into my throat and twisted itself around my voice, keeping me from even attempting a conversation.

Sooner than expected, the fierce storm rose to torment us once again. The whip-like attack of the sharp winds cut at our exposed skin. By the afternoon, both of us were exhausted and freezing.

I had started to lose feeling in my right foot, which didn't bother me too much because I knew I could heal from any injury brought about from the hike. Instead, it made me worry more about Luna's well-being. I knew she was a fast healer, but frostbite wasn't exactly something you bandaged over. If something happened to her here, I didn't know if I could get her back to the lodge in time. I threw the tent up again and did my best to warm her icy skin. Her chattering teeth were a constant reminder of what was just outside, waiting to punish us once more.

When the third day donned, we found our tent half submerged in harsh snow. It was an unwelcome change to have to dig through the powdery ice before we could even brave the painful flurry that lay just beyond. The trend of wading through snow and wind continued without relent. It got to the point where I only knew night had arrived when the bright light from the Lake of Gold shone behind us.

When we woke up to the new morning, we were blessed with the clearest skies thus far. Luna built a small fire and we shared a warm cup of spiced tea before taking to the trail once again. Our pace was much quicker in the calmer weather. We moved swiftly across the powdery surface, leaving one hand on the rocky guiding wall until, finally, something on the horizon caught our eye.

Through the white cloud, I could barely make out the entrance to a cave. Hope rose up inside me, and Luna removed her head from the crook of my elbow.

A silhouette walked out into the ice field and waved to us.

"Someone's waiting for us," I whispered to Luna. As we moved closer, I was able to make out the figure.

She was a tall, muscular woman with tanned skin. Golden curls cascaded down to her shoulders, framing her strong face. She wore a white tank-top that clung dangerously to her chest, accentuating her large breasts. Her hips curved sensuously from her waist and swayed seductively as she strutted forward. She wore long, green camouflage pants tucked into a set of black leather boots. Powerful arms brushed the hair from her face revealing a pair of golden eyes glinting like newly-minted coins. She exuded power and sexuality. It was pretty obvious she didn't belong out here.

"Well, hello there, sugar," she called in a sweet, southern accent. "I've been waitin' for ya'll to get here. Was wonderin' if you were gonna make it."

The golden eyes ignited a memory within me—it was the same girl who had been arguing with Dom'roqe the night we had arrived at the Lake of Gold. I found it strange she had been more warmly dressed in the lodge than she was out here.

"She is definitely evil, Noah. Be careful," Luna whispered into my ear with a twinge of jealously. I could feel the blush of her cheeks on my neck. I didn't need to see the future to know she was right. I could sense the cloud of memories mingling with the falling snow.

"Who are you, and what do you want?" I called out to the woman.

"Name's Millie, darlin'," she cooed. "I'm Number Two, the Chronographer of War, and I just wanna play a little. I tried to convince the landlord of that dive to let me have you there, but he would have none of it. It's 'kay, though. I figure this setting is much more dramatic. So, whattaya say we start the fun?"

Before I could respond, she whipped her hands from her sides and two green spheres sailed into the air. I realized what they were too late. I pushed Luna away from me as the two grenades hit the snow and sent the pair of us soaring in opposite directions. Luna, along with my backpack, were buried by a wave of icy snow.

I struggled to my knees and summoned my own nostalgia. I pulled the fitful cloud to me just as a leather boot hit me square in the jaw. I rolled over, stunned, and crawled to my feet once again.

"C'mon, sweetie. Try and fight back. I know I'm supposed to be roundin' up your girlfriend, but you gotta at least make this fun."

Millie pointed two polished fingernails at me and two .45 pistols took shape from the mist. I dove toward a deep memory— two knights engaged in a friendly tournament and a large crowd gathered to watch their battle. I reached deep into the cloud and pulled an iron shield from the air. Bullets rang shrilly as they clanged against the sheet of metal.

When I peered over the edge, the Chronographer's shoulder collided with the shield. The impact was otherworldly—a meteor ramming into a brick wall. Unable to defend myself against the earth-shattering strike, I felt the ground leave me, sending me tumbling backward over the snow.

This one had strength—raw, physical strength—unlike all the others. If I tried to fight her pith to power, she would tear me apart. But if she was anything like her brothers, this boldness of hers would work to my advantage. She advanced on me again with a swift kick and a solid punch.

I focused hard on what Chip had taught me: anticipate the movements and use the opponent's momentum to create openings. At first, it went well. I nimbly ducked a fearsome right hook and lowered myself under the strike, but as I moved in under her jab, a low roundhouse slammed into my chest, pushing me back against the rocky cliff wall.

She pulled a large, round mace from a snowflake and charged like a bull. That was when I saw my opening. With the rock wall providing support, I focused on the knights again. Mist began to form in my hands but I begged it to wait. It stirred restlessly in my grasp.

Millie raised the club, killing intent frolicking in her gilded eyes.

I could see the sun's glare hitting her pearly teeth as she snarled. That's when I let the eager memory become solid. Nine feet of steel shot from my hand as a medieval lance moved from nothing into reality. The nauseating sound of flesh being torn asunder and bones splintering into fragments echoed off the rough stone walls as the blonde tigress halted in mid-stride—her mace clattering harmlessly against the rocks.

She stood motionless with polished steel cleaving through her midsection. She peered up into the sky and curled both hands around the metal shaft. Then, she exhaled a breath of pure ecstasy. "Mmmmmmmm," she moaned as her golden stare locked onto mine. "That's it, stallion. Hurt me."

I stood—stupefied—as she tightened her grip around the lance and pulled herself down the cold, steel column. The wet sound of blood pouring steadily onto the snow assaulted my ears as she slid sickeningly closer. Her eyes rolled back into their sockets and with every pull, she let out another cry of joy.

"Yes," she gasped. "That's what I need. It's been so long since someone could please me."

She was inches away from my face now, blood trickling from her ruby lips. She leaned in close and kissed me hard.

Heat rushed to my face as she gently licked the inside of my lips. Dumbfounded, I let my concentration slip. The weapon I held began to turn back into smoke, and with the sound of cold steel hitting soft skin, she belted me with the mace that had been leaning against the rocks. My whole body went limp as I collapsed. Black spots crowded the edges of my vision, blurring my surroundings.

Millie stood above me, sanguine fluid pouring from her wound. She pressed her hands against her hips and caressed her sides. Her hands moved slowly up her torn abdomen until finally arriving at her breasts, which she pushed together with a quiet, seductive growl. Where her hands had been, white bandages now curved around tanned flesh, keeping her insides from spilling out onto the snow.

I pulled myself away from her and pushed against the ground with my feet but they just buried themselves in the fine powder.

She was on me before I could move an inch. She leapt gracefully onto my chest and wrapped her legs tightly around my waist. "We're just gettin' started, hun. You can't leave yet." She pulled a six-inch dagger out of thin air. I met her gaze and saw madness. She slowly pushed the pointed blade between my ribs, savoring the agony on my face until it was buried to the hilt in my side.

I screamed in pain as fire consumed my mind.

She gripped my throat with her free hand, imprisoning my voice along with my breath. Her eyes were wide with passion. Blood dribbled from my lips as I coughed for air. She wiped it with a delicate finger and suckled on the sweet tip.

I thrashed about under her weight. The world began to go dark. I could feel my muscles tiring from the cold and the struggle. A heavy object barreled into Millie and I felt frigid air flow into my lungs, burning down my throat.

Luna pulled me to my feet as Millie sprang from the snow.

"What's wrong, Moon Child? Jealous I can show your man a better time?"

"Shut up, bitch!" Luna roared in a way I'd never heard before.

I hadn't even been sure she could curse.

Millie tugged at a cloud, unholstered guns from the air, and wildly unleashed a hail of bullets. She laughed with the sound of machine gun fire.

Luna helped me stumble away while applying pressure to the wound in my side.

I tried to raise a concrete wall between Mille and us, but the beating I'd taken had done severe damage to my concentration and it was reduced to rubble shortly after its construction. I pushed and pulled on all the memories I had, trying to construct some stalwart defense while Millie psychotically rained bullets around us. With what strength I still had, I called on the same prison I had used to trap Chip. The snow shook with the sudden presence and the padded cell erupted under Millie's feet, devouring the vixen like a shark swallowing a minnow.

"Nice thinking," Luna panted.

"Thanks," was all I was able to return.

Before our enlightening conversation could continue, the steel walls of the cage began to bend. With a crack, the structure erupted into hail of stone and metal, which dissipated back into smoke mid-flight.

Millie's blond hair was tussled—she dropped a large sledge hammer into the snow. "Did y'all think a silly little prison cell was gonna hold me? I'm the crusher of nations! I'm the atom bomb! I'm the hatred that sits in every man's heart. I AM WAR!" The mountain shook with the weight of her words before she once again advanced toward us.

Even during this moment of impending doom, I couldn't help but notice her smooth skin, the rhythmic sway of her hips, and the soft bounce of her chest. It was as though she was created to distract men from their thoughts.

Luna tugged on my arm to pull me away, but Millie saw the move first. She waved a manicured hand, launching Luna several feet into the air—as if blown away by a strong gust of wind. "Now, Noah, I need ya to do this favor for me. Please... hurt me." She bounded forward, summoning a silvery long-sword from the inky nostalgia.

I reached into my white mist and began throwing the explosive black powder I'd used against Astrian her way. It burst into brightly-colored flames, but Millie skillfully darted between the blazes. I tried to backpedal away, but her speed was something Olympic runners would trade their first born for. Faster than I could think, she ducked in next to me and prepared to strike me down with her weapon. In defense, I threw the coarse sand at our feet. Heat rose from the ash, sending us both reeling away from the epicenter of the fiery explosion.

I raced over to Luna and fought to dig her out of the deep snow. Her eyes were cloudy and she was bleeding from a large cut above her eye. I tried to shake her awake. I needed to get her to safety while that homicidal maniac was distracted.

Singed camouflage pants rounded the still-burning pyre, sinking steadily in the snow from the resounding heat. "Why d'ya constantly gravitate to her?" Millie whined. "I won't be ignored!" She bent down and patted the snow. White flakes rose into the air and the black mist wrapped its smoky tentacles around the ice. It hardened the snow, solidifying it into two enormous siege cannons. They glistened under the bright sun. Images of fleeing armies were carved into the polished iron.

Millie fanned her arms back and two fuses lit with a fleeting spark. As the deafening explosion shook the mountainside, two heavy, black spheres rocketed toward us. I dropped Luna to the snow and focused on my memories. I haphazardly conjured a thick barrier by piecing together chunks of metal and concrete from whatever I could reach first. The cannonballs collided with my wall. Despite the defense I'd erected, the impact was still enormous. The concrete and fused metal I had raised imploded in front of me, sending rocks and sharp metal tearing through my skin.

The loud noise roused Luna and she looked up at me from the ground. As the rubble settled, I smiled at her. Her eyes went wide and I felt several hot stings pierce through my back. I fell to the ground and heard the tank-like roar of laughter. "Noah! Oh, my gods! She shot you!"

I opened my eyes as cold hands wrapped around me. "Yeah, I think she did."

Luna pulled me closer, pushing my half-buried backpack out of the way. The contents spilled out over the snow and she became fixated on a small object. "When did you get a rabbit's foot?"

It was an odd time to talk about the trinkets I'd picked up on our journey, but since I was pretty sure I was dying, I obliged. "Back at the rest stop—before you guys left me." The simple act of speaking sent an icy chill through my body. My breath now seemed a precious commodity. I coughed blood over the white powder as my lungs struggled to pull in air.

"Lay still, Noah. I know what to do."

Luna snatched the rabbit's foot from the snow. She grabbed my arm and turned it palm up. She pressed the rabbit's foot claws deep into my skin and dragged it from the bottom of my palm to my elbow.

A new pain surged through my entire body—like some acidic poison was being pumped through my veins. The numbness in my body fled from this new assailant. The muscles in my arm cramped and seized. The area where she had scratched me felt like a thousand tiny needles were prodding my flesh, and just before I felt like I would scream, it subsided. In fact, all the pain had melted

231

away. A renewed energy embraced me and it seemed like the battle had just begun.

Luna pushed me forward. "Now go!"

I stood and stumbled forward, not yet used to the new strength flowing inside of me.

"Oooh," Millie sighed. "I love it when a man hits his second wind." She threw her arms back again and two cannonballs screamed toward me.

I tapped into a deep memory—one I could barely sense. A pounding wind curled over my arms, tearing against my skin with its strength. With the power of a hurricane, I batted the heavy spheres away like ping-pong balls. I raised my hand and a white pillar sprang from behind the Chronographer of War. It slammed into the back of her head with a wet thud. She let out a high-pitched wail and stumbled forward.

I summoned a memory of a submerged, oceanic city. I pushed the mist toward the falling Millie and a golden, Atlantian trident sprouted from the snow. It cracked with magical electricity as it bore deep into her shoulder.

Millie squealed as the shimmering current erupted from the staff. Black smoke rose from her burned flesh. She struggled to pull the spear out, shaking as waves of lighting passed through her body. Finally, she tore the barbed prongs from her severed tissue, throwing it aside where it hissed and sank into the snow. "There's the tiger I was looking for."

She charged again, pulling a broadsword from the smoke and dodging nimbly through streams of flaming black powder that I had sent sailing her way. Her blond hair whipped around as she swung a sword at my hips with a warrior's cry.

Two chain-link gloves wrapped around my hands and I caught the blade as it spun.

She twirled away from the block, landing a kick to my ribs and sending me tumbling ten feet backwards. She had caught me off guard, but the attack had given me an idea. She was too quick to hit with the black powder, but if I could use her aggression against her—like I had with the lance—I might have a chance.

She stalked toward me, dragging her sword through the snow. Blood poured from her shoulder and the now reopened wound in her chest. It cascaded down the shining metal and left a crimson trail in the dreamy clouds that settled on the mountain.

I could feel the warm trickle of my own wounds. The rabbit's foot hadn't healed them, so what had it actually done? I decided it didn't matter and pushed the thought aside. I had to stick to the plan. I staggered to my feet, purposefully limping away from her advance like a weakened animal.

She giggled with delight at the pathetic display.

I flicked my hand into the air and tugged at the mist blanketing the ground. A white pillar sprang vertically from the earth, as tall as an evergreen tree.

Millie nimbly hopped away from it, avoiding the strike. "Nah uh, stallion. Those tricks only work once." She lifted her blade and cut through the shaft like it was warm butter. Gallons of black powder poured from its hollow center, covering Millie from her hair to her boots.

"I wouldn't pull the same tricks on a pretty gal like you, Millie," I spat at her in my best southern drawl.

She watched in horror as black soot streamed down from her golden tresses. After a moment, her features softened. She winked, blowing a sensual kiss in my direction.

The explosion was unlike anything I had seen before. A pillar of crimson flame shot fifty feet into the air. I stumbled backward from the shockwave. As the pyre danced brightly before my eyes, I tried to shield myself from the intense heat that clawed at my skin. My body felt like it was weighed down with steel. I choked on the blood pooling in my throat. Pain surged through my entire body and the sting from the holes in my chest returned. My head fell back into the ice. It felt warm.

I let the comforting blanket take me, wrapping me in its dark embrace.

FIVE

I was resting against the edge of a column from the original Cathedral Basilica of St. Augustine. That is, before I burned it to the ground. Yes, they rebuilt the damned thing, but I figured I would one day return to finish it off.

Burning a church? When did I do that?

I pushed these thoughts aside. I knew they weren't my own, but they came so naturally now.

I looked up and saw Prometheus. He paced around a maze of chipped and broken sculptures. He stopped and brushed a hand across a stone relief of a tall, muscular man with the head of a bull. The half-bull sat on a large rock and cradled his head in his thick hands.

A beautiful young woman held him, her arms barely reaching around his wide torso. I was familiar with the story of the Minotaur, but didn't understand the sculpture. The beast of the labyrinth never had a lover, right? Prometheus withdrew his fingers from the delicate carvings and turned to the person standing with him, who immediately spoke.

"There's still time to turn back, Father. Just because things have come this far doesn't mean you have to complete it."

I was shocked by how flatly Art spoke to Prometheus. All the other Chronographers seemed to cower from his heavy gaze.

But as the ancient scholar looked toward Art, I saw a weariness I did not expect from my enemy. "But that is precisely why I must complete it, Number Four. Of all my children, I thought you would understand what I am doing. Yet now you speak in the familiar tone of those who have lived. None of the five senses can understand what the mind feels." There was a timeless sadness in his words.

I tried to make myself smaller around the pillar. I did not want to intrude on this candid conversation.

"But Father, are you sure this is what you truly want? Do you remember why you asked for your gift in the first place?"

"Of course, I remember why I made my deal," Promethues replied angrily. "Although, at the time, I didn't know that I was simply a toy for the gods to play with. As for my certainty on this matter, I would not have pressed them as hard as I have if I did not wish for this conclusion." He reached out and touched the relief again. The intricate carving began to smooth, until nothing remained but a sleek, rectangular stone. "You know, I do not take joy in playing with lives as mine has been played with."

Art bowed in a gesture of humility and rose again to meet his master's eyes.
"I'm sorry I questioned you, Father. I just... had my doubts."

"As I have seen with your meddling," Prometheus jested. "I don't like the interest you have taken in the boy."

"I beg your pardon. I won't continue to aid him."

"I assume you will also not fight him?"

"You know I'm not one for violence."

"I know, Four. I wish you would visit me more often, yet I know there is little time remaining. You may leave."

Art nodded and turned down the long, dark corridor.

Prometheus stood, watching him go.

Candles flung sharp angles of shadow in the gloom, illuminating several other sculptures in the chamber. All were of things I had never seen before. A pair of feminine arms lay discarded on a table, and in one corner sat several half-carved slabs of granite depicting figures cowering from some unseen terror, as if fused in stone mid-gesture.

Prometheus stood in the darkness for what seemed like ages. Finally, he turned to face me.

I felt my consciousness dip into those ancient blue pools as they examined my broken body.

"Get out," he ordered as he, too, walked into the darkness. "You're getting blood on my carpets."

XXVI

Something warm pressed against my temple. My eyes fluttered open to the darkness of Prometheus's chamber. But as I scanned the darting candlelight, I could no longer see the half-carved sculptures. This wasn't the same place I'd just been. I was awake. It wasn't as cold here as it was outside, but it did share a familiar wet feeling. As my eyes adjusted to the lack of light, I saw the rocky walls that covered every side of the room. I tried to speak but the words came out as an unintelligible grumble. A heavy weight fell on me.

"Oh, Noah. You are awake! I was so worried." She wrapped her arms around me and every part of my body hurt.

"Ow, Luna. Ow-ow-ow!"

She eased her grip. "How can you still be hurt? You have been asleep for two days. I guess the rabbit's foot had a greater effect than I thought."

"That's funny," I groaned. "I thought it was the severe beating and the bullet wounds that did it." I sat up against the rock wall. We appeared to be in some kind of cave and I could see a tiny speck of light in the distance. A fire burned excitedly in the damp corridor.

Wait a minute, had she said *two days*? Usually, my injuries healed in a single night—at most—and here I was still aching after two whole days.

"Luna." I shrugged off a dull ache in my ribs. "What the hell does a rabbit's foot do, anyway?"

"Oh, they are quite powerful charms. They grant the user a kind of invincibility as well as speed, strength, and incredible luck. Of course," she lowered her voice, "that is in exchange for a price."

"What price?"

She cautiously leaned away from the annoyance in my voice. "The life of the person who uses it."

I stared at her, dumbfounded.

"I was almost positive it would not kill you. Besides, it practically guarantees victory to the person using it so long as it does not kill him first." She looked toward me again and then turned away. "Look, it has different effects on different people. You have heard of Achilles, right? His mother scratched him with a rabbit's foot when he was but an infant and look how long he lived. He won quite a few battles in his time, as well. I knew someone as strong as you would be able to withstand its touch."

"Thanks..." I sighed weakly, "I guess."

"You are welcome. Now, here." She handed me a slice of dried meat. "You have not eaten in days. Once you are ready to move, we can continue this journey."

It wasn't until I bit into the tough meat that I realized the voracious hunger eating at the inside of my stomach. I stuffed the rest of it in my mouth, swallowing it whole. Luna handed me a canteen of water and I downed it in a few gulps.

"Is there any more?" I asked greedily.

She shook her head, frowning. "No, we have been out here for almost a week and most of our equipment was destroyed."

I nodded. Millie did have a strange penchant for random explosions and collateral damage.

"When you feel a little better, I think we should head deeper into the cave and get whatever it is we are supposed to retrieve. There is a strange light in the recesses of the cavern and I believe what we seek is there. I would have gone earlier, but I did not want to leave your side. You were whimpering in your sleep."

"I have bad dreams." I braced myself against the cave wall and got to my feet. "We might as well go now. I'll feel better once I move around a little."

Luna threw my arm over her neck and helped me through the dark cavern. The glow from our fire slowly became but a firefly's glimmer as we continued to move forward. In the distance, a faint blue light called to us.

The cramped tunnel gave way to an enormous open chamber. Strange plants grew from the smooth, rock walls. They stretched several feet from the sheer face, drooping inward with long, orange petals. Each piece of the overgrown vegetation emitted a bright blue glow from somewhere inside the thick, translucent stems. The glow ran down the plants' bodies and into their roots, which covered the cavern walls like a system of shimmering arteries. This web of light filled the massive room, illuminating every corner in its shining phosphorescence.

A few feet from where we stood, a crystalline pool of water spread out across the entire cavern. It was hard to tell how deep it went, but the bluish glow that covered the walls and ceiling could be seen from somewhere under the tranquil surface. A polished stone bridge lead out over the water to a small isle in the center of the expansive room. The bridge seemed sturdy enough, so we proceeded across it together.

As we moved over the lake, I felt a stirring in its depths. My steps carried me closer and closer to the edge of the bridge. It was like something was calling me from under the surface. Around us, the cerulean lights frolicked across the still water. I felt my arm slide from Luna's shoulder as I stumbled forward to get a closer look. Those bright lights probably made it warm. I bet I could jump in for a moment, just long enough to sooth these sore muscles. I lowered myself to my knees and peered through the clear surface. Somewhere near the bottom, I could see the glowing plants reaching out.

"Noah." Luna tugged at my sleeve. "What are you doing?"

I swatted her arm away from me. *Annoying girl, after all she had put me through since we'd met. She wouldn't even let me cleanse my body in this calm spring. I would only be a second, and then we could get whatever stupid thing we came here for. She was so selfish sometimes. This whole quest was her idea to begin with, and all I wanted was one short dip in the soothing, clean liquid. I'll just splash some of the water on my face. She can't get upset at that. It looks so refreshing, with its bright lights and calming aroma...*

"NOAH!" Her voice was laced with hysteria and sounded muffled, despite her being so close.

I looked back to see what she wanted but she was no longer standing behind me. Somehow, she had gotten way above my head. I had no idea she could fly. Her arms grabbed my shoulders and pulled me into the sky. I broke the water's surface and she pulled me onto hard stone. She looked down at me and her eyes flashed with a strange power.

Suddenly, I couldn't breathe. I opened my mouth and vomited onto the rocks. My throat burned from the strain and I heaved in gasping breaths, pulling as much fresh air into my lungs as I could. I was soaked from head to toe. The chill in the cave amplified the uncomfortable feeling.

"What were you doing? You just... walked into the lake."

"I... I don't know," I replied, perplexed. "I don't even remember going in."

"I think it is these plants. I can sense they are alive. They must have some kind of hypnotizing qualities."

"Why didn't they hypnotize you?"

"That kind of power does not work on the celestials."

"Great," I complained, spitting more water onto the stone bridge. "Even with all this power, I can still be tricked into drowning myself by a salad."

"Well do not do it again." Luna helped me to my feet and, with her support, we traveled the rest of the way to the small island.

I did my best to keep my eyes off the welcoming waters of the underground spring.

The island wasn't very large—maybe the size of a tennis court. Thick, white, stone pillars rose from the smooth rock and continued upward until they met with the ceiling high above. These naturally-made columns were covered in bright flowers. Many of these native plants had grown over the island's surface as well, reaching out in various directions toward no discernible source of sunlight.

We hobbled to the center of the small island. There stood a single podium made from the same ivory that covered the walls.

Luna approached it, pushing aside a bundle of long, orange pedaled flowers that had grown across the path. The stand was about four feet high with a flat top.

"There is nothing here." Luna looked at me in disbelief. "It looks like something was here recently, but now it is gone."

I examined the top of the small podium. It was covered in dust and cobwebs except for a neat rectangle the color of the natural stone at its center. Luna was right; until recently, something had sat on this rock.

"Lookin' for this, darlin?"

We spun toward the southern voice.

Millie stood at the center of the bridge. She was wrapped from head to toe in the long fur coat I had seen her in when we had arrived at the Lake of Gold. Apparently, she hadn't healed as well as I had. Black and red scars ran up the sides of her face and the corners of her once plump, red lips were fused together and scarred. The shoulder of the coat slipped from her side as she began to trot toward the lone island. Underneath was bare skin, seared black from the blistering flames. For once, I had no desire to see what was under her clothing. In her left hand, she held a brown, wooden box with thin, gold engravings down the sides. She winked at me when I met her gaze and brushed her blonde hair over the gnarled side of her face.

"You did quite a number on me back there, tiger. Been thinkin' a lot about it."

"Give us the box," Luna snarled, "or I will make you give it to us."

"Big words from a spoiled princess. Here, you can have the box. I can't figure out how to get the damned thing open anyway." She threw the box to Luna who caught it in her nimble hands. "Thing's worthless to me. I just wanted to see him again." Her golden eyes locked onto me and she smiled with her wrinkled, burned lips. "That was quite the show you put on. Never imagined you'd use a rabbit's foot. Dangerous move, even for a Chronographer."

"Guess I'm luckier than the rabbit."

"Yup, and today's your lucky day. Why don't you come along with me? I bet I could show you some things that this little girl never could."

I looked Millie up and down. From the corner of my eye, I saw Luna's face flush. I snickered. Both women looked at me in confusion, and my snicker became a laugh. My laugh became a bellow and that bellow bounced off the walls in a cacophony of sheer, unadulterated hilarity. I wasn't sure why, but the sheer absurdity of the offer was the final straw. An undercurrent of rage dug its way into the laughter.

"Don't be so stupid." I laughed at the Chronographer, dressed in her worn coat. "Don't pretend you have feelings like a human. You're a shell and no matter how hard you try, you will never feel anything but emptiness. You know what? I pity you."

Shock covered Millie's face. She took a few steps back onto the thin bridge. Then, her burned skin crackled under the guise of anger and she took one heavy step forward. Her bare foot made a wet slap against the stone and it echoed over the high cavern walls. In a matter of seconds, all the emotion drained from her charred face. The result was even more disturbing than her burned appearance. Void of all emotion, her eyes became dead circles. It was like staring at a vacuum. Light rippled on her skin but was absorbed into an unsettling gray. She spoke in a slow monotone.

"I won't forget this, Noah Lane. What we lack in feelings, we more than make up for with a long memory. If Father doesn't see you dead, I'll take the truest pleasure in your slow torture." Silence filled the cavern again and Millie's dull eyes met mine through her dangling veil of hair. She stepped off the bridge and the shadows seemed to consume her. She vanished before even hitting the water.

I glanced toward Luna.

She looked back at me with fear.

I realized that I still wore a twisted smirk and felt the acid that had been in my voice just moments before slip down my throat. "C'mon, Luna. Let's get back to the fire. I need to dry out these clothes."

She nodded. "We will head out at first light."

Together, we limped across the cavern and through the dripping darkness to the dying embers of our campsite.

XXVII

After kindling the fire back to a healthy glow, we sat in silence. The flames sent shadows fleeing from the light over every surface in the cave.

"Is it true?" Luna asked quietly.

I didn't understand the question.

"Is it true they cannot feel?"

"Yeah, it's true."

She lowered her head and let the rising tide of silence wash over us once more. Eventually, she spoke again. "How do you know that?" Her voice was hesitant, like it hurt her to ask the question.

"I talked to one of them while I was alone. He told me that the Chronographers were similar to hu— I mean sons of man." I stopped for a moment to remember the walk Art and I had taken and the conversation we had shared as an abandoned mill full of vampires burned to ash. Aside from Luna, he was the only other person I thought I could trust. "He told me the Five had been made from the same mold as us, but their souls had been burned away so they could create memories and take their places at Prometheus's side. It rendered them emotionless. Apparently, it's also their weakness." I looked at Luna but she refused to meet my eyes. The fire reflected off her red hair and when it parted, I saw that she was crying.

"Do you think it will happen to you?" The words came spilling out, as if their implications were a burden—too difficult to make real by acknowledging them. "Will you forget about me... about us?"

"No." I put as much certainty into my answer as I could. "I'm still me, Luna." I moved closer to her, taking her face into my hands and raising her heavenly eyes to meet my placid mortal ones. "Even if this... this... *disease* eats away at my humanity, I will *never* lose what I feel for you." I wiped a tear from her cheek with my thumb and kissed the spot where it had been.

She wrapped her arms around me and let loose a heavy sob. "When I found you, I only thought you would protect me from Colere. I never imagined you would mean this much to me, Noah. I do not want to lose you."

"Don't worry, Luna," I whispered into her red tangles. "I will never leave you."

* * *

The sun peered through the entrance of the cave and we collected whatever belongings we still possessed. The trip back to the Lake of Gold was much easier than the trip toward the cave. The sun sat high in the sky and a pleasant wind blew through the valley. I wondered whether it would begin to storm again if I turned around and tried to return to the cave, but thought better not to chance the good luck we had been bestowed.

As we walked, I examined the wooden box. I held it between my hands, testing its weight. I couldn't imagine what rested inside it. The box weighed almost nothing. It was engraved with gold carvings and strange symbols I'd never seen before—one on the front sort of resembled Quel'ren. I gently rubbed my fingers over the smooth surface of the rectangle. I could find no latch or opening—every inch was seamless. Whatever was inside, I didn't think we'd see it until we made it back to the lodge.

We camped under a low overhang that night. Our tent had been destroyed and we had eaten the last of our dried meat. Luna picked some herbs and made a bland soup of roots and melted snow. It wasn't as revitalizing as previous meals, but I was simply glad to have something in my stomach.

The small alcove we used as cover shielded us from the night's wind and the clear skies painted a beautiful picture of shining stars. It was a good change of pace from the constant blizzards and dank cave. But despite the peaceful scenery, my attention kept wandering back to what Luna had asked me. Art said I was still mortal, and yet the rabbit's foot had not taken my life in exchange for its power. If I saw him again before we reached our goal, I would have to ask him how long I would remain human.

The next morning, we set out early to continue our trek. I was amazed that by mid-afternoon, I could see the bright yellow roof of the Lake of Gold. Had the distance we'd traveled really been so short? Had the storm been that impeding? I decided to count our blessing. We quickened our pace.

As we approached the building, we saw both Quel'ren and Dom'roqe waiting for us. Fluffy smiles graced the faces of the two liaths, and as soon as we were in speaking distance, Quel'ren gave a yell. "Hello, strangers. How goes the adventure?"

"Good, friend. We've got the box." I lifted the box into the air for them to see. Their eyes doubled in size. Dom'roqe whispered something into Quel'ren's ear and he went dashing into the house on his long, thin legs.

"Come, come, my guests." Dom'roqe beckoned with a wave of his branch-like arm. "Come inside and have a meal before you faint. We will discuss what must be done next and tonight, your room is free."

* * *

I stepped out of what might have been the best shower of my life. I looked down and watched the misery of the last week spiral into the drain. I rubbed the moisture out of my hair and threw on a pair of jeans. When I looked into the mirror, I was surprised at what I saw. Where once was a soft college student, now stood a lean warrior. Small pink scratches played across my darkened skin and my flat chest now rippled with sinewy muscles. So much had changed over these past few weeks. Without a second glance, I stepped away from my reflection.

Luna had already gone downstairs to see if our hosts needed any help. I had sat on the bed while she bathed, listening to all the hope she had of the coming days.

"We are almost there, Noah," she had declared passionately. "Once we solve that silly puzzle, we will be at the very foot of that monster's lair."

We really were so close to our goal. I walked out of the steamy bathroom and put on the white, cotton clothes left on the dresser. They were very similar to the clothing Luna had worn in the garden the night we had arrived. Warmth flowed through my body at the thought.

I stumbled down the stairs—two at a time—and swung into the small dining area. There was a large slab of meat on the table along with fresh vegetables and an assortment of other exotic foods. Apparently, our return had been deemed worthy of a celebration.

Luna was already talking amicably with Dom'roqe, and his younger sibling was adding the last touches to the meal. I threw myself into a chair and did my best to hold back the wave of drool that was threatening my mannerly appearance. After a toast to our success, we were bid to eat. My willpower vanished. I dug into the delicious meal with a ravenous appetite brought on by the cold and a diet of dried meat and fruit.

Luna watched me, embarrassed, but laughed when I smiled at her with a mouth full of cake.

The two liath just shook their heads disapprovingly.

Once everyone had eaten their fill, Dom'roqe cleared the table. He set the polished, brown box in the center of our gathering. "As asked, you have retrieved the artifact. That is not, however, the end of the trial. In order to gain entry to Prometheus's lair, you must solve the puzzle handed down from generations of liath." He swept one long claw around the perimeter of the rectangle. Everywhere his pointed nail touched traced a golden line. He continued until the engraving bisected each side. Then, with a gentleness I did not expect, he lifted the lid from the box.

The inside was covered in velvet and was form-fitted to the object within. Dom'roqe set the lid aside and with equal tenderness and removed an object from the velvet womb. The treasure was a small, perfect cube made of a strange silvery metal that seemed to emit a faint light. Every face of the cube was divided into nine smaller faces, each with different symbols and colored in separate hues.

Luna lifted the cube into her hands and examined it. Wonder filled her features as she prodded the box.

"The sides move," she announced as she turned one of the quadrants clockwise.

"Be gentle, please. That is an ancient artifact." Panic rose in the older liath's voice as Luna continued to twist the sections of the box back and forth in her hands.

"It looks like it is supposed to do it. Have you not seen this item before?"

"Well... um... that is to say," Dom'roqe stammered.

It was Quel'ren who finally finished. "The item has been sealed and hidden since its creation. Those at this table are the first to lay eyes on it."

"I guess you would not know what these colors mean, then." She held the box up to the light and recited the colors while spinning the sides of the ornate cube. "Yellow, white, red, green, orange, and blue."

It was at that moment that the realization dawned. "Wait," I blurted out. All eyes turned to me. "It's a box with six colors and six sides?"

"Yes. Is that not what I said?"

"Then there are also nine squares of each color."

Luna took a moment to count the white markings on the cube and nodded in shocked silence.

Even the two liath had taken a new interest in me.

I had to strain to keep from laughing aloud. "Can I see it, please?"

Luna passed me the ancient metal block and I began rapidly twisting the sides around with my fingertips. "What you have here, my friends," I began with confidence and dexterity as I quickly shifted the colored sides, "is the classic problem of a three-dimensional geometric pivoting cube."

The three of them sat in awe as I spun the device about, barely glancing at my movements.

"However, it is more commonly known to those ages six and up as a Rubik's Cube." I set the completed puzzle on the table, every side its own, solid color. "My mom gave me one for Christmas once—I was kind of a nerd."

Luna clapped her hands to her open mouth and the two innkeepers gaped at the object.

The box gave a faint shimmer and split in two. From the center fell a battered, bronze key. Dom'roqe stood and clapped his large hands together.

"Very impressive, young man. I might have underestimated you." He swept the key up with a swift flick of his arm and buried it in his palm. "In the tradition we follow, I bid you stay the night. We will see you off in the morning." He did an about-face and strode from the room.

Luna rose to stop him, but Quel'ren put a thin arm out in refusal. "We have traveled very far and done all you have asked us. I will not be denied that which we have come for by two resort owners. I demand you make him bring that key back!" Luna was furious, but the frosted giant simply shook his head.

"I understand you have waited quite a long time for this, Princess, but you cannot fathom how long we have waited."

Luna shrank back into her seat, seeing that this was a point she would not be able to argue.

"Please allow us puppets to play our roles all the way through. Besides, you have journeyed long, and for two people going to their deaths, I would think you'd wish to enjoy your last night on this plane in peace." He went to follow his brother then stopped. He spoke again in the calm whisper that the liath seemed to possess. "Your destination is very near and I promise the weather will not be a factor. I recommend you dress in what you would like to be buried in."

We stared at each other until Quel'ren left the room.

"Don't listen to them, Luna." I rested my hand on hers. "We'll set things right tomorrow. We'll make Prometheus pay for what he did to your family. Then, we'll come back here and tell them exactly how we did it."

"Thank you, Noah." Her voice was frail. "I suppose I should get some rest."

That night—in the darkness of the room—I sat cradling Luna's head in my lap as she slept in a tight ball. Everything had changed so much. With luck, these changes would make me powerful enough to protect her—to put an end to all of this. I made a promise to the still, black night that I would make sure she made it out, even if I had to give myself up to do it.

XXVIII

I gave Luna a gentle shake when I heard the light knocking on our door. She looked up at me and rubbed the sleep from her eyes with two balled up fists. I was struck by how adorable it was.

"Stop!" She yawned while rolling out of the bed. She stumbled across the room and shut the bathroom door behind her. I heard the faint sound of falling water as the shower started. I dug through my luggage and decided I wanted to be buried in my Saskatchewan shirt. Lots of good memories lived with it. "Yes, I've been to the prairie province of Canada. Did you know it has a population of 1,023,810? Such a beautiful countryside." Saying it aloud again brought a smile to my face.

Luna came out of the bathroom in a familiar blue dress. Her hair was tied back in a tight bun with a crystal comb holding it in place. A platinum chain hung from her neck with a black gemstone set into it. I stared stupidly at her.

"What do you think? James let me keep it when we left the farmhouse. I wanted to look like a princess when we meet the man

254

who destroyed my kingdom and this is all I had." Her delicate frame and pale skin made it seem like she had come fresh from heaven.

"You look like a queen." I beamed at her.

Luna smiled and gave me a soft kiss. "Thank you, Noah. You are too kind to me. Come, let us finish this."

I followed her down the steps and watched the hem of her blue dress leap joyfully about her legs. Not realizing the stairs had ended, I stumbled over on the last step, almost falling to the floor.

Luna giggled. "My hero."

Dom'roqe was waiting for us in the lobby. He wore decorative stone bracelets with precious gems set into the rock. His pointed ears peeked from behind a colorful woven headband. He crossed his gangly arms as we came to meet them. "Are you sure this is what you want?" he asked in a last attempt to sway our decision.

"I have never been so sure of anything," Luna replied.

The frosty behemoth tapped his crooked fingers against the front desk for a moment, and then nodded and led us through a door marked, "Employees Only." The room was cramped and reminded me more of a storage closet than an office. Old lamps and broken chairs were strewn about the crowded floor. Dust and cobwebs had settled on most of the objects, and the single flickering light in the center did little to brighten the space. Quel'ren had his back against a large bookcase and was straining to push it aside.

"Little help here?" His voice seemed heavier in the tight space, but no less gentle.

I walked over and together we moved the bookcase with ease. Behind it stood a tall, rusted metal door with no knob. It seemed sturdy and looked as though it could probably survive a small explosion.

Dom'roqe pushed past us and set himself in front of the thick barrier. He produced the old key from his palm and inserted it into the metal lock. A shrill grating echoed off the dusty walls and old paintings as he turned it over. The sound was followed by the slow moving metal bearings. With a strained creak, the door swung open.

The corridor beyond was pitch black. The mottled liath stepped aside and a dark shadow crossed his foxish face. I could see why these creatures had been associated with fear. On a dark hillside, the sleek frame and sharp teeth would probably not be a welcomed sight. Still, their comfortingly soft voices made it easy to look past their physical appearance.

"You have proven your strength and wisdom to the liath tribe. When you enter the door, I will have to close it behind you. There will be no turning back." Deep furrows creased Dom'roqe face and I could tell he felt he was damning the two of us by allowing us to enter the lightless hallway.

"We will have no reason to return, lest we defeat the man who has terrified the world for eons. I will let no others suffer the fate of my family—my kingdom." Luna stiffened her posture and walked on.

I hobbled after her.

"Um," Quel'ren stepped in front of us. "I will keep your luggage safe for you, just in case." I nodded. "G-good luck." He stepped out of our way and leaned back onto his brother, who draped a long arm over his shoulder.

Luna and I stepped into the shadowy tunnel. It was a strange darkness. It felt like it had a life of its own—like it knew someone stood in it. It crept over the walls and poured over every surface. Even when I lifted my hands to my eyes, I could not make out their silhouette through the impeding gloom. I looked back and saw the light from the hotel forty feet away. But how could that be? We had taken no more than a single step over the threshold.

I went to grab Luna's shoulder but she was no longer there. The grating of metal sounded behind me and the faint light extinguished like a candle accosted by a heavy wind. A latch clicked and the darkness grew thicker.

I set my hand against the stone wall and stumbled forward. I groped for Luna with my other hand but found nothing. I called out to her, but the words spun around me in the thick air, devoured by the murk. I waded forward and it pulled me back with its inky tendrils. I screamed and the sound wrapped around my neck like a noose. I gave up my grip and began to run. The weighty shade swirled about me as my footsteps fell silently. It raked my back with its nails, snapping with its rayless jaws. I closed my eyes and continued to dash until I crashed into something solid and went sprawling across the ground.

My eyes hurt when I opened them. A light shone out and the lurid blackness was nowhere to be seen. It all seemed so inconceivable—just a moment ago I was being swallowed by a black beast and now, here I stood. A green meadow stretched out as far as I could see and a cloudless, blue sky met the earth with a gentle touch.

Luna stood with her arms outstretched. A curling wind set her garment aflutter.

"Luna?"

She turned and looked back at me. "Is it not wonderful? A single step into darkness and this place rests on the other side?"

I pushed myself out of the grass and looked around. No door and no black cavern—just miles of green field and blue sky. I let the breeze invigorate my skin. "What do you mean a single step? I was walking for quite a while."

Luna paused from her sunbathing and looked back at me, addled. "You were behind me the whole time, Noah. We walked through the door and into this meadow. You less gracefully than I, it seems."

"Oh... Where are we?"

"The end of the world, I believe. And such a wonderful place it has turned out to be!" Luna spun around with delight, her skirt spiraling about her until she tumbled onto my back, draping her arms over my shoulders. She laughed and her warm breath sent a shiver through me.

I coughed. "Uh, so where do we go next?"

"I am not sure. I guess we should start walking." She sauntered around me and took my hand, leading me forward. She swung our hands between us and skipped as she walked.

I had never seen Luna so upbeat before.

We strolled casually through the meadow for the whole morning and on into the afternoon. Still, I couldn't help but be a little irritated at Quel'ren and his cryptic directions. My mood would probably have been fairly sour on this hike regardless, but Luna's humming kept my spirits afloat.

I scanned the horizon line and was not surprised that it was all familiar. No matter how far we walked, we saw the same scenery— green grass and blue sky. If it weren't for the crunch of the grass and Luna's exuberant tugging, it would have seemed as if we hadn't moved from the spot we had started from. It made me think of the black tunnel. I could still feel the darkness curling around my body and it sent an electric pulse through my veins.

The mid-afternoon sun was high overhead yet the air remained cool. A mild breeze blew past us and carried a wondrous bouquet on its throes.

Luna stopped to look at me. "Are you okay, Noah? You have been quiet for most of the day."

"I'm fine, Luna. I'm just… distracted." I did feel a little strange. The day had washed by like a calm stream. I couldn't remember a day like it, actually.

"Well, then. I think we should take a break." She pointed to an upturned oak lying on its side. I was pretty sure I hadn't seen it on our approach. With a little hop, she sat in the grass with her back against the trunk and her legs outstretched. She patted her hands against the top of her thighs and grinned up at me.

"Come on. You have allowed me to rest on you quite often. It is time I returned the favor." She waved me down and patted her lap again.

I shrugged and lowered myself to the ground, resting my head against her leg. She slowly ran her pale fingers through my hair. I hadn't realized how long it was getting until she curled a few strands around her index finger. We sat like this for a while. I closed my eyes, breathing in her sweet scent against the warm, midday sun.

"Today has been very nice," Luna muttered dreamily.

I grunted my agreement without opening my eyes.

She rubbed my temple. "Um, Noah?" Her voice was timid. I looked up into her concerned eyes. "I have been thinking… Since we came here… to this place…" I sat up and she leaned against me, looking at me with her vibrant, shifting eyes. "What if we really are fools? We have both lost everything and here we are, charging into what everyone has deemed suicide, for some modicum of revenge or redemption."

I looked intently at her. "What are you saying, Luna?"

"I am not sure all of this is worth losing you or our lives together. What if we gave it all up right now and lived here? This place is so nice, and I know we could find shelter, once we get out of this meadow. If there is one tree, there must be others around somewhere. We could make a home away from all the chaos and danger. We could stay here and be together."

I had to think about what I was going to say for a moment. What she was offering... it was all I really wanted. But what about everything else? What about those left behind and the ones already gone? I steadied my resolve. "Luna, I'm flattered and... well... I really care about you, too... but I don't think you could be happy without putting your parents to rest. Besides, think of all the good we could do for the world if we got rid of the Chronographers."

She turned away from me, crossing her arms. "I do not know if I feel that way anymore, Noah. Why can we not just be together?"

"Because I don't feel like I can belong to you until I get rid of whatever's inside me." I spoke with conviction. "Every time I use this power, I see those who've suffered as a result of a single man's greed for knowledge. And every time I look at you, I see that same pain."

"But what if I do not make it out alive? You have the strength to fight Prometheus, but I do not."

I thought about this for a moment. She had a point; I couldn't fight someone like Prometheus and protect Luna at the same time. "You're right."

She looked up at me, tentative joy washing across her face.

I stood and looked down on her as the smile faded. "You stay here, Luna. I'll go find Prometheus and do this for the both of us."

"But how do I know if you will come back?"

"Because I promised I would." I backed away, watching the pain on her face, until I couldn't bear it any longer. I gave her one last glance and circled around to walk toward the horizon.

But someone stood in my way.

"Well I'll be a swamp-rat's mother. It's usually the heroes that give in the easiest, an' here you are walking away." Hosef's broad frame took a few steps back as he looked me over with his bloodshot eyes. His leather jacket was frayed at the bottom and he wore a pair of wide suspenders to hold up his tattered pants. As he paced about, his torso shifted from side to side, almost falling off his lower half.

"You bastard. I... I killed you!"

"I reckon that's not quite correct, lad. If'n my memory serves me right, 'twas the historian who sliced me up like a catfish." He made a wide gesture to his bisected abdomen, held together by staples and stitching.

I reached out to call the mist but when I snapped my fingers, I felt nothing.

"Simmer down, youngin'. It's not my fault you refused to take the high road. Too stubborn for happiness, that's what you is."

"Shut up, you piece of trash!"

"Or what? You'll kill me again? With what powers?"

"I don't need powers to take down some undead scum."

"Well, for one thing," the large vampire held up one fat finger, "I'd be double undead. An' two, I ain't the one you should be worryin' about. It's yer girl whose frightnin' away all the wildlife."

I looked back at Luna who was kneeling over in the dirt, a shroud of red hair draped over her face.

"Hosef, what did you do?"

He was gone. A fierce wind began to blow as the sun rapidly fell behind ashen storm clouds. I backed away and ran toward her, sinking to the ground and grabbing hold of her shoulders. "Luna," I pleaded. "Luna, what's wrong."

"Why?" she whispered as rain started to patter on the grass around us. "Why will you not love me?" She looked up and I staggered backward. Her pale face was covered with thin, blue veins. Her familiar satellite eyes were shrouded in crimson hue. She sprang at me with a shriek and I deftly rolled aside. Her delicate hands now harbored a pair of black, gnarled claws. A shrill hiss revealed a set of dangerously sharp fangs.

"Luna, what's happened to you?"

She lumbered toward me, her bloody eyes fixed on mine. "Why will you not love me?" She snarled again and leaped. I tried once more to call forth the nostalgia, but nothing happened. Thunder echoed overhead as one of Luna's quick swipes made contact with my arm. Searing pain surged through my body and blood poured from the wound. The pain was worse than when I'd been shot. It was the familiar sting of being a weak, fragile human.

I turned to run but she was too fast. With a sweeping claw, she launched me into the air, splitting my side open. Blood rained from the attack as I rolled feebly across the ground. Luna pounced on me once again, pushing a sharp claw deep into my shoulder. Her movements were more animal than person. I tried to call out to her, but she wrapped a grotesque hand around my throat and began squeezing the air from my lungs. I had forgotten how much pain hurt. I struggled futilely and the muscles in my face began to ache.

Luna looked down at me and spoke through dagger-like fangs. "Why could you not just be with me?" A bloody tear fell down her cheek.

I felt my strength leave me. My struggling began to weaken until finally, I just gave up. I closed my eyes, accepting the opportunity to die as a human.

With a flash of light, everything around me exploded into dust. I felt a pull from afar as heavy tendrils fled my body. I gasped for air and rolled over in the dirt, clutching my throat. My arms and chest burned from deep, phantom lacerations. I pulled myself up under the night sky. My eyes darted about for Hosef or the meadow or the vampire Luna, but all I saw was dirt, dark sky, and a stone archway built into the side of a rock face.

"You're lucky," Art called, tossing a paint-stained towel to me. "I was just on my way out."

XXIX

I sat, stupefied, on the barren ground, looking up at the man in the brown duster. "What-what happened? I was walking through that dark tunnel, and then I was in a meadow with Luna. Where's Luna?"

Art put a finger to his lips to quiet me. He pointed to the woman heaped in the dirt. "She's fine," Art said softly. "It appears she chose the happy ending. I think we should allow her to enjoy it for the time being. Come. Get up." He reached a hand out and I took it. With his help, I scrambled to my feet.

"What do you mean she took the happy ending?" I asked, wiping the dirt and sweat from my face with the old towel.

"The gods never wanted anyone to find this place so they installed certain safeguards to keep everyone out. The darkness in that cave is alive. It latches on to you and attacks your mind. It gives you what you want the most and—while you enjoy living out your dream—it devours your life energy."

"Oh," I stammered. The meadow with Luna and her willingness to give up her quest to stay with me—that was what I wanted most. "I didn't take the happy ending."

"As I can tell by how close you were to death when I found you—if you deny that which you most desire above all else, the darkness simply destroys you—"

"—with your greatest fears," I finished the sentence for him. "But why go through the trouble of making the illusions? Why not just kill me?"

Art shrugged his broad shoulders, his dark curls bouncing at the movement. "I guess it likes to take its time."

"What about Luna?" I asked, looking down at her sleeping figure. "She's still unconscious."

"I sent the creature back. She's in no danger now. Just be glad you had the foresight to push the both of you out of the cave before you fell unconscious. If you would have fallen inside, there would have been nothing I could have done for either of you."

I remembered the object I'd stumbled into just before I'd entered the meadow. I looked up and saw Art heading in the opposite direction.

"Thank you, Art, for everything."

"If you truly want to face my father, I wish you luck. And if I never see you again," he called back, "knowing you has been a pleasure."

"You, too." I waved as he walked down the rocky path.

"Remember what I said," he yelled without turning around. "Prometheus may make up the rules, but he still has to play the game."

He turned a corner and walked out of sight.

I took Art's towel and wiped the dried blood from my arms and back. It had stained my shirt, but that had become commonplace by now. I leaned down and put my hand on Luna's shoulder. Her breathing was steady and her lips twitched into a calm smile. I rocked her gently, calling to her. "Luna. Hey. Get up, Princess."

She rolled away from my touch and her eyes blinked open. "Noah?" She yawned and stretched. Then, upon taking in her surroundings, her brows furrowed. "What is going on?"

"We've been asleep all day, Luna. Something in that cave knocked us out. It showed us our greatest desires to keep us distracted." I left out the part about it wanting to devour us.

She looked up into the night and sighed heavily. "How did you get out?"

"It showed me you but you were acting strange. I disagreed with the dream and woke up." Once again, I left out the more gruesome details. Luna just sighed again. I put my hand on her shoulder. "What did it show you?"

Color flushed into her face and she grinned—just slightly. After a moment she responded. "I dreamed of family." She raised her arm to me and I stood to help her up. Luna dusted off her dress and scoffed. "It was so nice, too. Oh, well. What now?"

I pointed up the small hill. "I believe it's right over that ridge."

Together, we trudged up the dirt knoll. Dark trees littered the landscape around us but no vegetation grew on the path. There were no clouds in the night sky, and yet I couldn't make out a single star. As we headed for the outcropping on top of the hill, I reached over and took Luna's hand. She looked at me and smiled. There was no moon in the sky here, but I found the radiance from her stare comforting.

The top of the hill was no different from the rest, just a large clearing of dirt and dust. No wind blew in this strange place, but the dust still seemed to stir on the barren earth. We scanned the area for some sign of inhabitants, but there was scarcely shade, let alone the castle or fortress that no doubt awaited our arrival.

"I think it is there." Luna pointed to a dim object near the edge of the clearing.

We moved closer to the shadowy structure. It turned out to be a dilapidated shanty, its rotting wooden boards somehow standing despite its rancid odor and obvious decay. I could see the dark interior through the gaping holes in the walls, and the bowed, rusty tin roof did little to supplant the title of shelter.

"There's no way Prometheus lives in this." I poked the moist surface with a finger. Wet mold fragmented from its side and I wiped it on the side of my jeans.

"Do you see anything else up here? This can be the only place." She reached out and pressed against the door, which steadily gave way. The musty scent of decaying wood permeated the opening. Luna stepped through the frame and I followed close behind. As we entered the small shed, our footsteps created an echo. The building was so small and rotten, they should have been more of a thud. As the sound bounced off the walls, small flares of color exploded behind my eyes. We took a few cautious steps forward and the eruptions became fiercer until, finally, a last step sparked a bright, blinding light.

When my vision cleared, we were in new surroundings. Luna stared in awe at its extravagance, but the scene was all too familiar for me. We stood in a vast amphitheater constructed of architecture from every era imaginable. An assortment of pillars lined the central nave and a wide, regal carpet had been laid down the center, traveling deep into the cavernous depths of the chamber.

Luna continued to scan the area. "It is incredible! Oh, my Gods. I believe that staircase over there is from my family's castle, and that column is from Wolf Hall. It is like every architect was pulled together to create this place."

I looked at the endless room. All the sides trailed off into the far darkness so that no walls could be seen. Ambush would be easy here. I wondered, for a moment, if there actually were any walls in this place at all.

"Don't you mean how many architects were murdered to create this?" I said dryly.

"You are right, Noah. But just look at this place! Over there is a..."

I knew Luna was talking, but her words started to fade until I could no longer understand them. It wasn't like I was ignoring her. It was just that something was calling for my attention so fervently that I could not partition enough of myself to hear her words. I felt a gentle pull in my chest. It steadily grew stronger until I moved a single step toward it. That step felt good.

Really good.

So good, in fact, that I felt another was necessary. But before I could claim the ecstasy a second time, cool fingers wrapped around my hand. The steady tugging grew taut for a moment, and then shattered like glass.

"Noah, are you listening?" Luna pulled at me in annoyance.

"Um, sorry. I was just looking at everything."

"Well, it *is* quite amazing, but we should get going. We have a task to complete."

With my hand in hers, she dragged me down the path. Our footsteps fell dully on the soft carpet beneath our feet and for a time, I felt comfort in knowing our approach would not be heard. As we passed some large, stone statues and a single Gothic spire growing from the floor, I started to notice the plants.

They were scarce, at first—a few plain pots with red flowers inside. But as we traveled deeper, I noticed the pots were lumped together. Eventually, roman amphora, burial urns, and large, decorative vases covered the floor next to the endless carpet, stretching out as far as one could see. Roses sat next to red tulips, and crimson sunflowers mingled with auburn dandelions. Somewhere in the distance, I saw a cherry tree. It was a strange, red garden built at varying levels inside an assortment of carriers. I wondered how many pots there could be. Thousands? Millions?

When I looked back at the trail, I noticed the carpet had ended. A smooth, white floor stretched from its end, and a young-looking man stood several lengths from us, enshrined by a wide circle of pots. He wore a black robe, tied at the waist with an ornate, red sash. Even with the new clothing, there was no way I could forget the piercing blue gaze that now looked at us.

"I was beginning to get worried," he began, his voice full of raw energy. It seemed more solid in this place, more dominant. "I lost track of you when you passed through the door. I feared you had succumbed to the darkness."

I was gripped by his presence. I could feel the creeping hollowness that had kept me chained and mute so many times before in this place.

Contrarily, Luna strode confidently forward and spoke. "Prometheus, of the Old Ones, I have come to make you pay for what you have done to my family and my kingdom, as well as the worlds around it. You will not be permitted to cause destruction for your gain any longer."

"Bold words from someone doomed to fail. More so now that you have brought to me what I desire." He took a step toward Luna, who stood her ground. She didn't even flinch as he continued to close the gap between them.

I used her courage to find strength of my own. I pushed in front of her and called on the Chronographer's power. The tug of reality was stronger here, and the mist that emerged was as thick as dense clouds. It blanketed the floor between Prometheus and me. "I won't let you touch her, Prometheus. You will not take her ability as your own."

Prometheus stopped, looking puzzled. "You haven't realized it yet, have you? I have no desire for a dethroned celestial and her fortune telling."

Luna pushed in beside me. "Do not try and trick us. I know that with the full power of my family's vision, you intend to escape from this prison."

Prometheus looked at Luna, amused. It was as though the thought had never even occurred to him. He chuckled at first, but it soon progressed to a loud, booming laugh. He clutched his sides and wiped a tear from his old eyes. "If only it were that simple, girl. I knew you had some sort of delusions to seek me out, but I never imagined them to be so ridiculous. I admit, I needed you for a time, but your usefulness ended the minute you met him." Prometheus pointed a finger directly at me.

I looked back at Luna and saw a twinge of panic behind her calm features. "I-I do not understand."

"Then allow me to fill in the blanks, my dear." Prometheus bowed low. "It's true I sent Colere to take your kingdom into the nostalgia that fateful night." He said this with such nonchalance and I could hear Luna seething behind me. "But with the memories he claimed came a vision so powerful it brought me to my knees. A series of incomprehensibly unlikely events was about to occur if spurred along properly. A son of man—on his day of birth—was about to walk into an area where the barrier was weak and a celestial with heightened emotions—on the brink of death—was going to pull him through. In this transitional dichotomy, he would be able to escape the binding clutches of the gods themselves."

"It still does not make any sense! Noah killed Colere that night. He took his powers and struck a blow to your ranks."

"Indeed he did, and that event was the beginning of something as of yet unseen. My children are empty vessels, unable to experience the fruits of life. There are certain things they cannot bring to me—the gentle touch of love; the miracle of life; the final embrace of death. That is, until Noah killed Colere in that impossible moment where he was able to defy even the gods' creations." Prometheus looked at me with hunger and triumph as he continued. "Inside you, Noah, is what I need to escape this room. Colere's last memory—his memory of death."

Luna remained silent.

I stood, shocked. All this time, I had thought I was delivering some kind of justice. But it turned out I was the package, not the courier. I mustered some strength and pressed him for more answers. "So how will you gain any kind of knowledge with the memory of death?"

"Gain knowledge?" He spat the words. "Do not speak to me of that nonsense."

"Isn't that why you're here?" I asked with more confidence, after seeing him lose some of his control. "Didn't you ask the gods for all the knowledge? Isn't that your gift?"

Prometheus slouched. Grief and anger radiated from him like a crashing tide. "I wanted what I thought my people deserved." He paced restlessly about the small circle, like a captive wild animal. "Those bastards didn't give me a gift—they cursed me! They locked me in this box and turned my words against me. I know everything, but I have *experienced* nothing. At least my children can walk through the world and feel the wind against their backs. Everything I touch turns to dust. I sit in this chamber and watch life ebb by." He stopped and lowered his head, plucking a petal from a red sunflower. It dissipated into mist as it touched his fingertips. "I have lived countless lifetimes and have never known that which brings life to the living. What the gods gave me was an endless torture."

The realization hit me like strong gust of wind. "You don't want to know everything, you want to destroy it. The people, the animals—all of it!"

"And when there is nothing left, there will be nothing left to learn."

With a swipe of my hand, I brought the nostalgia to my fingertips. I launched a thick cloud toward Prometheus. It steadily transformed into coarse, black powder as it soared through the air. He turned and walked toward the attack. As the explosive ash grew near, it reverted back into smoke and harmlessly rose away.

I reached out to conjure something else but heard the thundering stomp of Prometheus's foot. My hand moved lazily through the memories, as if they were a thick fog.

I felt nothing.

With little more than a focused look, Prometheus sent the cloud circling about me. It pressed hard against my skin and I could feel it cutting through my flesh. I cried out in agony as the last of it crammed itself into my body.

A powerful hand grabbed my neck. "Did you think you could use the nostalgia against me? Did you think you ever had a chance at all? The only reason you destroyed Number One was because I let you."

A fist flashed past my eyes and sank hard into Prometheus's jaw. He barely flinched.

Luna stood in horror as he removed her fist with his free hand.

"How I wish I could have felt that. Oh, well." He pushed against her hand, sending her soaring through the empty space. She crashed against a clay jar, shattering its contents onto the floor.

He returned his attention to me, releasing his grip from my neck. I moved forward to strike him, but my arms pulled taught against invisible tethers. I felt my knees give way as the cords crushed me under the pressure. I dangled helplessly from puppet strings that weren't really there. These shackles didn't connect to any true thing; they were a part of me.

Prometheus stepped back to examine his prize. The dark robe made him look as if he were gliding. "The problem with you, Noah, is that you're still mortal. I had hoped that having my sycophants attend to you would mature Number One's power. With time, I thought forcing you to use the nostalgia to defeat my children would burn the mortality away. But it seems if you want something done right—" He closed in on me again, leaning up right against me, resting his head on my shoulder. He whispered into my ear, "—you do it yourself."

His hand clamped onto my forehead and I felt fire engulf my skull. A pain unlike anything I could describe surged though my body, sending me into a wild seizure. My eyes rolled back as the heat devoured my whole being, circling around some hidden prey within myself. It looked for something I had never felt nor knew existed until this moment—something I had carried with me all my life. And when the heat found what it sought, it ripped it from me like a rabid dog.

Abruptly, Prometheus removed his hand and my whole body tugged forward, like a fish caught on a hook. I felt a sickening pull as something broke free of my body and shot into Prometheus's hand. The fire subsided and my muscles relaxed.

"That's better," he chided as he dusted off his hands. "Now, my last Chronographer, give me the power of death."

Prometheus raised his arms to the sky, awaiting my gift.

I felt no urge to oblige him. In fact, I felt no pull at all. I felt more in control now than I had felt since the day I killed Colere.

He lowered his arms and examined me. He took my chin in his hand and looked deep into my eyes. "I don't understand. You are no longer burdened by mortality. Why can't I tap into your memories? You should be a soulless vessel."

I heard Luna move from the edge of the potted garden.

I glanced at her as she struggled to her knees.

Prometheus followed my gaze. Without warning, he spiraled away, laughing jovially. Really?" He stumbled about—his voice almost childish. "Oh my, this *is* rich!"

I looked back at Luna who was watching the strange display.

"You love her, don't you?"

The question surprised me.

"You gave her part of your soul, you sly dog."

I felt the beginnings of a smile on my face. "You can't take it, can you?"

"No." He sighed. "As long as you love her, I can't. Damn! Isn't this poetic?" He leaned up against my shoulder and looked at Luna. His new demeanor reminded me of David—smug but quick to point out a mistake.

I chuckled under my breath.

"Well, I guess I'll just have to improvise." He raised a hand toward Luna.

Her eyes grew wide as Prometheus snapped his fingers. Quickly, she turned toward me. "Noah, I love yo—" Luna fell limp as blood erupted from her body.

Pots shattered and dirt soared into the sky, showering downward in a storm of red petals. Drops of scarlet liquid sprinkled my face.

Prometheus reared back and howled with laughter. I couldn't hear him over the screaming. It took me a moment before I realized it was my own.

"Now," Prometheus began tartly. "You have two choices. You can live forever without the woman you love, or you can destroy it all."

I sank into my invisible shackles—a puppet with his strings tangled, a doll for gods. She was the one thing that had made my life seem right. I had promised to protect her and had been helpless to do anything to save her. With all I had been given, I was still helpless. I looked up at Prometheus's calm face. "I'll give you what you want, Prometheus." He grinned as I closed my eyes, focusing on the smallest fragment of mist still left in the room. I dove deep inside it, looking for that last memory. I felt a gentle pull and sunk toward it. I let it carry me all the way inside...

And there it was.

XXX

It opened to me like a book.

I was a man moving through the world as a shadow, clinging to the tiniest spark of interest. I had followed a girl across half this country—all because my father told me it was necessary—because this girl was the key to everything. I'd toyed with her—letting her think she was getting away. I usually found this kind of thing a chore, but this time it was different. It seemed... fun. At least I assumed this was what fun felt like. I stalked her—like a great cat—as she fled through dank tunnels... and I found myself smiling.

I caught up with her in some dreary city. Somehow, she acquired a son of man. I pitied him, lost from his world of color and music and stuck here—food for the vampires. I felt a push from a great distance, the familiar hand of my father pushing me onward. I buried my thoughts and carried on, calling forth the thick tendrils of the nostalgia. I attacked the girl, and she fled with the son. I gave chase, erecting monoliths around them. They darted through shrouded streets and into alleyways. The pursuit was nothing too difficult.

After a brief chase, I cornered them in a dilapidated old building. Why do the sons of man build such things and then leave them to rot? What's the point? Of course, I already knew why. I mean, I *am* Culture.

The girl was unconscious; she would be easy to take now. The son of man squared off against me, a crude weapon in his hand. It was a comical sight.

"Do you even realize what you are doing, Son of Man? What forces you are facing? I do not wish to learn from you, but I am sure you could impart some of your knowledge on me."

The boy had an amusing fire in his eyes. He tried to sound intimidating, but it came off as pathetic.

"I won't let you touch her."

I laughed at the poor, misguided creature. I tried to convince him that what he was doing was foolish. He had no part in these matters.

The child spoke of fairness and justice. Funny how these animals always gravitate toward these two ideals.

He questioned my morals and I grew weary of his prattle. I had larger business to attend to. "Not right? Boy, right and wrong are not merely words with which to attack your enemy with. I take little joy in anything but the pursuit of knowledge, and now you are boring me, which is impressive for someone who has lived as long as I."

I tried to move past him, but he swung his cloddish weapon. Dodging it was as easy as blinking and the implement clattered against the door frame. I moved to destroy this annoyance, but felt that familiar pull. Father's touch was in the air.

"I'm sorry, Colere. This is how it has to be."

Father? My senses jumped from my body and wrapped around the son's weapon. Swiftly, it pulled it toward me. The feeling was strange—a sharp tingling in my neck. Why did I feel pain? I looked at the frightened creature in front of me and the edges of my vision became darker. Something washed over me.

Sadness? Impossible.

A coldness swallowed me and I looked hard at the son of man, but I did not see him—I saw the man I had devoted my life to.

"Father, why?"

* * *

I shot from the cloud like a rocket.

Prometheus stood, still grinning at me expectantly.

I had retrieved what he'd asked for—it was time to give it to him. I breathed in and blew black smoke into his face.

He staggered back, coughing. "What did you do?"

"I did as you asked, Prometheus. I gave you death."

He lost his balance and fell to the floor, clutching his chest.

"You really should work on how you phrase your requests. I thought you'd learned that by now."

He tried to crawl away, but there was no escaping the smoke. He lurched onto his back and stared at the distant ceiling. A dark cloud poured in behind his eyelids.

"At least... I... am free." His body went limp and he spoke no more.

I sensed a myriad of tiny strings, all from a great distance away. They suddenly grew taut and then shattered, including the one that connected to me.

I fell to the floor—my shackles destroyed. From the edge of the clearing I heard a noise. I rushed over to Luna. Massive gashes covered her body and her dress was more red than blue. Her torn abdomen shuddered with each struggled breath. She blinked up at me, but had no strength to talk.

"Luna, don't move! I'll do something. I don't know how, but I'll find a way."

She opened her mouth to speak but blood poured from her lips, streaming down her cheek.

"Oh, God. No!" I pulled her closer to me. "Don't move, my love."

Her bright gray eyes glinted in the light. "Noah." The blood bubbled and she coughed. "Remember... when I said... I dreamed of family?"

"Yes." Warm tears seared my cheeks as I held her closer to my face. "I remember."

"The family... it was not my family... It was... our family."

I lost all restraint. I buried my head in her blood soaked hair and cried. "Don't leave me, Luna. I need you. I love you. Please!"

She didn't respond.

"Luna!"

Her breathing grew quieter.

"Luna." My eyes burned. "Luna!"

Matted hair fell from her face.

"Luna..." I made a decision. I lowered her to the ground, the light rapidly leaving her luminescent eyes. I pressed my hand against her chest and concentrated. I dug deep and tried to feel her—who she was and what she had been. I tried to channel whatever it was I had learned back at the farmhouse.

I saw her as a child playing in strange, golden fields. I saw her parents scolding her for spending too much time with the werewolves. I saw her grow into a beautiful woman—clothed in extravagant dresses and complaining the whole time. Like a flash, I saw her desperation as her home burned, and the birth of a singular hope brought on from a vision. I ran with her through the murky depths of underground tunnels, silently pursued by a killer. I saw our time together—the good and the bad—and felt warmth. I saw a family that never existed and I saw myself looking down at her, crying.

I open my eyes and felt a tugging sensation flow through me. It singed my fingertips and ran up my arm, surging through my body before settling somewhere deep inside.

Luna's bright eyes became a cold gray.

I reached within myself and pulled at a small string. "Luna..." My voice echoed from somewhere inside my mind. "Luna, please."

"Noah? Is that you? Where am I?"

My mind filled with her voice. I smelled her lavender scent and tried to hold back the wave of emotion that battered against my will. "You're with me, Luna." I spoke to the voice inside my head. "I'll make this better, no matter what it takes."

I rose, lifting her body in my arms. It felt empty and still. I turned toward the wide, red carpet and followed it into the darkness—into the night.

EPILOGUE

I don't remember how long I walked. I don't remember how far. I knew the direction to take, but had no concept of the distance. The cold didn't bother me; neither did the sun. I could feel the immortality burning beneath my flesh and deadening my senses. Eventually, I reached the house. I knocked on the door and he answered it.

He was expecting me.

I sat on the couch and stared through the glass into the fishbowl.

The creature darted about the edges.

I reached into my jacket pocket and lifted the contents to the table for the fish to see. I let the sand slip through my fingers; small shells decorated the pile.

The fish swam to the edge of the bowl and examined my offering then he looked at me. Small bubbles popped on the surface of the still water. "You can do it, but it will be hard."

I had become accustomed to the drifting scent of lavender, but sometimes it still startled me into looking for its source.

She was letting me know I didn't have to do it. I shook my head. I looked back at the fish. "I don't care. I have nothing left."

"*You have me.*" The familiar voice whispered from somewhere deep inside me.

"Not yet," I whispered back. "But I will."

ABOUT THE AUTHOR

Trevor T. Faulkner is an American author from Tallahassee, Florida. He studied Digital Media at the University of Central Florida and currently resides with his wife, Heather and cat, Racer.

If you want to know more about the works of Trevor T. Faulkner, go to his website at: www.MEMORIESOFANOAK.com.